By Carlos Fuentes

Where the Air Is Clear

The Good Conscience

Aura

The Death of Artemio Cruz

A Change of Skin

Terra Nostra

The Hydra Head

Burnt Water

Distant Relations

The Old Gringo

Myself with Others

Christopher Unborn

Constancia and Other Stories for Virgins

The Campaign

The Campaign

The Campaign

Carlos Fuentes

TRANSLATED BY

ALFRED MAC ADAM

Farrar · Straus · Giroux
New York

English translation copyright © 1991 by Farrar, Straus and Giroux, Inc.

Originally published in Spanish as *La Campaña*

Copyright © 1990 by Carlos Fuentes

Copyright © 1990 by Mondadori España, S.A.

All rights reserved

Published simultaneously in Canada by HarperCollins*CanadaLtd*

Printed in the United States of America

Designed by Constance Fogler

First edition, 1991

Library of Congress Cataloging-in-Publication Data

Fuentes, Carlos.

The campaign / Carlos Fuentes ; translated by Alfred Mac Adam. —
1st ed.

    p.   cm.

Translation of: La campaña.

I. Title. II. Series; Fuentes, Carlos.

PQ7297.F793C2913 1991   863—dc20   91-9723 CIP

To my son, CARLOS,

braver than many warriors,

with all my love

Contents

The Campaign

1

The Río de la Plata

[1]

On the night of May 24, 1810, my friend Baltasar Bustos entered the bedroom of the Marquise de Cabra, the wife of the President of the Superior Court for the Viceroyalty of the Río de la Plata, and kidnapped her newborn child. In its place, he put a black baby, the child of a prostitute who had just been publicly flogged.

The anecdote is part of the story of three friends—Xavier Dorrego, Baltasar Bustos, and me, Manuel Varela—and a city, Buenos Aires, where the three of us were struggling to get an education, a city of smugglers too embarrassed to show off their wealth. Even though there are now about forty thousand of us *porteños*, as we inhabitants of the city call ourselves, Buenos Aires is drab, its buildings crouched low, its churches austere. The city wears a façade of false modesty and disgusting dissimulation. The rich subsidize the convents so the convents will hide their smuggled goods. But this also works to the advantage of those of us who love ideas and books: since crates containing chalices and ecclesiastical garments are not opened at customs, friendly priests use them to send us forbidden

books by Voltaire, Rousseau, and Diderot . . . Dorrego, from
a family of rich businessmen, buys the books; I work in the
printing shop of the orphanage, where I secretly reprint them;
and Baltasar Bustos, who is from the country, where his father
has a big estate, turns the books into action. He wants to be
a lawyer under a regime that despises lawyers, that accuses
them of stirring up endless lawsuits, hatred, and rancor. What
they're really afraid of is that we'll educate creole lawyers who
will speak for the people and bring about independence. That's
Baltasar's real problem: he's got to study without a university
in Buenos Aires and rely (like his two friends, Dorrego and
me, Varela) on smuggled books and private libraries. The authorities keep an eye on us. The last viceroy was right when
he said that the spread of "seduction" had to be stopped in
Buenos Aires; this vice, he exclaimed, seemed to be rampant
everywhere.

Seduction! What is it, where does it come from, where will
it end? Ideas are what seduce us, and when all this is over, I
will always remember the young Baltasar Bustos drinking a
toast in the Café de Malcos, bubbling with optimism, seduced
and now seducing us with the vision of a political idyll, the
social contract renewed on the banks of Buenos Aires's muddy,
swampy river. Our friend's fiery spirit made everyone stop
working, even the boys pouring river water into clay jugs to
make it drinkable and the cooks holding half-butchered chickens, capons, and turkeys. Baltasar Bustos drinks to the happiness of the citizens of Argentina, governed by human laws
and not by the divine plan incarnate in the king, and even the
wagons laden with freshly cut barley and hay destined for the
stables stop to listen. He proclaims that man is born free but
is everywhere in chains, and his voice grips this city of creoles,
Spaniards, monks, nuns, convicts, slaves, Indians, blacks, and
soldiers in their orderly ranks . . . Seduced by a miserly Citizen
of Geneva who abandoned his bastards at the door of a church!

Does Baltasar seduce? Or is he seduced by his audience,

real or imagined, in the streets of a city that has barely left the suffocation of summer as it is enveloped by the fogs that blow in from June to September? May is the ideal month to talk, to make oneself heard, to seduce and be seduced in Buenos Aires. We are seduced by the idea of being young, of being Argentine *porteños* with cosmopolitan ideas and books. But this isn't all that seduces us; we are also seduced by a new idea of faith in the nation, its geography, its history. The three of us are seduced by the fact that we aren't Spaniards who get rich on smuggling and run back to Spain; we are seduced by not being like the rich, who hoard grain to push up the price of bread.

I really don't know if we seduce one another. I am thin and dark, with a big upper lip I cover with a black mustache, whose bristles are so wiry they seem aggressive even to me, as if they were attacking my face pitilessly. I defend myself from this hairy assault by shaving my cheeks three times a day, using the mirror to contemplate the inflamed fury in my almost light (they really aren't) eyes set in all that blackness. I try to compensate for my savage appearance with calm gestures and an almost ecclesiastical composure. Xavier Dorrego, by comparison, is ugly, a redhead, his hair cropped close to his skull, almost shaved, which makes him look like something he isn't: a manhunter, a usurer, the kind of man who keeps strict accounts. The beauty of his skin, which is translucent and opaline, like an egg illuminated from within by an eternal flame, makes up for the rest.

And Baltasar . . .

The clocks in the plazas ring out on these May days, and the three of us confess how fascinated we are by clocks. We admire them, collect them, and feel thus that we own time, or at least the mystery of time, which is to imagine it running backward or speeding us to our meeting with the future, until we reject that idea and define all time as the present: the past that we not only remember but that we imagine, as much as we imagine the future, so that both will have meaning. Where? Only here, today, we tell each other, wordlessly, when we admire the jewels Dorrego is collecting thanks to his father's money: a clock in the shape of a carriage, covered by a glass dome; a ring clock; a snuff-box clock . . . I have my own special treasure, which I inherited from my father, who for some reason never sold it. A Calvary watch: the Cross presides over the entire works, and marks, as a memento mori, the hours of the passion and death of Christ.

"Citizens," exclaims Dorrego when I go into raptures over my religious clock. "Remember that now we are citizens." And that seduced us and bound us together as well: the name of our group is the Citizens.

And Baltasar?

He was educated on his father's estate by one of those Jesuit tutors who, though they were expelled by the king, managed to return in secular clothes to carry out their obsessive mission among us: to teach us that American flora and fauna exist, that there are American mountains and rivers, and, above all, that we have a history that isn't Spanish but Argentine, Chilean, Mexican . . .

Baltasar's father, Don José Antonio Bustos, sided with the Crown against the English invaders and now again against Bonaparte in Spain. Which is how he acquired the influence to get Baltasar, the law student, a job at the Superior Court during the impeachment trials of the discredited viceroys Sobremonte and Liniers. Sobremonte was accused of dereliction of duty and neglect in the defense of the port during the English invasions of 1806 and 1807, when he fled from the British attack, absconded with public funds, and abandoned the defense of Buenos Aires to creole militiamen. Those soldiers eventually repelled the English and gained prestige which grew like a tidal wave that would reach its peak during the revolutionary days of May. The irony of these two trials is that Liniers led the militiamen who defeated the English. But when events rapidly moved toward independence, Liniers lost courage, hesitated, fell out with everyone (except, it was said, his French mistress, Madame Pernichon), and went from being a hero of the defense against the British to being a nullity during the fight for independence.

As he listened to the charges against the former hero, my friend Baltasar, the young legal clerk, imagined himself raised to a glorious position thanks to the new spirit and the speed of events. He wrote all that down in a document he sent to me later, at a certain point in our long and unpredictable friendship. "Since Liniers is being tried in absentia, I have to imagine him sitting here, his wig half powdered, forceful one day, feeble the next. Apparently, all we need is one demurrer to strip the hero of his honors and sentence him. You know, Varela, I imagine a fleeting fire passing through Liniers's eyes. I see it and wonder if we three friends from the Café de Malcos are up to events. I live these days intensely, but I'm afraid we are fated to enjoy an uncertain glory which our hasty spirits will rapidly exhaust. I write our three names. His, Xavier Dorrego. Yours, Manuel Varela. And mine, Baltasar Bustos. I can trace back our names. But I cannot give them a final fate. And thinking of Liniers's fortunes, a hero one day, a traitor the next, I want to avoid such a deviation of destiny. Yet I also ask myself a troubling question. Can we expect anything at all except knowing that we have a destiny yet are unable to master it? Wouldn't this be the saddest destiny imaginable?"

I received these notes from my friend and imagined him carrying out his tasks as clerk in the trials of the viceroys with praiseworthy patience.

What I didn't know is that Baltasar was meticulously rehearsing quite a sequence of actions.

A dry, old, cynical man, the Marquis de Cabra, presided over the sessions in the courtroom. He never even glanced at the clerk Baltasar, but Baltasar took careful note of the president of the court, seeking to read his thoughts, observing his every movement. Above all, as we shall see, Baltasar envied him.

Baltasar continued writing and pretending that he was sorting papers after the day's session was finished. When asked to leave the hall, he apologized, acting very busy, and left by a side door, giving the impression by his gestures that he knew his way around the building better than anyone else. The main doors were locked; he would have to walk down the corridors and exit by a door at the back.

He walked along one of the halls to the noisy rhythm of his gold-buckled, high-heeled shoes, hugging the documents against his cambric shirt and scattering between the tails of his frock coat the crumbs that had accumulated in the lap of his nankeen trousers, the remains of a roll he'd eaten surreptitiously. Instead of leaving the building, he went into the now empty library, hid in the stacks, and waited patiently for the lights to go out. His father had told him a secret: behind the thick volumes containing the works of the church fathers, there was a hidden passage through which the presidents of the Superior Court passed unseen and unhindered into their private chambers.

He waited another half hour, then poked his finger hard against volume 4 of St. Thomas's *Summa Theologica*. Slowly and silently the stack slid open—the hinges, Baltasar noted, as always were perfectly oiled. The passageway led to a patio shaded by peach trees. But a gray, dusty vine allowed an agile man to climb from the patio to the balcony. It was almost as if the ivy invited the young body to come up and celebrate the arrival of May and the departure of the humid, unbearable heat of summer in the Río de la Plata, heat that turns clothing into a clammy, undesirable second skin.

Now, however, a cool breeze with a touch of ice blew off the Plata, as if to quell the ardent spirits of the revolutionary city, itself rejuvenated by the speed at which events were taking place. On the thirteenth of May, an English (always the English!) ship had brought the news: the French occupied Seville; Napoleon held not only political control over Spain but economic control as well. Spain was no more. King Ferdinand VII was no more. What would Spain's New World colonies do? The Argentine viceroyalty had only one strength, the militias forged to repulse the English invasions and replace viceregal ineptitude: Riverside Men, Plainsmen, Patricians—such were the names of the regiments that on the twentieth of May withdrew their support for the viceroy, Hidalgo de Cisneros, saying: "You represent nothing now." And then they rallied around Cornelio de Saavedra, commander in chief of the Patricians, giving him the power to rule. On May 21, Saavedra's ally, a fiery Jacobin orator, Juan José Castelli, appeared in the Plaza Mayor with six hundred hooded, well-armed men the people dubbed "the infernal legion," and forced the viceroy to hold an open meeting at the City Hall, where Baltasar Bustos deliriously applauded Castelli's speech . . .

"His style is dazzling, his demeanor intrepid, his spirit daring," observed our friend that night in the Café de Malcos. "And his message is crystal-clear. There is no more sovereign power in Spain. Thus, sovereignty reverts to the people. To us. Castelli is the creole incarnation of Rousseau!"

"No"—I dared to break in on his enthusiasm. "That idea was invented two hundred years ago by Francisco Suárez, a Jesuit theologian. Look behind every new idea and you'll find an old one, which might even turn out to be Catholic and Spanish—painful as that would be to us."

I smiled as I said it; I didn't want to wound my friend's enlightened sensibility. But that night nothing could diminish his enthusiasm, which was more philosophical than political.

"Saavedra has demanded total power for the Municipal

Council. Castelli demands general elections. What are we going to do?"

"What is it you want?" interjected our third friend, Xavier Dorrego.

"Equality," said Baltasar.

"Without liberty?" Dorrego argued, as was his custom.

"Yes, because we might end up proclaiming liberty without having eliminated the problem of inequality. And if that happens, the revolution will fail. So: equality above all!"

Baltasar Bustos was repeating his own sentence when he stopped, just for an instant, in the center of the patio adjacent to the residential wing of the Palace of the Superior Court, in front of the vine that reached to the balcony outside the rooms of the president and his wife. The door of the service wing opened, and a pair of black hands proffered a living bundle, asleep but breathing and warm.

"I don't understand why you have to make things so complicated, young master," said the voice of the black woman. "It would have been so easy to come in through the service entrance and take . . ." The woman sobbed, and Baltasar, the child in his arms, headed for the vine. What he was going to do wasn't easy for a robust, overweight, not to mention nearsighted man. The ivy may have been an invitation to a young body to come up and celebrate the coolness of May, but the body of this friend of mine, Baltasar, at the age of twenty-four was the product of a sedentary life, febrile reading, a willful isolation from action, a proud disdain for the country life which had been his as a child and which continued to be his father's and sister's out on the pampa. Bustos, in short, had cultivated a physique which to him was at once cosmopolitan, civilized, intellectual, and a rebellion: the antithesis of the barbarous customs of the country, the colony, the Church, and Spain. He admitted ironically that his was not the proper physique for what he was doing: climbing a vine right after midnight with a bundle in his arms. In other words, he saw himself as urban and urbane but hardly romantic.

Barely had he set foot on the first tangle in the vine than he realized that if no one had noticed his earlier explorations of the terrain it was because no one could even imagine something as daring as what he was attempting; no one would examine the vine to see if it had been climbed. Ivy grew all on its own and did not need to be tended or watched over. Lawns had to be cared for, peach trees had to be pruned. But no one inspected the ivy, abandoned to its parched dustiness, to discover exactly what Baltasar Bustos did on the night of May 24, 1810: he climbed up to the balcony of the wife of the President of the Superior Court of Buenos Aires with a black baby in his arms, entered her bedroom, took the white, newly born child of the president and his wife, and in its place put the black infant, also newly arrived in this world, though his realm would be one of kitchens, beatings, and curses.

[2]

The announcement that Ofelia Salamanca, wife of the President of the Superior Court, the Marquis de Cabra, had given birth was forgotten during the disturbances that May in Buenos Aires. When the English ship arrived with the news that Seville had fallen, three centuries of custom, of fidelity to the Spanish Crown, of subservience to commercial plans made in that very Seville and its Indies Trade Office, floated in midair for one astonished instant and then crashed to the ground: if there was no monarchy in Spain, could there be independence in America?

The child was born without grief or glory but to the manifest anguish of Ofelia Salamanca, who reproached her husband for having taken her from the captaincy-general of Chile, where she had her comforts, her mestizo servants, and her Indian midwives, to hand her to these Buenos Aires black servants. And this on top of the voyage from Santiago to the Río de la Plata, which took almost two months!

"And all to try two viceroys already condemned for incompetence and for failing to maintain order," Ofelia Salamanca rebuked her husband.

Leocadio Cabra had acquiesced to his beautiful, independent Chilean wife's wish to retain her maiden name. She explained why:

"First, my dear, because we have to start defending the right of women to their own name; that is, their own person. Second, because if I use your name, people will end up calling me la Cabrona, and I don't want to be known as a son- or even a daughter-of-a-bitch."

"Chilean to the bone!" exclaimed her exasperated husband. "Don't delude yourself: Salamanca is your father's name, not yours, and it was your grandfather's. There's no way you can escape having a man's name, you goose."

"There's never been any Ofelia Salamanca but me," the beautiful Chilean creole proudly pointed out. Baltasar Bustos was seeing her naked for the first time through the vaporous curtains of the bedroom, curtains that were merely the first veil over a universe obscured by successive layers of muslin blindness: the permanent drapes over the canopied bed, as well as the summer mosquito netting the servants had neglected to take away; the translucent cloth over the dressing table where Ofelia Salamanca was sitting, naked, in front of the mirror, offering to the nearsighted but dazzled eyes of Baltasar Bustos a body shaped like an hourglass, a white guitar, her back turned to him but stunning with the round perfection of her firm buttocks, twin fruits below an even firmer and slimmer waist, as if there could coexist in a single human being not that many but such unique perfections: a slender waist, round buttocks soft yet hard, but not as much as the waist, and not one pore that did not exude perfume but also wholeness, perfect harmony, with no flab, buttocks that were carnal twins of the moon. And to think she had given birth just seven weeks before!

She powdered herself without the help of chambermaids, and the powder kept him from seeing her breasts clearly, so

Baltasar Bustos fell in love with her back, her waist, and her buttocks. With her profile as well, since Ofelia Salamanca, as she powdered her breasts, presented only half her face to the ecstatic contemplation of the young *porteño*, the perfect reader of distant ideals. He would have wanted to see a romantic turbulence in her features; but the classical perfection of her clear brow, straight nose, full lips, her oval chin and long, swan-like neck foiled such wishes. It was like seeing Leda in the myth: the rice powder was the swan that enveloped her, possessed her, and veiled her from the eyes of her admirer, turning her into what he most desired: an unattainable ideal, the pure bride of pure desire, untouched.

His impassioned readings of Rousseau mixed with the cold teaching of the church fathers: Baltasar Bustos's intellectual hero was the Citizen of Geneva who asks us to abandon ourselves to our passion so that we can recover our souls, whereas St. John Chrysostom condemns ideal love that is not consummated, because the passions become all the more inflamed.

The saint knew that once we attain our carnal objective, habit will ultimately cool any passion. The distance between the balcony from which Baltasar spied, desired, and entered into conflict with his own feelings and the rotund object of his desire, at that moment covered by a haze of gauze and powder with which she was unfortunately more intimate than she was with him, distant witness of the unattainable beauty of Ofelia the president's wife, only succeeded, it was true, in increasing his passion.

That was the first time he saw her, spying from the balcony, rehearsing the act he would commit for justice's sake.

The second time, she was accompanied by her husband, who paced impatiently around the bedroom, pushing aside gauze veils as she got dressed, again without the help of a maid. Perhaps the subject of their conversation called for privacy: the marquis was complaining because Ofelia wasn't breast-feeding the newborn child, lamenting that his son had been turned over to one of these black Buenos Aires wet nurses.

He missed Chile and its Indians; the Río de la Plata was filled with blacks—almost half the population. I don't want our son to grow up surrounded by blacks, said the old creole, who had reached his present position through his fervent devotion to the Crown. Don't worry, said Ofelia Salamanca, black children don't go to school with white children, not here or anywhere. In Catamarca, not long ago, a mulatto was flogged when people found out he'd learned to read and write.

The marquis, who seemed made of porcelain, said to his wife: "If your reprehensible appetite for novelties and horrors—the same thing, in my opinion—requires stimulation, let me tell you, my dear, that just two months ago, right here in Buenos Aires, a black hetaera sick with the French pox was sentenced for daring to have a child. To cure her of her malady, her profession, and her maternity all at the same time, she was condemned to a public whipping."

"I'm sure that cured her of prostitution and syphilis," said Ofelia Salamanca with cold simplicity, as she finished dressing, much closer this second time to the eyes of Baltasar Bustos, who used every means to preserve the beatific vision of the first occasion. Seeing them together, he realized that she was the same porcelain color as her husband.

Ofelia Salamanca wore Empire dresses, but she went against fashion by zealously covering her breasts and revealing instead her legs and the curve of her posterior. That wasn't what excited Baltasar Bustos most in this second vision; it was two elements in her toilette. The first was her hair, cut in "guillotine style," shaved to the nape as if to make way for the quick slice of the revolutionary blade. The other was the thin ribbon of red satin tied around her neck like a thread of luxurious blood, as if the guillotine had already done its work.

Ofelia Salamanca said something in a low voice to her husband, and he laughed. "Patience, sweetheart, we'll make love after we stamp out the revolution."

"Well, then, get on with trying your viceroys so we can get back to Chile as soon as possible."

"It's very hard to hold a trial when the entire country wants to kill them. The time is not ripe for justice."

"So, commit an injustice. It wouldn't be the first in your career. And let's get out of here."

"We're comfortable here, and you've just given birth. Do you really want to travel with a two-month-old infant?"

"We could bring the nurse."

"She's black."

"But she's got milk. It's like traveling with a cow. Besides, this building frightens me. I hate living in the same place where you work. You sentence too many people to prison and death."

"I just do my duty."

"And I don't like weak men. I only have two complaints, Leocadio. Your past weighs too heavily on you. And in Santiago at least the court and our residence weren't under the same roof."

"Perhaps a gift would cheer you up, darling."

"Anything but flowers. I hate them. And think what you like about me."

"What would you have me do?" said her husband impatiently. "They brought me here from Chile because I'd be impartial and free of local influences."

"For God's sake, I know that tune only too well. Justice for friends. The law for enemies. You're right. There is a difference. And I'm getting bored."

"Well, what can I get you, if you don't want flowers?"

"Put twenty-five lighted candles around my son's cradle, one for each year of his mother's life. Perhaps that way we can scare the ghosts away."

"As long as you live?"

She said yes. "You really take the long view of things. The older I get, the more afraid I'll be."

"Poor child. And when you die?"

"The candles will all go out at once, Leocadio, and my son will be a man. Look at him."

Baltasar inscribed these conversations on his soul. But on

the third and final visit the child's parents were not there, although the twenty-five candles were around the cradle. They had replaced the black nurse who had handed Baltasar the black baby in the patio.

Bustos, nearsighted and panting, parted the curtains and walked into the bedroom. He moved quickly: he put the black child next to the white one in the cradle. He contemplated them both for a few seconds. Thanks to him, they were fraternal twins in fortune. But only for a moment. He took the white baby and wrapped him in the rags of the poor child; then he swaddled the black one in the gown of high lineage. With the white child in his arms, he returned to the balcony, blind, tripping, just as the child—which one?—began to wail. But the cries were drowned out by the pealing of the bells and the thunder of the guns at midnight, between the twenty-fourth and the twenty-fifth of May 1810.

When Baltasar's feet touched the ground, he shook his full head of honey-colored curls—his best feature, along with his passionately sweet eyes and Roman nose. Unfortunately, the image he projected was that of an overweight, myopic man. How would that splendid woman ever fall in love with him? He, in any case, adored her already, despite what he was doing or, in some obscure sense, because of what he was doing: kidnapping her son, his most fearsome rival, but giving himself over to the passion that claimed him; he sought no explanations, convinced that the passion we don't seize by the tail and follow all the way will never again show us its face, and instead will leave an eternal void in our soul.

Branches scratched him. The child's smock was covered with dust and dead leaves. The black hands reappeared, this time trembling, at the service entrance, and Baltasar Bustos followed them, turned over his burden to them, and said simply: "Here's the other baby. Let him live his own fate."

[3]

Baltasar retraced the secret route he'd taken to mete out what he thought was a most severe form of justice, an act others might consider criminal. He wanted to avoid leaving by the service door this time because he was afraid to know where the black woman had taken Ofelia Salamanca's son. As the black wet nurse had said, he was once again complicating his life. He went back into the library, where he fell asleep, not knowing that throughout the night the debate in the Municipal Council had aligned the high-ranking creole merchants and Spanish administrators against the lawyers, doctors, military men, and philosophers like himself. Even if he hadn't been chosen to represent the general will in the assembly, he had done something better: he'd put revolutionary ideas into practice. He did in real life what had been proclaimed (or declaimed) so often at the tables of the Café de Malcos, which was our meeting place, the scene of the most agitated political and philosophical arguments in early-nineteenth-century Buenos Aires.

It was there the three of us—Baltasar Bustos, Xavier Dorrego, and I, Manuel Varela—savored ideas along with pastries and hot chocolate. We knew we were citizens of a city whose wealth as a port was based on the smuggling of blacks, hides, and iron; the blacks and the hides would, as they used to say, "get lost" en route and reappear on the docks, in the courtyards, mills, and markets; the iron came from France, because we have no industry; there aren't even mines, as there are in Mexico and Peru. All we have is fraud—leather, wool, salted meat, and tallow abound, but they can be marketed only according to quotas set in Madrid, so even exports turn into contraband in Buenos Aires. But no one talks about great fortunes here; it's important to complain and pass ourselves off as the poor relations of America, so we don't reveal the fraudulent basis of our wealth. The Crown prohibits universities in active ports where ideas circulate rapidly, and this absence of an educational system virtually invites us to cheat. So the three of us are self-taught; we all share the same political dream whose name is happiness or progress or popular sovereignty, or laws in accord with human nature.

We argue a lot, either in the heat of events or because of our individual positions. Around us, at the café's marble tables, the main subject is the number of political options open to us after Napoleon's invasion of Spain. There are two parties: one proclaims its loyalty to the Spanish monarchy; the other insists there no longer is a monarchy. The latter talks about de facto independence while hiding behind the "mask of Ferdinand"; that is, past loyalty to Ferdinand VII, who is held under arrest by Bonaparte. Those loyal to the Crown support Carlota, Ferdinand's sister and the daughter of Charles IV, who has taken refuge in Brazil with her husband, John VI of Portugal. She could govern us while her brother is Napoleon's captive.

Bustos, Varela, Dorrego—the three of us are above these political subtleties and dynastic conspiracies. We talk about the ideas that live the long life of the *stoa*, not the ephemeral struggles of the *polis*. Dorrego follows Voltaire; he believes in reason but thinks it should be exercised only by an enlightened minority capable of leading the masses to happiness. Bustos follows Rousseau: he believes in a passion that would lead us to recover natural truth and bind the laws of nature and the revolution together like a sheaf of wheat. They are two faces of the eighteenth century. There is one more: mine, the printer Manuel Varela's. I follow Diderot's smiling mask, the conviction that everything changes constantly and offers us at each moment of existence a repertory from which to choose. The quotient of freedom in this possibility to choose is equal to the quotient of necessity. Compromise is imperative. I smile tenderly as I listen to my dogmatic, impassioned friends. I will be the narrator of these events. Baltasar will need me; there is in him a candid gentleness, a vulnerable passion that requires the hand of a friend. Dorrego, however, is as insistent and dogmatic as his master Voltaire, and nothing inspires more scorn in him than the news that in Mexico and Chile there are priests who share our ideas, start discussion groups, publish revolutionary newspapers. He's adopted Voltaire's anticlerical motto: *Ecrasez l'infâme!*

Which is to say that the Café de Malcos was our university, and in it circulated, now openly instead of in secret, *La Nouvelle Héloïse, The Social Contract, The Spirit of the Laws*, and *Candide*. There all these books were read and meticulously discussed by the young men who were now opposing the Spanish administrators and the Argentine conservatives.

"In the City Hall they talk about the general will of the people!"

"You should have seen the faces on the Spaniards!"

"One even said you'd never hear nonsense like this in a Spanish assembly!"

Baltasar Bustos declared, in opposition to his friends, that the general ideas of Voltaire, Rousseau, and Montesquieu were all well and good, but it was up to each individual to put them into practice in his personal and civic life. It is not enough, he exclaimed, to denounce the general injustice of social relations or even to change the government if personal relationships aren't also changed. Let us begin by revolutionizing our behavior, Bustos suggested; but at the same time we should change the government, suggested Dorrego and Varela.

"Why are laws valid only in one country and not in all countries?"

"You're right. They must be changed. Human law is universal."

"That's what Argentina should do—we should universalize the laws of civilization. We must assume the risks of the human race."

We laughed at him a little, affectionately. Everyone knew that Baltasar Bustos had read all the books of the Enlighten-

ment; we called him the Quixote of Reason, but we didn't
know what to fear most: his eloquent confusion of philosophies
or his foolhardy, quixotic decision to test the validity of his
readings in reality.

"Now, Baltasar, I hope you're not going to . . ."

"Baltasar, act politically, with us . . ."

"With you, I'll never find out if the law can really encompass
all classes and not just one. The three of us are sons of ranchers,
merchants, viceregal functionaries. We risk confusing our freedom with that of everyone else, without being certain that's
the way things really are."

"The government has to be changed!"

"The new government will change the laws!"

"We'll see to it that your ideas become reality!"

"All revolutions begin in the individual conscience. Everything else derives from that."

"So, what are you suggesting, Baltasar?"

While he was putting his plan into action that night in the
bedrooms of the aristocracy, Dorrego and I, Varela, were proclaiming a junta headed by Cornelio Saavedra, hero in the
defeat of the British invasion of 1807, a born military leader,
but in fact a conservative man. According to Bustos, Saavedra
wanted freedom for the creoles but not for the blacks, the
poor, the downtrodden. The other leader of the junta was
Bustos's personal hero, Juan José Castelli, a man of ideas and
an activist as well, who diligently sought to make law and reality
coincide. Biologically speaking, neither was young any longer:
Saavedra was fifty and Castelli forty-six. The young man of
the revolution was Mariano Moreno, beloved by all, indomitable, radical, who at the age of thirty had made the greatest
economic demands possible for the nascent Argentine revolution: free trade was necessary for the well-being of the people
in the Río de la Plata. The young, ardent, fragile Mariano
Moreno inspired love in everyone; we had heard strong and
serious men say, "I am enthralled by Mariano Moreno." His

portrait appeared everywhere, always retouched to eliminate the smallpox scars on his face. But Bustos shared the doubts his father, a landowner on the Pampa, had about Moreno: he was afraid the commercial interests of the port of Buenos Aires that the young economist defended in the name of the nation's well-being would sacrifice the well-being of the interior.

"Who's going to buy products from La Rioja if he can get the same things cheaper from London? Even a poncho, my boy, even a pair of boots: the English (they're crawling out of the woodwork!) can make them cheaper," said Baltasar's father, José Antonio.

Baltasar shook his mane of honey-colored curls and paid no attention to economic or political arguments: it was not, he declared during our nights at the Café de Malcos, the price of ponchos or commercial competition between Spain and England that was the revolution's main problem, but equality and justice. Why aren't there laws valid for all nations and all classes? Why are there laws that take from the people who work and give to people who are idle?

"That"—his eyeglasses steamed over—"is the problem of the revolution."

But now the revolutionary junta presided over by Saavedra, Castelli, Moreno, and Belgrano gave all power to the military and the patriots in the professions. The Spanish functionaries were removed from office; the viceroy and the circuit judges were expelled to—where else?—the Canary Islands. History was moving with incomparable speed, but Baltasar Bustos slept with his head resting on a desk in the library, isolated from the decisive tumult in the streets, satisfied that he'd done his duty.

What he'd dreamed was now a reality. A black child condemned to violence, hunger, and discrimination would sleep from now on in the soft bed of the nobility. Another child, white, destined for idleness and elegance, had lost all his privileges in a flash and would now be brought up amid the violence, hunger, and discrimination suffered by the blacks, whom the creoles called "the damned race."

"Equality is valid for all classes," the young hero declared to us, his friends in the Café de Malcos. "Without equality, there is no freedom: not for trade and not for the individual." Surrounded by the sanctioned volumes approved with the *nihil obstat*, which gave off a peculiar aroma of incense and which became part of his *cauchemar*, Baltasar Bustos, using his arms as a pillow, tried to fall into the sleep of reason. The nightmare of reason reverberated like the bells and cannon shots of the morning of May 25 in Buenos Aires. And if this minor hero of equality could justify, in the name of justice, what he had done, passion, soul, the other side of his Enlightenment conviction told him: "Baltasar Bustos, you have mortally wounded the woman you think you love. You have committed an injustice against the most intimate nature of that woman. Ofelia Salamanca is a mother, and you, a vile kidnapper."

He woke up with a shock because his nightmare took place just as a flood of May light poured in through the building's tall latticed windows. He woke up asking himself why in his dream he had used the French word *cauchemar* instead of *nightmare*. Because it sounded better in French? The glare behind him kept him from answering. He looked at the letters in the title of the book he'd fallen asleep over as if they were flies: from a distance of centuries, St. John Chrysostom condemned unconsummated love because it sinfully exalted desire.

[4]

He thought he'd slept for a long time—the length of a nightmare—but it hadn't even been ten minutes. He had carried out the most audacious act of his life without calculating the full effect of his actions, without anticipating, above all, that the vision of Ofelia Salamanca would captivate him with all the force of the inevitable. He dreamed about her—the sweet part of his dream—the way Tantalus dreamed of the fruit and water that continually eluded his grasp. A tantalizing woman: he desired her, desired not to possess her, so he could go on desiring her, desired not to have done what he had, desired— dreaming all the while—never having to stand before her, saying: "Here is your son, madame. I ask you to love me despite what I've done."

He didn't have time, because he looked, sensibly, at his watch, which resembled him (blind crystal, round body, gilt glitter), and realized that it was only twelve-thirty at night. The glow at his back was, nevertheless, that of daylight. But that was the heat not of May but of February. And the books began to crackle suspiciously. The threatened leaves in the sacred books were reverting, becoming, *tout court*, dead leaves. The creak of the bindings and the shelves was not only a hint of what was to come but also the result of the leaves that really were burning outside: Baltasar Bustos ran, opened the library door, scurried to the hall that led to the patio, and saw his fiery curls reflected in the courtyard in flames. The ivy blazed, the muslin blazed, the bedroom was ablaze. The servants gathered in the patio shrieked. Baltasar Bustos instinctively, cruelly looked for the black wet nurse among them. There she was, just for an instant, lulling a swaddled baby, which he could not see, in her arms. But then she was gone. Baltasar Bustos couldn't decide whether to follow her or to stay where he was, which is what he did, mesmerized by the sight of the fire vomiting out of the balcony of the presiding judge's quarters.

Twenty-five candles blaze, one for each year of the mother's life. The flammable drapes blaze. The cradle blazes. The child is consumed by the flames. Disfigured, burned beyond recognition, the black child seems to be just a child killed in a fire. Even white children turn black when they are burned to death.

[5]

"What will happen here," declared the Marquis de Cabra, the judge appointed by the king to preside over the Superior Court convened to try the two viceroys, Sobremonte and Liniers, "is that instead of enduring the distant authority of Madrid, Argentina will endure the nearby tyranny of the port of Buenos Aires. You," he went on in his after-dinner chat to the illustrious assembly of creole and Spanish merchants from the port, "will have to decide whether to open the gates of commerce or to close them. The Crown had to make that decision about its colonies. If you close those gates, you will protect the producers of wine, sugar, and textiles in the far-off provinces. But you will ruin yourselves here in Buenos Aires. If you open the gates, you will become richer, but the interior will suffer because it will not be able to compete with the English. The interior will want to secede from Buenos Aires, but you need economic as well as political power, so there will be civil war. In the end you will be governed by the military."

"The military? But they're all revolutionaries, allied with that pack of scheming lawyers, doctors, and pamphleteers who've popped up out of nowhere," Don Adolfo Mugica, a grain merchant, indignantly observed.

"The military men won prestige by defeating the English in 1806, and they will derive even more prestige from fighting the Spanish now. Their allies are the Buenos Aires professional class—unimportant people: clerks, poor priests, God knows what," said Don Ricardo Mallea, famous for his donations to convents that expressed their gratitude by hiding his illegal merchandise.

"Let them all defeat Spain, and then they'll have to decide between defeating Buenos Aires—that is, all of you—or defeating the merchants from the interior, who will demand protection from Buenos Aires's port commerce," concluded the president and judge, whose authority was clear to everyone by the deference with which even the viceroys treated him. After all, tómorrow he would be trying the viceroy himself. But on this May night there was no viceroy in Buenos Aires: there was only the judge, Cabra himself. No further proof was needed to determine who was who.

"And what does your lordship advise?"

"You must try to create a new class of landowners out of the manufacturers from the interior and the Buenos Aires merchants."

"What are you saying? The landowners are our enemies, and in any case they're ignorant gauchos, virtually savages," exclaimed Mugica with a *frisson*.

"I would advise you to divide up the public lands," Leocadio Cabra went on elegantly, confidently, "to encourage cattle ranching and grain production. Then you will get rich on export, and the interior will have to submit to you even if it wants to break away. Problems in Tucumán or La Rioja can be put off, but meanwhile they'll have enough to eat and time to get used to the idea. As long as this abundant land produces, gentlemen, everyone can be content . . . You've got to castrate this country with its own abundance," said Cabra, making a sudden, bitter grimace, which, because it was unnecessary, he corrected instantly.

"You are a wise man, your lordship. If only you'd govern us and not that mob we hear outside . . ."

"Rogues."

"Deluded fools."

This meeting showed that, between the disappeared viceroy on the one side and the revolutionary assembly on the other, the Spanish monarchy and its most loyal subjects were standing firm, proudly isolated from the reigning confusion. But that chaos was not slow in entering the salon where, even before English commerce, English manners were establishing themselves in the Río de la Plata.

After dinner, the ladies had withdrawn so the men could

smoke cigars, drink claret, and talk politics. But the cigars hadn't yet been snuffed when the rules were broken: the women fluttered in like sea gulls, resplendent in the fashions of the detested Empire, the daring revelations commonplace in Paris modestly covered up—in great agitation from a shock bordering on grief but fully consonant with the uproar, the cannon blasts and ringing bells of that long night of independence.

"It's on fire, it's on fire!"

The porcelain marquis, stiff and fragile, stood up: "Where is my wife?"

"She's fainted, your lordship."

"The court building is on fire . . ."

"By which you mean, madame, the mob has set it ablaze."

"Meddlers."

"Deluded fools."

"What's that you said, Mister President?"

"Twenty-five candles." He laughed, provoking all manner of scandal. "One for each year . . ."

[6]

Baltasar had to call on us to help him look for the black wet nurse in the tumult of that May night, inquire among the hysterical, weeping servants of the burning palace, run to the less respectable neighborhoods in the port, threaten, ascribe to ourselves nonexistent functions and nonexistent missions to tear like savages though bordellos where men were dancing the fandango with women of uncertain race, or among the multitudes of working-class children, born of free love, who would be brought up with and like animals, without homes or school. For Baltasar Bustos, it was the saddest city in the world that night when all was celebration.

In any case, we did not overlook one half-sunken shack at the edge of the marshes, one whorehouse shaken by its roaring clientele where a wet nurse might give comfort to a worn-out, sick sister who in turn would lull a blond baby. We searched every yard, every corner, every hut along the river.

The café was closed at that hour, on that exceptional day, and the city sad; it was only in the printing shop at the Orphan Asylum that we could rest, drink our foamless hot chocolate, and go on doing what held us together: talk.

Dorrego, the rationalist, had asked Baltasar why the black nurse herself hadn't exchanged the babies in the cradle, since she had direct access to them. It was right after committing the act, when Baltasar had told us, his two intimates, not to make us accomplices—that was not Baltasar's intention—but because we were his confidants in everything he did.

The black baby was the nurse's nephew, that's why—our friend explained—the child of a flogged prostitute impertinent enough to give birth. He was afraid that at the last moment the nurse's hand would tremble and she'd be overcome by emotion. I said I thought that when Baltasar found out about the flogging he'd decided to take justice into his own hands. But my friend said it wasn't that at all, that if things went wrong he didn't want the black wet nurse to be punished, to add injustice to injustice. He wanted to be solely responsible.

"Not anymore, since you've made us party to your crime," said Dorrego, to provoke our friend.

I intervened to calm things down. Baltasar thought the philosophic basis of his acts demanded that he himself commit them. I gave Dorrego a severe look and added seriously that the responsibility of a free man excluded complicity with those who deny freedom.

Dorrego smiled. "Why are you afraid that things will go wrong, Baltasar? Well, just think: they did. Your black baby is dead, burned to death. And your white baby, even if he's to live in misery, is alive and kicking."

Baltasar did not deign to answer. He knew that Dorrego liked to have the last word and that it didn't matter to us; it didn't mean Dorrego was right. Baltasar and I understood each other better than ever in silence. We were very young, and life was going to be an endless series of moral decisions, one after the other.

"One child is dead, the other alive. Long live justice," exclaimed Dorrego, adding rapidly: "The chocolate's cold."

"I'm going home" was all Baltasar Bustos said.

2

The Pampa

"If you find me dead with a candle in my hand, it means I've finally admitted you were right. If you find my hands crossed over my chest, entwined in a scapulary, it means I held fast to my ideas and died condemning yours. Try to win me over."

In Baltasar's mind, these words were sufficient to characterize his father, José Antonio Bustos. He remembered him standing in the midst of corrals, stables, coachhouses, warehouses, workshops, flour mills, and gauchos bidding him farewell. Or solitary in a nightfall that was in itself an imitation of death, sitting on a chair made of hides, four stakes, and a cow's skull. Greeting him.

And this time, would he be there to say, *How are you, son, welcome home, you're always welcome here, Baltasar?*

Or would he say, instead, *Goodbye, Baltasar, I've gone, I'm not here anymore, don't forget me, son?*

It was twenty-four leagues from Buenos Aires to the pampa, and twenty more to Pergamino, where he would leave the stagecoach. News and travelers alike arrived late. From Pergamino to his father's land, on the other side of One-Eyed

Deer, he'd have a good way to go by mule. But now Baltasar Bustos watched the passing of the carts laden with blankets, ostrich plumes, salt, bridles, and fabric on the deeply rutted road that would take him back to his father.

Would he find him dead or alive? Both forebodings took hold of his mind and heart little by little as he made his way to the paternal home. An abrupt, somber, mysterious, abysmal world seemed to close in around him, suggesting either alternative—life, death—news of which a slow or nonexistent mail service (word of mouth often outstripped paper) did not bring very often.

Lulled by the rocking of the stagecoach, Baltasar Bustos tried to find a meaning in the city he was leaving, and saw only an apparent contradiction: Buenos Aires was twice born. It had been founded first by Pedro de Mendoza with the ill-gotten gains he'd derived from the sack of Rome, with his fifteen hundred soldiers lusting for gold, with the women— some disguised as men—who had stowed away with the troops, all of them good at making campfires and keeping watch. But, ultimately, all of them, men and women, were defeated by the nightly Indian raids on their log fort, by the absence of gold and the presence of hunger: they ate the boots they were wearing, and some say they even ate the corpses of the dead. Finally the conquistador without conquest, Mendoza, died of fever, and they tossed his body into the Río de la Plata. The only silver anyone ever saw in that misnamed river was Mendoza's rings as they sank to the bottom.

It wasn't El Dorado. The city was abandoned, burned, leveled. Forty years later, Pedro de Garay founded it a second time. Seriously, Castilian-style, like a chessboard, using the surveyor's cross: it faced the Atlantic and the mud-colored river into which bled the exhausted veins of Potosí, the mountain of silver. It wasn't El Dorado. This was a city dreamed up for gold and won for commerce. A city besieged by the silence of the vast ocean on one side and the silence of this interior ocean, equally vast, on the other. Baltasar Bustos was crossing that interior sea at top speed, lulled by the long, sturdy strides of the horses, dreaming of himself in the middle of this portrait of the horizon which is the pampa, having the sensation of not moving at all. The horizon was ever present. It was eternal. It was also unreachable.

And here he was, in the middle of the pampa, with his baggage in his hands, suddenly surrounded by a herd of wild horses, tens of thousands of them, which populated the plains like a mob spreading over the entire planet, the natural descendants of the horses abandoned by the first, vanquished conquistadors. They bred haphazardly, like the blacks in the port, savagely growing and multiplying, wild, tall, untamed, and he was captive in the midst of these beasts, unable to move, smelling their glittering sweat, the pungent foam on their dewlaps, the acrid urine of thirty or forty thousand masterless horses overrunning the face of the earth, preventing him from moving a single inch, forcing him to abandon his suitcases crammed with volumes of Rousseau, as he implored his patron saint, the Citizen of Geneva, for aid: "I find myself on the earth as if on a strange planet . . ."

He woke with a start; the coach horses were galloping at half speed, imperturbable. The travelers fleeing Buenos Aires were quite perturbed. They were Spanish merchants going out to save what they could in Córdoba, Rosario, and Santa Fé or to take refuge in those bastions against the revolutionary tidal wave they could see coming, stirred up by the oratorical storms of Moreno, Castelli, and Belgrano. The wealthy Spaniards could not imagine a revolution in the traditionalist interior; all evils came over the sea to Buenos Aires—they were ideas. But all goods also entered there—that was commerce. This contradiction drove the conservative merchants mad, as did the contradiction disquieting Baltasar's soul as he left the city, his friends, the revolution, all to return to nature and in nature find "the solitude and meditation" that would enable him to be himself, without obstacles, truly be what nature wanted him to be.

They were racing across the treeless pampa, but whenever they chanced on a solitary ombu, the only thing the passengers could think (and often said) was: "We'll all end up hanging from its branches!"

Baltasar, on the other hand, felt a boundless freedom on the vast plain. His soul and his nature seemed harmonious reflections of each other, mutually attracted like lovers. As Baltasar emerged from the bad dream of the herd of wild horses, that was the sensation he sought and appreciated with greater intensity. He regretted the presence in the coach of the complaining, chattering Spaniards, who kept him from consummating his marriage with the landscape. He let the rumble of the wheels over the stones and ruts of the road to Córdoba deafen him so that the desired communion could take place despite all obstacles, in the unassailable silence of his soul.

What would these men he didn't know who were traveling with him say if he told them what he was thinking?

But instead of irritating them with a sonorous "Welcome to the pampa, you Spanish bastards!" Baltasar began to feel sorry for himself. Having identified himself with that face of infinity which is the great Argentine plain, he would have wanted to achieve his ideal in a flash: the identification of Baltasar Bustos's soul with immortal nature. The reader of Rousseau knew that the soul, reunited with itself after discarding its useless baggage, can finally enjoy the universe and possess the beauty that enters the spirit through the five senses.

Now alone on a mule, on the road to his father's wretched estate, he finally had the opportunity to envision what the noisy presence of the contemptible Spanish bastards had blocked out during the trip from Buenos Aires. Yet the hubbub around him and the dream of the wild herd had allowed him a communion more certain, though thwarted, than had this solitude on muleback in which the pampa, its creeks, its peach trees, its leagues and leagues of hard lime soil inhabited only by maddened ostriches seemed to him so many bleak, opposing accidents. The pampa was no longer the mirror of God on earth. Now, instead of the much desired communion, all he saw on the horizon were problems, contradictions, untenable options, all crowding his overly receptive spirit.

He left Buenos Aires carrying little baggage. A wicker suitcase, an umbrella, and three or four of his favorite books: *La Nouvelle Héloïse, The Social Contract, The Confessions, The Reveries of the Solitary Walker*. The kidnapped child was not in his luggage. The wet nurse had disappeared along with her sister, the flogged mother of the black baby. He'd searched for her with his two friends, but their attempts had all failed. The two women had carried out their promise to Baltasar Bustos: the child of the Marquise de Cabra would live the life of the son of a sick, publicly flogged black prostitute. Justice, for Baltasar, would thus be carried out. In the suffering of the white child's mother? The banks of the road darkened when he tried to justify his action (to himself, not to win sophistic arguments with his polemical friends: alone on a mule, with an umbrella, a wicker suitcase, and books by the Citizen of Geneva—with no one to speak to except nature, with which he sought to become one, freely and joyously). The goal of justice is not universal happiness. The person punished suffers so that the person rewarded may rejoice. That's the norm. But it was a penal norm, worthy of the celebrated Italian Beccaria, not of the totally free Genevan, Rousseau. And the norm was even less sure in its application to the sufferer, in this case a woman for whom Baltasar Bustos—alone, twenty-four years of age, riding a mule—felt a passion that daily grew more unbridled.

Didn't the woman Ofelia Salamanca deserve a more immediate devotion and selflessness than that called for by the ideas of Baltasar Bustos (and Jean-Jacques Rousseau) on Nature and Justice? The shadows of the banks pierced his soul when he replied to himself that this was true. He would never find nature or justice except through a real person, a beloved person moreover, especially if, as it became clearer with every moment in his memory and his desire, that person was Ofelia Salamanca. Yet he couldn't see himself tearing the child away from the nurse and her sister to return it to the Marquise de Cabra, especially since the black baby was dead. There was nothing to give them in return for the plea: It was all a mistake. Things will once more be as they were before. Forgive me.

He didn't find them. But they would have spit his words in his face: nothing can ever be as it was. We slaves are more slaves than we were yesterday, poorer, more humiliated. The masters are more arrogant, crueler, more insensitive. They deserve this pain you've inflicted. The child stays with us. It doesn't matter that the other child is dead. Blessed be his fate: he's in heaven. Now this son of an expensive whore will live the life of the son of a cheap whore.

What could the wretched Baltasar say to that?

But I'm in love with Ofelia Salamanca.

He heard the laughter of the black women between two screeches of a screamer bird. He heard the laughter of his two friends, Dorrego and me, Varela, seeping out of his wicker suitcase. Even the mule stopped and brayed, laughing at him with its huge teeth as white as new corn. The Devil, goes the gaucho saying, dwells in cornfields.

[2]

This time, José Antonio Bustos was waiting for him at the entrance to the estate. Baltasar was grateful and relieved. What did it matter, in the end, if his father waited for him dead with or without a candle, with or without a rosary. He had bade him goodbye sitting on that throne of death the gauchos prefer for conversation, drinking maté, and warding off grief. But his father was waiting for him like this, on foot, amid workshops,

warehouses, horses, gauchos, chickens . . . As long as he had
come to stay.

"How did you know I was coming?" the traveler would have
wanted to ask his father.

José Antonio Bustos's eyes, somber and hollow, set in flesh
which was once pink but which ranch work and the pampa
sun had turned to leather, precluded such a question. It would
have been redundant. José Antonio Bustos *just knew*. The son
felt ridiculous sitting on the mule, out of joint beside the proud
elegance of the father. The young man was the object of mock-
ing glances from the tough, sinewy gauchos with hungry faces
who watched him as he arrived.

He dismounted and led the mule to the grand gate that
separated the road and the outside from the inner world, the
property of José Antonio Bustos and his children. The house
was constructed like a fort: it was surrounded by a moat to
thwart Indian attack and had a watchtower at its center. The
watchtower was the only high place, and it looked out over a
vast, indifferent, dangerous world. The gallery was at once the
warm and cool apex of the austere compound. There Baltasar
had spent the long afternoons of his childhood (when he had
a childhood), but now José Antonio preferred to take his strolls
at the back, around the well, near the windows of the house.
From there he could contemplate a small clover lawn. The old
man was remembering. Keeping watch. Baltasar walked toward his father.

José Antonio took one step beyond his property and his
legs failed him. His knees buckled, and he clutched a post as
the gauchos watched him without any change of expression.
Baltasar ran to his father to help him. The mule shied and
headed for the road. A gaucho halted it, laughing to himself.
They were all laughing at him, Baltasar realized, and at his
father, the man they said they loved and respected. Baltasar
had fled from this savagery when he was seventeen, to study
in Buenos Aires, to become a man of his times, to save himself

from this gaucho savagery—it seemed appropriate that the word *gaucho* resembled *gaucherie*, the French for error and clumsiness.

"See? Death starts in your legs," José Antonio said with a smile as leathery as his skin, as he leaned his weight on his son.

"You come with me, Papa," said Baltasar. Then he ordered the gauchos: "Bring my bags to the house."

He liked to give them orders and feel their humiliation. His father rebuked him mildly for it. Charity begins at home. If you want to be just, begin with those who serve you. But Baltasar saw the gauchos as a Mongolian horde. Each one was Genghis Khan, with his own personal history of violence, superstition, and stupidity, the kind Voltaire had condemned for all time. Baltasar simply could not conceive of a future with gauchos in it. They spoiled his idyllic vision of nature. They had no compunctions whatsoever about slaughtering a steer, lassoing a horse, or murdering a fellow human being. They were the agents of an unproductive holocaust which left the countryside littered with corpses. And they offended Baltasar's sensibility even more because they were nomads who would never take root anywhere, mobile negations of the sedentary life he identified with civilization.

What about nature, then? For Baltasar, nature, provisionally, consisted of his episodic visits home. A salutary return to his origins. A spur to move forward toward a happy future, free, prosperous, and without superstition. Only thus would nature be saved from those who exploited her: Spanish bastards or brutish gauchos.

That was the subject of the prodigal son's conversation at the dinner table on his father's estate. The two men alone, so different physically, come together to have supper by candle-light, which flashed in Baltasar's dim eyes with the memory of the twenty-five candles around the cradle of Ofelia Salamanca's newborn. A memory; also a foreboding. That of the single candle in the dead hand of his father, who would be saying to him from eternity: "Son, you were right."

At table in the paternal house, it was not that way. No one was right. Baltasar was young, impulsive, convinced, and dazzled by the ideas he'd so recently encountered. The father was like his physical posture: sitting on a cow's skull but animated and vital in his opinions; standing at the entrance to his estate, at the frontier between what was his and what belonged to everyone, standing straight but already vanquished by death, which came to him through the earth and which started in his legs.

"I hope that's how it works and that it takes its time in reaching my heart and mind. I still want to see what's going to happen. I want to see if you're right, son."

Baltasar imagined his father as a man on the threshold between life and death and also between reason and unreason, between independence and colonialism, between revolution and counterrevolution. He asked himself sometimes whether he would have preferred a brotherly father, a correligionary, to share his ideas and enthusiasms. He simply did not know the answer. Finally, he accepted this father of his, transformed by the sun, stripped over time of his European complexion to become what he was: the patriarch of a savage band of gauchos, and the impresario of a budding industry. A threatened industry. Perhaps this style of coexistence with opposites gave José Antonio Bustos his austere, just tone and his Solomon-like sympathy. He was a benevolent judge in a land and time that cried out for tolerance. And if Baltasar was demanding justice in the cities and was capable of implementing it as he did on the night of May 24 in Buenos Aires, what could he say to his father, landowner and judge in the barbarous territories of the interior? If the son had to be implacable in the city, the father, perhaps, had to be flexible in the country. It was the difference between the porcelain skin of the Marquis de Cabra and his wife and the leathery, tanned hide of José Antonio Bustos.

Plump, myopic, and with bronze-colored curls, Baltasar Bustos, looking at his reflection in the gilt-framed pier glass that lugubriously extended the dining room, saw himself as a hybrid between the two, formless and, barely outside the city, in need of the help of others to survive. He needed the mule because the post coach did not stop here. He needed the gauchos if only to order them to bring his bags to the house. He needed the servants because he did not know how to make his own bed, sew on a button, or press a coat; he needed the cook because he did not even know how to fry an egg. He needed his father to attack his ideas, not as an enemy, but as an affectionate, Socratic interlocutor. But, frankly, he did not know if he needed his sister, Sabina, whose presence would be ghostly if it weren't so obstinately real.

Sabina resembled her father. Except that what in him was austere nobility was pained severity in her. Sour, Baltasar wanted to say when he hated her (which was quite often, especially when they were together); vinegary, premature old maid, born an old maid, a frustrated nun . . . But his sense of justice made him rectify that opinion (especially when he was far from her, in Buenos Aires) and tell himself that, trapped as she was out in the country, a woman alone in a houseful of men, condemned to live among savage gauchos, her character could not be other than what it was.

She would not sit at table with the men. No one stopped her, only she herself. And she insisted on serving them. Thus, she was both present and absent at the meals of the father and the son. Sometimes Baltasar paid no attention to her; other times, Sabina's presence determined the tenor of his arguments. He knew what she was going to say, standing there with the platter of roast meat trembling in her hands, holding the serving tongs with a coarse napkin decorated in a red checkerboard pattern:

"We've got no protection. You and your ideas have left us at the mercy of the elements. We used to have a refuge, being a colony. We used to have protection—the Crown. We used to have redemption—the Church. You and your ideas have left us at the mercy of the four winds. Just take a good look, brother. What harm your side is doing to ours!"

These things, said between servings, did not help Baltasar Bustos's digestion. In vain he searched in his sister's severity for his father's equanimity. Yet Sabina and Baltasar were both the product of the drive for equilibrium that characterized José Antonio Bustos.

Attentive to everything that went on, blessed with an extraordinary sixth sense for finding things out, some by induction, others by deduction, José Antonio Bustos could make use of even the most insignificant piece of information that came his way from reading a newspaper (rarely), from letters (occasionally), or through remarks, gossip, or anecdotes (for the most part), at times even from gaucho songs, to tie loose ends, remember or come to some conclusion—to anticipate and take action. The basis of his knowledge was the wandering network of gauchos he protected as they roamed the pampa. They told him more than anyone. When he was young, as soon as he discovered the idea of the age, he applied it to the economic reality of country life in several ways. On his own property, he established a small textile and metal industry; at the same time, he expanded his holdings in case of a boom in cattle ranching. He prepared himself to endure or enjoy the opening or closing of trade with the outside world. He looked to Buenos Aires as a market for his goods, but he feared the foreign competition that would make them too expensive.

He remained open to commerce with Upper Peru, the source of the metals necessary for the workshop where he made spurs, carts, axles, and keys. And he married a young Basque woman, a child of the so-called second conquest that in or around 1770 multiplied the number of Spanish merchants in the port of Buenos Aires, merchants spurred on by Bourbon reforms in favor of free trade. The arrival on the pampa of the young, golden-haired, somewhat plump, and decidedly myopic María Teresa Echegaray—Mayté—did not transform the social life of the distant province. It was the province that absorbed her. A homebody but vain, Mistress Mayté refused to use spectacles. She had to look for everything—an egg, a ball of yarn, a cat, a needle, her slippers—by bending down to peer at close range, and that posture eventually became natural to her.

Bent over and blind, José Antonio Bustos's wife stopped talking with her fellow humans, all of whom stood up straight in the distance, and instead sustained long monologues with ants on her practical days, and on dream days she chatted with the spiders that approached, swinging before her eyes, teasing her, making her laugh with their silvery ups and downs, forcing her to imagine, invent, wishing sometimes she were entwined in those viscous, moist threads until she was caught in the center of a net as seamless as the fabric in her husband's shops that went to make ponchos, shirts, and other gaucho clothing.

The ants, on the other hand, brought out her diligent, practical side, and that was when she and Sabina would become suspicious and check over the supplies stored in the cupboards and calculate the level of thievery among the maids, associating everything with the collapse of authority, the degeneration of customs, the lack of respect for the Church, and, finally, the dissolution of colonial authority. Napoleon in Spain, the English in Buenos Aires, and the terrible consequences: King Ferdinand dethroned, the English defeated not by the viceroy but by the local Argentine militia (gauchos, no doubt). All this news finished off the ant in Mistress Mayté, and not even the spiders in her were able to compensate for so much horror. Actually, the spiders betrayed her, and in her dreams she saw a world without Church or king, a world adrift. She would curse herself for having abandoned Spain, but then she would remember that Spain was in the hands of Napoleon and his drunken brother "Joe Bottle," and her heart would sink.

It sank permanently one hot afternoon in the summer of 1808, and Sabina inherited all her mother's certitudes and agonies. Except that the daughter, stronger, standing upright, alien to ants and spiders, turned them into dogma and battles.

"She feels unprotected," José Antonio reiterated, "but she doesn't know how to express her ideas in complex terms. She talks about Spain, the Church, and the king as if they were the roof of the house. Her fear goes deeper. We are leaving a traditional empire, one that is absolutist and Catholic, for a rationalist, scientific, liberal, and perhaps Protestant freedom. You should try to understand our fears. She's right. It is like being left to the mercy of the elements."

Baltasar regretted that, instead of accepting tradition, he had brought revolution to the house (unprotected, from now on without a roof). He would have wanted, though, to ask his father: Can one exist without the other? Can there be tradition without revolution? Doesn't tradition die if it isn't renewed and shaken? He wasn't able to formulate something he barely intuited, because Sabina was already there, precipitating everything, presenting him with the final option: Are you loyal to your family or loyal to your revolution? His sister, a dividing force, offered herself as the representative of "what will keep us together." Baltasar was left in the position of the one who divides. Their father did not seem displeased with the role that fell to him: that of arbiter between brother and sister.

"You taught me all I know."

He managed to say that much to his father; the intention was affectionate, but mixed with the affection was some fine malice. José Antonio Bustos trembled as he listened. His son had had a Jesuit education. Julián Ríos, an aged member of the Society who had discarded his habit and returned to Argentina, where he'd been born, was the young Baltasar's mentor. The Jesuits, expelled from Spain and her colonies in 1767, left an immense void behind them. People protested the expulsion, demonstrated in the streets, wept . . . And the Jesuits of the Americas had their revenge on Spain. They sailed to the coast of Italy and asked the Pope for asylum. The pontiff, fearful of offending the Bourbons, at first forbade them to disembark. The holy brothers remained on board for weeks, at the mercy of waves and tides, seasick, unable to sleep, unable to believe what was happening to them.

In the end, the Pope accepted some good advice. Kings might well scorn the intelligence of the Jesuits, but the Pope could take advantage of it. Often it happens the other way around; now let Rome open her arms to what Madrid and Lisbon have rejected. It was said that the ex-Jesuit Julián Ríos returned to Argentina without his priestly vestments the better to fool the colonial authorities. Like all New World Jesuits, he taught national history, national geography, the flora and fauna (and the form and fame) of the nascent nations, from New Spain to Chile, from the Río de la Plata to New Granada.

And, besides giving his pupils a national awareness, Don Julián, the defrocked, also gave them books banned by the Church and the authorities: *The Spirit of the Laws, The Social Contract*, Diderot's *The Nun*, Voltaire's *Candide* . . . That was Baltasar's education, but not his sister's. She was left to the distracted instruction of her mother and the affectionate virtue of her father. But she was stubborn; she envied her brother; she read more than would be expected of one imprisoned at home. In contrast to her brother, she read breviaries, Catholic pamphlets, sermons . . . On her own she created a counterculture the better to challenge her younger brother.

He wanted to see her a different way, prettier, tenderer, better. He wanted to be generous. She would not allow it:

"Decide: are you loyal to your family or to your revolution?"

She ceased to be the swan he wanted to find; she became once again the ugly duckling she would always be, thus giving her father the opportunity yet again to be generous and evenhanded.

"Your sister means that there may be options less brutal than this one we are living through. Try to understand her."

[3]

Baltasar walked out into the open country to think what those options might be and how he might undo what had already occurred. He accepted the fact that history, the conglomeration of ideas, facts, and desires which he fought for or against, came to be only in the company of others, in something shared with others. It irritated him that he so often felt that the *we*, the *others*, were the *excess*, the *superfluous*. But then his reading of Jean-Jacques would come to his rescue (the same way the romances of chivalry served as models for Don Quixote, said his friends, Dorrego and I, Varela, laughing), to tell him that feeling uneasy in society, or seeing society as an excretion, an excess, was not a sin but a virtue. It showed that society was in a bad way.

Here on the pampa, he looked into the distance, toward Mendoza and the mountains: the great range seemed South America's sleeping beast, a lion-panther with a vast white back and black belly, lying in wait for its ferocious chance. He accepted the fact that, though he was born here, he was returning not to stay but to rest; from this spot he would move toward those mountains, where, perhaps, history could be made so that nature and society might once again be united.

I will be free in society only when I no longer need society because I myself have transformed it.

Unfortunately, he was tied to his society. He was not its master; he was mastered by it. He had thrown himself into the Argentine revolution and carried out a daring, highly personal act of justice, as vital for him as writing a manifesto was for Mariano Moreno or dethroning a viceroy for Cornelio de Saavedra. Baltasar Bustos had traded the destinies of two children. But he wasn't fooling himself. He had only substituted one injustice for another. His most radical act, followed by his most private crisis of conscience, spoke to him thus. So, after having dinner with his father, served by his sister, he invoked the imperfect loneliness of the Argentine countryside, itself a prologue to the mountains and their pure solitude. He imagined the Andes an echo chamber for his soul, liberated and reconciled with the natural order.

Then things began to happen.

The first was the vision of Ofelia Salamanca pursuing him. The woman desired interposed herself between him and nature, occupying all physical space. She was an enchanting chimera. She always sat with her back to him, but in his vision tonight she was no longer seated but standing, a white flame, total, shimmering, bending over little by little, spreading her legs slowly to reveal, from the rear, the most irresistible vision of her sex, womankind's genital catholicism, which is adored, imagined, and penetrated from all angles. The mountains were impenetrable: the vision of Ofelia Salamanca, naked and offering herself from the rear, wasn't. It invited, invited . . . And then the woman whirled around and gave him, not her dreamed-of sex, but her feared face: she was a Gorgon, accusing him with eyes as white as marble, transforming him into the stone of injustice, hating him . . .

When Baltasar Bustos turned away from that vision floating between his eyes and the mountains, he felt for the first time a warning from his own soul: *Ofelia Salamanca knows everything. She hates you and has sworn vengeance.*

Besides, he found himself staring into eyes as wild as those of his would-be lover. There were other Medusas in the world: these gauchos who had gathered around him in the darkness, when all he wanted was to be alone with nature and the image of Ofelia. Their presence confused and bewildered him and set him up not against the mountains or the night or his desire for a woman but against other men. What were they doing? They offered him a light, but he wasn't smoking. He wished he were offering them the flame of a match like the one Xavier

Dorrego elegantly carried inside a watch during their sessions at the Café de Malcos. But his hallucinated imagination only took from the sky a candle like the twenty-five around the cradle of Ofelia Salamanca's kidnapped child. It was doubtless because of this series of hallucinations that Baltasar Bustos offered the gauchos an imaginary light, taken from the night and protected from the mild mountain wind by the cupped hands of the master's son, as if a flame were really burning there.

The gauchos did not laugh.

"Don't make fun of us, young master."

"Don't call me that. I'm just a citizen."

Now they did laugh, and as they laughed, Baltasar smelled in their collective breath a ravenous stench, like that of young stray dogs. There were bits of food in those bushy black or copper-colored beards that began at the neck and climbed almost to the eyebrows—an extension of the hair covering ears and cheeks, leaving open only the mouths, which were like wounds of a paradoxical abundance. Red and as bloodied as the meat they ate, they revealed the hardness of an uncertain country where the people eat everything they have, never just what they want. Today there's more than enough, but tomorrow we may have nothing.

He felt a profound compassion for his homeland. But one of the gauchos kept him from extending that compassion to these men. The young gaucho, who knows with what intention, took him by the hand Baltasar had used to shield the imaginary light. The young citizen tried to pull himself out of his daydream, plant his feet on the rough earth and the roughness of the customs of this world. What was he surprised at? It was all familiar to him. He belonged to this land of dust as much as he did to the land of ideas that was Father Julián Ríos's or the land of smoke of the gatherings at the Café de Malcos. He raised his eyes and found neither the mountains nor the Medusa, neither nature nor that forbidden sex. What he found was a mirror. The young gaucho holding him by the hand looked like Baltasar. A filthy, bearded, hungry Baltasar, even though sated today with the flesh of a dead steer. His round face, distant gaze, his hair with its curls burnished by the same elements that frightened his sister, Sabina.

Baltasar stared at that atrocious twin and had the presence of mind to return the squeeze, take the gaucho's wrist, wrench back the man's sleeve, and reveal the cruel wounds on his forearm. Baltasar's country education, rejected and savage, came back to him, and he felt disgust at having allowed himself to be overwhelmed by his detested origins—especially because it was rural wisdom that would save the civilized presence.

The young gaucho, so like Baltasar, emitted a suffocated grunt, wrenched back his arm, and covered it with his sleeve. First the others looked at the young gaucho with scorn, then with pity; and they bestowed the same sentiments on Baltasar Bustos, but in reverse. First pity, then scorn. He knew what he was doing. He had showed the other gauchos that this one, who dared touch him, was, if not a coward, at least an incompetent who let himself be cut easily in fights on the ranch or at the general store. Did his companions already know that, keeping what they knew to themselves, insulted because an outsider, which José Antonio Bustos's son was by now, had come back to tell them: I know that this man has no talent for knife fighting? He's a fool of a gaucho, the boss's son had just said to the other gauchos. He doesn't know how to protect himself. Didn't you blockheads know that? What kind of joke is this?

José Antonio Bustos appeared at the door of the house, wrapped in his yellow poncho. Who can know how much a gaucho knows. Who can know if they really were comrades. They were all tramps. Perhaps they'd just met a few hours earlier; a few hours later, they'd separate, scattered in the immensity of the pampa. Baltasar Bustos had united them in support of the young gaucho whose ineptness he'd just shown, whom he'd just humiliated, because now the man's secret did not belong just to the gauchos. Perhaps it would end up being sung by a bard, maligning the stupid young man with the round face and the coppery curls. Could he also be a bit blind without knowing it? In the country there are no optometrists. They couldn't resemble each other so much, Baltasar and the nameless gaucho: a pure, dissembled wound.

The erect presence of the old man in the yellow poncho prevented any sequel to what had happened. The gauchos drifted away muttering and grumbling. They'd meet another day. Baltasar looked at his father and was amazed that the mere presence of the old man could dominate at a distance, dispersing these country toughs, even if they went reluctantly. Could what they said in Buenos Aires be true? *The ranchers from the interior are as ignorant as their gauchos. Inferior people, second-class creoles. Can't compare with the urbane city merchants.* He looked at his father from a distance. José Antonio Bustos was not like that. And it was not just that Baltasar was his son and loved him as he was. José Antonio Bustos was not like that. But his authority, demonstrated just then, reminding the gauchos that he was always watching, that he was the father, that he was the only authority, could that be more than a symbol of power in a land that ignored the laws of the distant cities, a land that let itself be governed by a patriarchal figure? He looked at his approaching father as someone he'd never understood before. A patriarch stronger than the laws of today and tomorrow. Baltasar didn't know if all the liberal constitutions in the world could be stronger than a simple patriarchal presence.

"Don't come out at night. It's too cold. You might get sick," Baltasar said affectionately to José Antonio, using the familiar form of "you," forgetting for a moment to treat his father with the usual deference: the old man was so full of dignity, so strong, and at the same time so vulnerable, at the mercy of the elements, as Sabina had said, that at that moment his father was in fact his son. Which is what he wrote to Dorrego in Buenos Aires.

José Antonio Bustos overlooked his son's lack of respect. He attributed it to what he'd just seen. The unprecedented physical contact, between his son's hands and the gauchos'. He did not want to admit that old age turns parents back into children.

"Don't worry. When the doctors say I'm sick, I just make believe, to be polite. If I don't, they get discouraged and go back to being, I don't know, to being gauchos." The old man laughed to himself. "You've got to respect people's titles. It costs them a lot to get them. Anyway, we lead a healthy life around here. We don't need doctors, people live a long time, and the only things that kill the young ones are knife fights and falling off horses."

"It's good to see you looking so well, papa," said Baltasar, reverting to the proper respectful tone.

"All I've got left are the small pleasures of old age. Like walking out to see the stars. Nights here are so beautiful. When I was a child I counted the stars, I couldn't understand that they were uncountable. Then, when I was a little older, I went on to count the nights when there was a moon, until I found out it was in the almanac. So what are we left with? Who knows."

"You aren't the way people in Buenos Aires say ranchers are," Baltasar said awkwardly. He felt as inept as the gaucho with the wounded arm.

"Savage rancher? Barbarous creole? No. I think I've had a few ideas. I don't want to lose my faith altogether. How good it is that you keep yours strong."

The son took the father's wrist, the way he had taken the gaucho's a moment earlier. "You've kept your senses, papa, along with your faith."

Now José Antonio laughed openly. "Five of them left me a while ago. The sixth stayed, but it's pure memory."

"Then let me add a seventh, which is your intelligence."

The father was silent for a moment and then said that old age offers small pleasures; not everything is lost. Arm in arm, they walked into the house.

Sabina seemed to be waiting for her brother after he left the old man asleep in his bedroom. He was surprised; he tried to see the beauty in her ugliness; he hadn't given up on that score.

"Hasn't he asked you yet?"

"What?"

"Whether you want to be a merchant or a rancher. The poor man has his illusions. Didn't he mention the small pleasures of his old age?"

"Yes."

"That's to set the scene. He wants you to choose."

"I can't."

"Of course you can. This damned revolution will be your career."

"And what about you?" asked Baltasar, furious, seeing her uglier than ever.

"You know the answer to that, too. Don't play the fool. While you go to your revolution, I stay here taking care of the old man. If I don't, who will? Someone has to."

Baltasar felt the reproach. Sabina's eyes that night were filled with a burning desire.

"How I'd like to go off somewhere far away, too."

Afterward, a pause during which the two of them looked at each other like strangers. To see if they could love each other only that way: "How I wish I could be like Mother—all she knew was how to make sweets. She who spent more on candles for the church than on food for the children. How she worried about which things she was going to leave us, how many cups, tea sets, or sterling-silver platters. And not only us. She thought about the generations to come. And at the same time, how sure she was that, once she was buried here, underneath the ombu, she would come back to see what had happened to the pot of honey, the biscuit, the silver teaspoon."

"Why don't you leave, then?" Baltasar asked her, understanding the comparison she was making between their lives, as well as the fear that lurked behind his sister's words.

"Our father doesn't say it, but he'd rather give me to some creole as a mistress than see me married to a half-breed. The problem is that in all this immensity there are no creoles."

She looked at him with disdain and a bitter coquettishness, unconsciously rubbing her thigh.

[4]

"If my friends could just see me stuck here on this ranch, they'd be happy for me and pity me at the same time," said the old man with humor, perhaps recalling the days when he was politically active in Buenos Aires, when he felt it was necessary to defend the Spanish Crown against the English. Not even the viceroy's ineptitude could make him change his mind; the creole regiments were defending the same thing the viceroy defended.

"I fought against English Protestants, not Spanish Catholics. That would have been like fighting against ourselves."

During his stay, Baltasar tried to observe and understand his father's life. A life he did not want for himself: feudal, isolated, without recognized laws, and with no authority other than that which the patriarch managed to win for himself. Unlike other landowners, José Antonio Bustos was too elegant a man to resort to theatrics and demand his patriarchal rights. He exercised them discreetly, with an admirable sense of personal honor, and, as a result, his chaotic world took note and even obeyed him. It wasn't easy, he said one day to Baltasar, not to brag but to teach his son, it wasn't easy to gain the respect of men whose livelihood was smoking beef, of roving town criers and horse drovers, judges and royal attorneys,

scribes and court clerks, horse dealers and common criminals
. . . For each one, he said, one had to have a good word, a bit
of pity, and some reason to be feared. Without the patriarch,
José Antonio Bustos suggested, they'd all devour each other.
And not out of hunger, but out of satedness. That was the
enigma of this land as well as its paradox.

"Is there anything this country doesn't produce?" said José
Antonio. "A man can get a return of more than twenty times
the value of his labor here. There are no forests to clear, as
there are in North America. You can plant twice a year. The
same field yields wheat for ten years without being exhausted.
The only thing you have to be careful of is planting too much
in one spot. If you do, the harvest will be overly abundant.
And the cattle graze on their own."

The father paused with a smile and asked his son: "Aren't
you worried about a country like this?"

"On the contrary. You confirm all my optimism."

"I'd be more cautious. A country where all you have to do
is spit for the land to produce may turn out to be weak, sleepy,
arrogant, self-satisfied, uncritical . . ."

What Baltasar feared was that his father, the patriarch, a
power so discreet and at times so ironic, would have to make
a show of strength in a dramatic, forceful, theatrical fashion
to regain his authority.

The opportunity came that winter, when the news was
spread by two scouts on horseback, from the country to the
general store, to the workshops and the fort, that the cimarrons
were back. Baltasar remembered his dream on the stagecoach.
He knew that a herd of wild horses could surround a man for
days, not letting him pass, or drag along post-horses, endan-
gering the lives of passengers and drivers. This was worse, José
Antonio said. What? Come see tonight.

The old man gathered a small army of his best, his fiercest
gauchos. He rounded up his men, ordered them to bring in
the scattered cattle, tie the animals to the fence, and then have

a squad of gauchos collect the old, useless horses. They were to slaughter the nags by the ravine just beyond the front of the ranch, so the cimarrons couldn't miss the scent of the fresh blood.

José Antonio Bustos himself, mounted on his best horse, rode out. He ordered Baltasar to ride a barely broken stallion so the gauchos would look on him with respect. The troop of gauchos followed them on their own fast horses, half with lances ready, the other half with torches, all headed for the hollow where the *caranchos*, the vultures of the pampa, were already circling the spot where the old horses had been slaughtered. José Antonio ordered the place to be surrounded as cautiously as possible and then had the men attack without mercy the pack of wild dogs devouring the fresh, bloodied meat. The dogs, startled and barking, blinded by the torches, their muzzles and eyes red, couldn't recognize a master but would attack with the same ferocity with which their terrorizing packs pursued the herds. Lanced and then clubbed to death, their bodies were tossed on top of the dead horses until there wasn't a square foot in the hollow unsullied by blood or death.

"Didn't I tell you?" José Antonio looked at his son. "There's too much abundance here. Meat is just left to rot on the pampa. The dogs run off because they eat better in the wild. In two years they regress two centuries. They're a plague. This hadn't happened for a long time here. Then they started coming closer to towns. They have lost any fear they may have had, so we have to teach them a lesson."

He ordered everyone to move on to the nearest caves.

There, José Antonio Bustos and his men found the dog cemetery packed with bones that glinted in the night. Cow and mule bones, but also the bones of dogs who'd died there, mad, wild, gorged with food. The patriarch ordered the cave sealed with mortar.

It was a rapid, efficient expedition. Baltasar understood the pride of the gauchos, and his respect for the old patriarch was renewed. The gauchos did not look at him. What had he done? Less than his sister, whom they found, when they got back to the house, standing in the drainage ditch. She was covered with blood, along with the servants and women from the farm, all engaged in an uncertain, dim action. Baltasar saw Sabina stained with blood, a knife in her hand, cutting the throats of dogs, which she then flung back into the ditch, which was filling up with carcasses. Watching his sister wield a knife with the strength and skill of ten men, Baltasar was suddenly aware that she loved knives. With what pleasure she sank hers into the throat of a dog, burying it right to the hilt, grasping the animal's neck between her thumb and index finger, her female fingers implacable and eager. With what delight she pulled it out and plunged it into the animal's guts, repeating the gesture of pleasure, feared love, closeness to the enemy body, to the heat of the beast.

"Sabina!" shouted José Antonio in horror when he saw his daughter. She passed her hand over her mouth, smearing it with blood, and then ran to the ranch—but without dropping her knife.

That night, Baltasar heard the muffled, wounded, strident voices of the father and the daughter: that echo of family combat neither time nor walls could silence.

He waited for José Antonio in the hall outside the bedrooms. The old man was upset when he saw him there.

"Want to know something?" Baltasar asked, grasping him by the shoulder and once more speaking to him familiarly. "I was always afraid of loving you a lot but not having anything to talk to you about . . ."

The old man sighed and squeezed his son's hand.

"Those weren't wild dogs. They were the dogs of the ranch hands; she ordered them brought here so that they would never become like the others."

Baltasar did not know what his father saw in his eyes, but

the old man felt obliged to say: "She did it out of goodness . . . She doesn't want anything bad to happen to us . . . She's a woman who keeps an eye on the future, just like her mother . . ."

[5]

José Antonio Bustos watched his son watching country life but not taking part in country life. He'd never asked the question Sabina had said he would ask: Have you decided? What do you want to be? Rancher or merchant?

He knew that his father considered him a raw boy, virgin, not very attractive physically, with a juvenile passion for new-fangled ideas, waiting for the right moment to settle down, strangely rooted in the thing he said he detested: this land, the gauchos, barbarism, his hostile sister. José Antonio wouldn't want to admit the reason behind his son's renewed sense of rootedness. Baltasar thought him old, so he was stretching out this time with him before making the decision that would take him away from here. Rancher or merchant? The news that began to reach the interior over the following months made Baltasar's decision for him. But, before that, José Antonio Bustos had decided to change his tone, to force his son's hand.

Xavier Dorrego wrote from Buenos Aires: The former vice-roy, Liniers, was executed along with the bishop and the treasurer. Liniers had organized a counterrevolution, and all the malcontents had joined with him. There were plenty—the expulsion of the current viceroy makes it clear that authority no longer resides in Spain but in Buenos Aires and the Argentine nation. The royalists have sworn revenge. The creole merchants are unhappy. Free trade is ruining them. They cannot compete with England. You in the interior should look at yourselves in that mirror. If the merchants can't compete, how will the producers of wine, textiles, and tools?

But our own people are discontented as well, Dorrego went on, because Cornelio Saavedra has imposed a conservative congress in opposition to Mariano Moreno's radical representatives. Those of us with Moreno have been forced to leave the government, and Mariano Moreno himself has been sent into gilded exile in England! Our ideas of progress and rapid transformations have been postponed.

This letter cast Baltasar Bustos into a deep depression, until another letter came from me, Varela the printer, telling him that Saavedra, the army, and the conservatives had created a Public Safety Committee to root out the counterrevolutionaries. "The Committee has attacked royalists, conservatives, and radicals equally. The royalists," I told him, "are now seeking armed assistance from Spain to reconquer the colony. The government has thus extended the persecution to all Spaniards; they've been arrested, exiled, and executed. The conservatives have conspired against the creole government; the merchant Martín Alzaga and forty of his close associates have been executed. And Moreno's radicals, now leaderless, are also being persecuted. Weep, little friend: our idol, the young, brilliant, kindly Mariano Moreno died at the age of thirty-two aboard the ship taking him to England. Who's left? Your hero Castelli has been sent to take command of the northern army, that's where they expect the Spanish attack to come from. And here in Buenos Aires, Balta, we young followers of Moreno are again meeting—after taking precautions—in the old Café de Malcos. We are preparing to support Bernardino Rivadavia, who seems to be the most radical embodiment of our ideas of progress. We miss you, Balta, old man, you should be here with us."

José Antonio Bustos watched his son, waiting for his reaction, waiting for his son to give him the news he already knew from his own sources. "The Buenos Aires centralist tyranny"— José Antonio did not mince words this time—"is at odds with everyone. It persecuted the Spaniards just for being Spaniards;

first it ruined the businessmen and then had them shot, it decapitated its own group of liberal thinkers at the same time that it strengthened the army and gave it political powers. Is that what you call a revolution for independence, Baltasar? Is this violence supposed to fill the void left by Spain?"

"Yes," answered the son, "but the revolution has also created a new educational system and proclaimed the rights of man, just as they did in France. And it has outlawed the infamous slave trade."

"And it passed a law called freedom of bellies which declares that all children of slaves born from now on are free," José Antonio said, his eyes fixed on the silver straw in his maté gourd.

"What's so bad about that?" asked Baltasar, astonished, incredulous, above all, that this argument was actually taking place. The father and the son never raised their voices; there was something more than the politics of the revolution at stake here.

"Just read what they say in the *Buenos Aires Gazette*." Now the father, embarked on this enraged recrimination, pulled the news sheet out from among the pile of papers on his desk. "The blacks should go on serving, because slavery, as unjust as it has been, has given them a slave mentality. Once a slave, says the paper, always a slave. And it says it to attack the Spanish slave laws, which is the most ironic thing. Just accept things as they are! We'll give you your freedom, little by little! The habit of slavery has marked them forever, won't allow them to be free, so we'll administer freedom to them with an eyedropper! Free bellies, but only when *we* say so. Those who were slaves before will go on being slaves."

Baltasar's only argument was that the laws regarding blacks also took care of the education of the race that had languished in subjugation for so long. "But they still have to stay in the master's house until they're twenty, even if they're born free," his father retorted.

Baltasar sensed a deep, dull pain in his father's words, as if he'd been bitten by a snake. There were thirty thousand slaves in Argentina, but for him they were summed up in a pair of black women, a wet nurse and her sister, who held Ofelia Salamanca's kidnapped child.

He was on the point of being honorable with his father: I kidnapped a white child. I left a black one in his place. What a surprise the judge and his wife would have had if they'd found him in that aristocratic crib! But, after their shock and rage, what would they have done? Would they have raised him as their own son or returned him to slavery? The creole republic was going to turn its back on the slavery issue; it was going to reform it only on paper. The reader of Rousseau had a premonition that split his skull like a lightning bolt. There will be freedom but not equality.

"The President of the Superior Court and the marquise returned to Chile. She looked splendid dressed all in black as she left the court in mourning for her son, burned to death in the sinister fire of May 25. No one thinks it was an accident. The counterrevolutionaries say a liberal mob entered the residence as part of the terrorism they attribute to us. If they only knew that all we did was try to face up to the many problems that lingered on without a solution for three centuries in the colony's cellars! What was better, to go on ignoring them or to bring them out into the light of day, acknowledge them and say: Look, there are problems, difficulties, contradictions. The revolution's sincerity gets mixed up with the revolution's terror, brother Baltasar. The same thing happened in France. Remind anyone who argues against us of that fact," his friend Dorrego wrote.

"The same thing happened in France!" exclaimed Baltasar to his father.

"I have real fears about the freedom of the nation and the unity of our countries," said the old man calmly. "I would have preferred the solution proposed by Aranda, Charles III's minister: that we form a confederation of Spain and her colonies, which would be sovereign but united. Strong. Not weakened by uncalled-for excesses and fatal dissension."

"Things would not have gotten better without a revolution," replied the son. "In France, neither the king nor the nobility would have given up an iota of their privilege if the revolution hadn't wrenched them out of their hands. It was the king who set off the violence. You're right—a civilized agreement would have been better. But it didn't happen that way, not there and not here. What matters to me is that we consolidate some rights for the majority, where, before, there were only many rights for just a few. If we put an end to a single abuse, a single privilege, the revolution will have been justified."

Old José Antonio Bustos applauded in silence, with a gesture but without actually clapping his hands, as yellow as his poncho, their lines accentuated by the fluttering shadows of the dying candles during one of the longest after-dinner talks they'd ever had. Those hands were as thin as wafers but as yellow as the patriarchal poncho, not porcelain-colored like the hands of Ofelia and her husband. The applause meant: "Bravo! You're addressing me as if I were a multitude." His words were firm but tender.

"I suppose you've made a decision, then," said the father in his usual tone.

"Yes," Baltasar lied.

He realized that his father's odd harshness in their political discussion had no purpose other than to oblige the son to reach a decision. Baltasar understood in that instant that his father wanted not to annoy or offend him but to force him to make up his mind. Obliged to review his options, the young Bustos had to choose, as he told us in a letter: "I am not going to stay here. It doesn't matter to me whether the merchant destroys the rancher or if the pampa takes control of Buenos Aires. I'm interested in two things. First, to see Ofelia Salamanca again. And second, to bring the revolution to those who have not yet been liberated. But I can't make an impression on her unless I act first. So I'll start by attending to the revolution. I'll join up with Castelli and the northern army to support the integrity of the republic against the royalist forces."

"Tomorrow I'm going to join up with the revolutionary army in Upper Peru."

The old man sighed, smiled, stretched out a hand that not even the candles could warm anymore.

"Do you believe so firmly in the final triumph of your ideals? I envy your faith. But don't fool yourself, or you're going to suffer a great deal. Have faith, but be sincere. Can you do that? Are you capable of modifying your own behavior before you change the world?"

Baltasar Bustos sat down next to the old man's armchair and told him what had happened the night of the twenty-fourth and twenty-fifth of May in Buenos Aires. "Don't let anyone tell you it was the revolutionaries who caused the fire. I did it, Father. It was my clumsiness. I knocked over a candle without realizing it when I was exchanging the children. I'm the guilty party. I caused the death of an innocent child."

[6]

Sabina was outside the door. One never knew if she was secretly listening, spying on father and son without any excuse, as if saying: Life has given me so little that I can take whatever I want. Less still could Baltasar believe that father and daughter were united in their siege of someone as insignificant in the eyes of his family and the world as he: a romantic idealist, a physically unattractive fellow, a fool in love with an unattainable woman, an agent of the blindest, most involuntarily comic justice. Might that act of sincerity with his father at least have saved him? He detested himself; therefore he detested the intrusive presence of his sister even more, as he imagined a net of possible complicities and actual indiscretions.

"He still hasn't asked you?" said Sabina, a candle in her hand.

"Asked me what?"

"Whether you want to be a merchant or a rancher."

"Don't be a hypocrite. You heard everything."

"The poor old man still has his illusions," Sabina went on, as if not listening to her brother, as if reciting lines in a play. "He wants you to choose."

"You heard everything. Don't go on pretending. You rehearsed this scene as if we were in a theater. Well, the first act's over. Say something new, please."

"I told you that I wanted to get out of here, too."

"But you can't. The old man needs you. Sacrifice yourself for him and, if you wish, for me as well. There's always one selfish child and one self-sacrificing child. Wait for the old man to die. Then you can get out, too."

She began to laugh. No, she was not the only sister who could take care of her father, sacrificing herself for him. The old man had dozens of children. What did little innocent Baltasar think? Didn't he know the laws of the country? A patriarch like José Antonio Bustos could have as many children as he wanted with the farm girls, if his legitimate wife wasn't enough, especially if she was as insipid as poor María Teresa Echegaray, who ended her days as bent as a shepherd's crook, peering at the ground until she forgot people's faces and died. She was plump and nearsighted. "Like you."

José Antonio Bustos had a regiment of children scattered over the pampa and the mountains. But country law was implacable: the patriarch could recognize only one son. As for the others, well, this vagabond land would swallow them up.

"You are the legitimate son, Baltasar," said Sabina, as if she were illegitimate or as if, having been born, she died every night in the bed to which she'd been condemned and had no time to be reborn the next day. "But you look just like Mother. That gaucho you challenged a little while ago looks just like you, didn't you see it? I'm the one who looks like Papa, not you."

"I don't know what you're talking about," stammered Baltasar in confusion. "There must be any number of Papa's kids who look like you and him."

He felt he was losing himself in the thing he detested most: self-justification. Even though he detested her, he preferred being as honest with Sabina, who was as dry and dark as their father, as he'd been with his father because he loved him.

"I know you heard everything. Think about it awhile and help me. I love a woman. I'll never win her unless I do what I must do. I'm going to join up with Castelli in Upper Peru, sister dear. But only now, talking here with you—and I thank you from the bottom of my heart!—do I realize that I have to do everything I can to save an innocent child. My friends in Buenos Aires will help me. I want to save that innocent child. I'll send him here to you so you can take care of him. Will you do me that favor?"

"What is all this about an innocent child? Do you want me to stay here, a captive, even after the old man dies? What are you talking about?"

This wasn't a complaint or even a question. It was simply a statement of the fatal, implacable fact that dominated her life. And when, in the days that followed, new information came, brother and sister would catch each other's eye during dinner or when Sabina would bring freshly pressed shirts into the bedroom where Baltasar was packing his bags. They only had eyes, in fact, for the corrals and fields, where the gauchos had become agitated because of the news. The government of Buenos Aires had passed a law against nomads. The gauchos were to abandon their barbarous, wandering, useless customs and settle down on ranches or farms or in industry. To that end, they would be given identification cards. In turn, they would have to produce employment certificates. Violators of the law would be sentenced to forced labor or military service.

José Antonio Bustos had to read this law aloud to the gauchos summoned to the entry gates of the ranch. The hairy men, with no break in their matted pelts other than the glint of their eyes and teeth, listened as if they were getting ready to fight, their hands on their belts or resting on the hafts of their daggers. Their blades, spurs, and belt buckles also glinted, blinding the old rural patriarch more than the tenuous rays of this winter sun that sank behind the mountain range early, as if bored with the laws of men. As he read the proclamation of the creole revolution, old Bustos looked into eyes that said: "Old man, you're useless to us. You are unable to save our way of life. Fence in a gaucho and you kill him. Let's see if there's someone here among us who will take charge and send you, Buenos Aires, and these laws straight to hell. Who do these people think they are? Do they really think they can dictate to us from there? Maybe we ought to go there and govern those sons of bitches. So who wants to take charge of the gauchos? Let's see who wants to be our chief. Whoever it is, we'll follow him to the death, against the capital city, against the law, and against you, to keep our freedom to roam as we always have, free."

It was then that Baltasar really saw death in José Antonio's eyes. The liberal law offended him as much as it did the gauchos, but it was a triumph for the son and his ideas: it was as if José Antonio, standing firm in defeat, were dead with a candle in his hand. In his features an autarkic world was dying, a world as slow as the carts in which it traveled, a world held together by carpenters, bakers, seamstresses, soapmakers, candlemakers, and blacksmiths; and the gauchos. Almost all of them were born and came back to die here, but that fidelity in the extremes of life was based on their freedom to move, to get on a horse and seek their fortune bearing their property on their backs or between their legs—the mare, their spurs, arms, and trinkets. Women were bought. Indians were tamed with alcohol and honey. But the gauchos always came back to their real master to be reborn or to die again. All that passed through the anguished eyes of José Antonio Bustos, standing there with his yellow poncho elegantly crossed over his chest, indifferent to the slow and invisible disintegration of his warehouses, stables, coachhouses, granaries, and chapels. His gauchos were always there when he needed them—on condition that he not force them to be there.

That night it was Baltasar who stopped before entering the dining room, to listen to the voices of his father and sister.

"Well, now that the gauchos are going to be locked in like me, why don't you give me to one of them . . ."

"Calm down."

"All locked in. Now we'll be alike."

"You can go to Buenos Aires or Mendoza whenever you want. We have friends and relatives."

"You must think to yourself with a laugh, Well, she's got her knives for fun; the poor thing amuses herself killing dogs with a dagger whose handle is made from a bull's sex . . ."

"I'm going to slap you, Sabina."

"You'd be better off kicking your wife's grave. The poor woman shriveled and shriveled until she disappeared. Do you think I'm like her and that I'm going to imagine that being small is my only greatness? Nothing can console me, Papa, nothing, nothing. Except a pesky idea I always have in the back of my mind, which is that my mother must have been capable of passion, just once, a single infidelity, having another child . . . That consoles me when I see a savage gaucho with my mother's face and his forearm covered with knife scars."

"Calm down, daughter. You're raving."

"Doesn't anything break your serenity? Do you ever say what you clearly mean—that you don't agree, that I'm wrong, that I'm crazy, that in my mind I'm a slut?"

"My behavior is my tradition, daughter. Calm down. You seem bewitched."

"That's it, Father. The world has bewitched me."

[7]

"The republic promulgates another good law," said Baltasar to Sabina as he packed his bags, taking the shirts his sister passed him. "Most of these gauchos will end up in the army for being rebels. Then they'll demand that careers in the military be open to all. The revolution's officer corps should come from all classes and regions. It can no longer be limited to the upper classes."

"You'll see that these thugs will all end up dead or in jail for desertion," said his sister, handing him a pair of old boots. "Take them, papa says they're a gift. They've brought him good luck. They're from here. Made from mules' rumps."

"He's starting to give me his worldly possessions." Baltasar smiled with some bitterness.

Then father and son parted with an embrace, and Baltasar said it was amusing to think that, while he went to war, the gauchos, by law, had to stay on the ranch for good.

"That way I'll never be alone," said José Antonio Bustos.

"Wait for me, Father." Baltasar hugged him tight and kissed his hand.

"Let's just see." The old man laughed dryly. "In peacetime, sons bury their fathers, but in wartime, fathers bury their sons."

"Then let them bury you next to me, Father."

"So, in that case, it might be you welcoming me with a candle in your hand?"

"No, because they're not going to bury me in holy ground."

"All right. Goodbye, Citizen Bustos. Good luck."

Then an order from the Buenos Aires junta came for Baltasar Bustos to join the army in Upper Peru, so what had been his own decision turned into an obligation imposed on him by others.

3

El Dorado

In the immense confusion of the armies, only nature—so naked, so harsh—could bring serenity to their souls.

The rebels and the Spaniards had defeated each other an equal number of times. The two armies had nullified each other and could count only on their military and political rear guards—the viceroyalty of Peru for the royalists, the revolutionary republic of Buenos Aires for the patriots.

"What advantage is there for us in this situation?" I asked in a letter that Baltasar Bustos received when, under orders from the Buenos Aires junta and with the rank of lieutenant, he joined the army gathering in Jujuy to prepare for the attack on Upper Peru. Baltasar wouldn't have known what to answer. He arrived between two victories and two defeats; he hadn't even reached the high plateau and already he was facing decisions he'd never made before. Dorrego and I had joined Alvear's junta—Alvear, we assured him, was a strong, decisive, and attractive man—and, thinking we were doing our friend a favor, we'd put him at the head of a revolutionary regiment. Military expertise? "Don't worry, dear Balta. You'll have the best advice. What you already have, however, is something no one else there has: revolutionary fervor and a sense of justice. Without such virtues, the revolution would be just another war." At that time, we did not know our orders coincided with his wishes.

It was a guerrilla war: Baltasar went on repeating this newly coined term—recently arrived from the Spain that rose up against Napoleon—as an orderly helped him put on his uniform of black boots, white trousers, short embroidered outer coat, and three-cornered hat with the tricolor cockade. The only forces the revolution had available to it to keep the road to Upper Peru open and to consolidate the revolutionary government in that region—which was inhospitable, unfair, but, because of its mines, essential to the prosperity of Buenos Aires—were the guerrillas who had spontaneously organized between Santa Cruz de la Sierra and Lake Titicaca. They would lend their support to the revolutionary force fighting the Spaniards. There was no other possibility. They interrupted the flow of supplies and food, ambushed the Spaniards, and cut lines of communication between the plateau and the pampa. Lieutenant Baltasar Bustos's orders were: *Collaborate with the guerrillas.*

Our inadvertent hero had no time either to protest or to rejoice: I lack military ability, I don't see well, I'm overweight, and my passion is justice, not war. "Why don't you come out here and fight?" he asked in a letter to Dorrego and me, Varela. "What the hell am I—fat, blind, and enamored of my books— doing in these savage and lonely places? What are you doing in Buenos Aires? Having your clocks fixed? Well, take careful note of this: we're in different time zones."

In reality, there was no time. Between his relaxed life on his father's ranch on the pampa and his tumultuous arrival at Chuquiscaca, there was more than mere spatial distance. There were other centuries and other dreams; no matter how much he denied them, they turned up in overflowing confusion on

Baltasar Bustos's route. There was no fighting. The improvised soldier of independence never had to command a battle formation, and more than once the word "Fire" froze in his mouth. There was nothing to fire on. The granite bulwarks of the mountains assumed human, enemy shapes, and the afternoon shadows could come alive in menacing ways. But barely had he ascended from the Argentine plains to the Peruvian plateau than Baltasar was thankful for the hostile, immobile solitude of that lunar landscape. It was, he told himself again and again, the only element of harmony and tranquillity in a world gone mad. The turmoil of the actors had nothing to do with the melancholy serenity of this stage. There was no one to shoot at in this phantasmagorical campaign.

Baltasar Bustos reached Upper Peru during the interregnum between Spain and independence. The Spanish forces had immediately executed patriot officers, and the patriots had shot the royalist officers. But the revenge grew: the colonial administration offered more and better candidates for the firing squad—quartermasters, wardens, judges (standing and circuit court), even lawyers, notaries, and mere scribes had been shot without a trial in the Potosí plaza. In La Paz, "unhappy and barbarous city," explosions, pillage, libertinism, and desertion were the norm. The women opted for the most fiery party, joining the ranks of independence as a "pretext to abandon religion and modesty, and to give themselves over to pleasure with the utmost wantonness."

"You must impose order," Dorrego wrote him. "The army of the revolution should not sacrifice its prestige by committing or condoning crimes." Order? Me? Baltasar Bustos burst into a bitter guffaw, as he sought a praiseworthy avenue for justice amid this chaos: the walls of Upper Peru were stained with the blood of creoles and Spaniards—white men like him, Baltasar wrote to our friend Dorrego—who were the officers and captains of the three armies—the Spanish, the guerrilla, and that of the Buenos Aires junta. The great mass of the soldiers were of mixed blood, and the Indians were the beasts of burden in all three armies. Even his myopic eyes perceived this, but he was in no position to mete out justice no matter what they'd seen.

The whites ran the war—the wars, the guerrilla wars—and killed one another off. The mestizos died in battle, and the Indians provided food, labor, and women. Everyone exploited, everyone recruited, everyone pillaged. When he reached the plateau, Baltasar Bustos repeated incessantly: Only justice can save us all, justice means order without exploitation, equality before the law. He was seeking a tribunal from which to proclaim his truth and set up the words, and also the acts, of justice against the chaos of blood spilled—and this he only reluctantly accepted—in order to allow the birth of a new world.

Arms captured from the Spanish forces entered the plaza of Santa Cruz de la Sierra at dawn, disturbing the coolness of the mountains. Horses released from the corrals invaded the streets of Suipacha at midnight, altering the rhythm of the planets. In the Cuzco marketplace, the guerrilla fighters of Ayopaya exchanged a confiscated crop of coca leaves for rations to be used by the guerrillas. The ranches abandoned by the rural oligarchy were occupied by the guerrillas and turned into barracks for the local warlords, petty chiefs who, from every mountain peak, canyon, and almost from every promontory on the road, seemed to proclaim their independence, their micro-republics, as Baltasar Bustos called them from his ridiculous calvary, his ascent to the roof of America.

There he was, under orders from the revolutionary, enlightened port of Buenos Aires to establish relations with a series of cruel, haughty, audacious, smilingly fraternal, egoistic warlords, who all felt they had a right to take anything—ranches, lives, women, crops, Indians, horses, stagecoaches and stagecoach routes—in the name of independence. But, as the caudillo José Vicente Camargo, who controlled the route between

Argentina and Upper Peru, said to him: "Our goal is to free ourselves from the laws and the oppression of Spain, not to exchange them for the laws and the oppression of Buenos Aires." And that is how it was in those years between 1813 and 1815. To bring Baltasar up to date, I wrote to him, "Every one of the valleys that spill their waters into the Pilcomayo River, every chain of mountains, every ravine, is a petty republic, a center of permanent insurrection."

However, it wasn't necessary to explain a thing. Between Tarija and Lake Titicaca, between Suipacha and the Sipe-Sipe River, Baltasar Bustos was made to feel that he was the representative of a new power as distant and despotic as Spain. The vindictive Miguel Lanza in the micro-republic of Ayopaya, the brave Juan Antonio Alvarez de Arenales on the Mizque and Vallegrande roads; the subtle and slightly mad Father Ildefonso de las Muñecas to the north of Lake Titicaca; the grand, generous patriarch Ignacio Warnes, who welcomed those who entered his impregnable refuge in the mountains; the reckless couple, Manuel Ascencio Padilla and Juana Azurday de Padilla—each declared his own independence, his own micro-republic, his own power against two equally vicious and distant powers: Spain and Buenos Aires.

All of them confiscated crops and cattle, recruited mestizos from the towns and Indians from the mountains, sacked ranches, raped women, but they also cut the Spanish Army's communication lines, deprived the army of supplies, attacked it at night here and there, unexpectedly; incapable of defeating it in a frontal attack, they bled it with small, constant, cruel, and sudden wounds. And they opened the road, provided rest areas, food, and supplies for the liberating army, which, without the micro-republics, the local warlords, and their troops of guerrillas, would have died of hunger at the very start, lost in the hallucination of that plateau so similar to the perpetually hidden face of the moon. There were also the Spanish counterattacks. Without food or communications, without replacements, incredibly far from their Buenos Aires base, the army in which poor Baltasar Bustos commanded two hundred recruits from Argentina's northern provinces wouldn't have lasted a single night if it hadn't been for the local warlords. But they rejected everything Baltasar Bustos brought to Upper Peru, as he sought, with a neophyte's impatience, the opportunity to proclaim it.

The moment was finally supplied by Father Ildefonso de las Muñecas in the fortified plaza of Arecaja on the northern shore of Lake Titicaca. The other caudillos wouldn't brook Baltasar's revolutionary rhetoric; their decisions, so implacable they seemed irrefutable, were made on the spot even if they were the result of long planning. They always knew what they wanted: horses, a crop. Unless their orders were carried out immediately, the war would be lost; it was that simple. Victory was the name of their satisfied demands. Having their orders carried out immediately: the souls of the guerrilla warlords seemed to be what independence was. Baltasar, speaking with them, watching them in the wake of the whirlwind these men stirred up, could not find in them that tiny crack necessary for doubt; and, without doubt, there is no discourse for justice.

"Round up a hundred Indians to move supplies," Manuel Ascencio Padilla would order on the road to Chuquisaca. "Shoot the whole administration of Oruro," Miguel Lanza would dictate from his jungle throne between Cochabamba and La Paz. "Drive all the cattle off of B———'s ranch and bring them down to my place," José Vicente Camargo, on the road to Argentina, would say, imposing his will. "Open the mountain trails to all wounded guerrillas who come to Santa Cruz," Warnes the magnanimous would order. "I want a woman," said Father Ildefonso de las Muñecas, clasping his hands and squeezing his lively eyes shut, "but I can't; it would violate my vow of chastity . . ."

Baltasar saw him arrive on a mule, like a vision out of Cervantes on a stage that resembled the central plateau of Spain:

dry, high, somber, and wrinkled. Spain was reiterated in its colonies: the Andalusian Caribbean, the Mexican Castile, Extremadura so like Cuzco. Ildefonso de las Muñecas also looked like his Spanish and American land, but if he was Castilian in physique, he was definitely Andalusian in gesture and eyes. A revolutionary priest: Baltasar smiled with shock, not his own but the shock he thought our Jacobin friend Xavier Dorrego would feel. Bustos's glance did not escape Father de las Muñecas.

"Do I stand out too much?" was the first thing he said. "I don't want to cause a scandal. But even my name attracts attention—after all, *muñecas* are dolls and I certainly like good-looking women. So why wouldn't my actions do as much? Do our names determine our character or is it our acts that give meaning to our names? Let Plato figure it out." And the guerrilla priest laughed.

"We should all be guided by the law," Baltasar Bustos said, jumping up and almost spilling the maté gourd he'd traveled with from the pampa. Who'd hidden it among the white shirts in his baggage: his father, José Antonio; his sister, Sabina; a friendly but facetious gaucho? "Your vow is an example to all, Father."

"And you, what do you want that the law forbids?" He opened one eye and looked at Baltasar with a mix of sarcasm and curiosity.

"I want justice. You know that, Father."

"It's not the same thing. Your desire and the law are not in opposition."

"But my desire and my reality are."

Now only curiosity glinted in the revolutionary priest's slit eyes. "If I give you an opportunity for justice, will you give me an opportunity for love, young man?"

Blushing, but without a second thought, Baltasar said yes, and Father Ildefonso de las Muñecas broke into uncontrollable laughter. "It just occurred to me that it ought to be the other way around, youngster. I should be imparting justice, and you should be learning about 'pleasure-giving females,' as Juan Ruiz, the Archpriest of Hita, a priest as hot-blooded as I am, said a few hundred years ago."

He tucked up his cassock, as he always did when he was making decisions that involved God and man equally, and he told the astonished lieutenant that he, Father de las Muñecas, did not know what the young citizen of Buenos Aires understood by justice but that he, the priest, did believe in the abundance of blessings the Scriptures associated with human or divine justice. He let his cassock drop to its normal length and then draped his chest with cartridge belts and scapularies.

The next day, Father Ildefonso summoned Baltasar to the main square of Ayopaya, where he found a mass of Indians waiting for him. Turning to Baltasar, the priest said, "On horseback, so they believe you. Get up on that horse, fool, if you want them to believe what you say."

Baltasar's astonished face pleaded for a reason.

"The horse is authority, numbskull. The horse defeated them. In this land, there is no word without a horse."

"I want to bring them justice, not more defeats," protested Baltasar, decked out for the occasion in his parade coat, with wide lapels and gold braid, epaulets, and three-cornered hat with cockades.

"There is no justice without authority," said the priest in a tone of finality.

Baltasar took a deep breath and looked up, as if seeking inspiration in the oppressive totality of the plateau: the mountains a single colorless color, brown, like the pure earth before the stains of snow, rain, the boots of soldiers, the picks of miners, even before grass. Earth without adornment, naked, as if expecting that on Judgment Day it would be reborn from the reserve of the Aymará mountains. Then he lowered his eyes, and there they were, the men, women, and children he'd only seen cooking, carrying loads, tending the fields, breast-feeding, pushing cartloads of weapons, their foreheads marked by the sweaty thongs of the sacks of guano, coca leaves, or silver that their shoulders carried and their heads balanced.

Baltasar Bustos had been waiting for this opportunity, and he thanked Father Ildefonso for giving it to him. A few republican officers came out of the barracks, and a few guerrillas as well. In the distance, some carriages had stopped, and men wearing high, shiny top hats poked their heads out. Some even took off the hats that protected them from the sun but that heated up their foreheads, gripped by the bands of leather. Their hats were like their heads, which now, with habitual disdain, they wiped with the sleeves of their coats as they smoothed out the velvety softness of the hats. Their foreheads seemed marked by those hats in the same way the heads of the Indians were marked by the rough straps on the sacks of manure.

He said to all of them, because for him that world at that moment was all the world there was, that the enlightened revolution was sending from the Plata—which the English invaders called the River Plate—the river of silver, a luminous river, to this land whose bowels were of real silver. The Buenos Aires junta had ordered him—he said after a pause, insinuating that the metaphor was only a preamble and the preamble merely a metaphor—to free the Indians of the plateau from servitude, something he was now doing formally. The horse, jumpy, wanted to twist around and did so, but Baltasar never turned his back on his audience; they were all around him, mute, impassive, patient. Thus, the orator felt powerful and at ease, talking about justice to an oppressed people while mounted on one of the marvels of nature, a black shining horse joined to an eloquent rider. Baltasar Bustos held up for all to see, grasping it firmly (although the stiff paper persisted in rolling up again, adopting the comfortable form in which he'd carried it, tied with a red ribbon, ever since Dorrego had it borne by messenger to Jujuy), the decree he read aloud: All abuses are abolished; Indians are freed from paying tribute; all property is to be divided; schools are to be established; and the Indian is declared equal to any other Argentine or American national.

Baltasar saw some Indians kneel, so he dismounted, touched their heads covered by Indian caps, offered his hand to each one, and told them, in a voice not even he recognized, an infinitely tender voice he was saving for the first woman he ever loved, Ofelia Salamanca, whose blond, naked, perfumed image blended uneasily with the reality of this ragged, inexpressive people, whom he raised from their prostrate position, saying to them: Never again. We are equal. Never kneel again. It's all over. We're all brothers. You should govern yourselves. You should be an example. You are closer to nature than we are . . .

Father de las Muñecas took Baltasar by the arm, saying, That's fine, that's enough, you've been heard. In that instant, Baltasar reacted with a strength he didn't know he had, just as he hadn't known the tenderness that had just manifested itself in him.

"That's a lie, Father. I haven't been heard. How many of these Indians even speak Spanish?"

"Very few, almost none, it's true," said the priest, without changing his expression, as he stared, not at Baltasar or the Indians, but at the coaches stopped at the edge of the plaza. "But they know the truth from the tone of voice of the speaker. No one ever spoke to them like that before."

"Not even you, Father?"

"Yes, but only about the other world. That's where I hope to find the justice you have just proclaimed. Not here on earth. You spoke to them about the earth. It's never belonged to them."

He shrugged and looked again at the coaches.

"It doesn't belong to those people over there either. But, on the other hand, I do think these Indians own heaven."

"Who are they?"

"Rich creoles. They live off the *mita*."

"What's that?"

De las Muñecas didn't even smile. He decided to respect this envoy of the Buenos Aires junta, respect him even if he felt sorry for him.

"The *mita* is the great reality and the great curse of this land. The *mita* authorizes forced Indian labor in the mines. A lot of them actually run away and seek refuge on the plantations, where the owners seem like Franciscans compared to the mine overseers."

The priest kissed his scapulary.

"No. This is a rebel cleric speaking to you. There is something better for these people. I only hope you and I can help them. On the other hand, look at the faces of those merchants and plantation owners over there. I think we've just lost their confidence."

"Why did they come?"

"I alerted them: Come and hear the voice of the revolution. Don't fool yourselves."

"But, when all is said and done, are you my friend or my enemy?"

"I don't want anyone deluding himself."

"But I depend on you to put the edicts I've just proclaimed into practice."

"You, my boy?"

"Not me, the Buenos Aires junta."

"How far away that sounds. As far as the viceroy in Lima, the king in Madrid, the Laws of the Indies . . ."

"I'm from the interior, Father Ildefonso. I know the maxim of these lands: We obey the law, but we don't carry it out. I recognize that here you are the law, just as Miguel Lanza is in the jungle, and Arenales in Vallegrande, and . . ."

The priest squeezed Baltasar's forearm. "Enough. Here only me. A rebel cleric is speaking to you. I and my boys, who number only two hundred—but not for nothing are they called the Sacred Battalion."

"All right. Only you, Father. Just see to it that the law is carried out here."

Father Ildefonso burst out laughing and embraced Baltasar. "See? You've just entrusted me with the law, but you haven't found me a woman. Unlike you, I keep all my promises."

He told Baltasar that the Buenos Aires puritans, just like the conservatives in La Paz, were horrified by the disorderly conduct of the women who confused the war of independence with a campaign of prostitution. He laughed, remembering some moralistic proclamations according to which the fair sex lost all its charms when it succumbed to disorder. To him, Ildefonso de las Muñecas, the conservative puritans and the revolutionary puritans seemed equally imbecilic. God gave sex to men and women not just for procreation but also for recreation. But to be human it is important to have sex with history, sex with sense, with antecedents, with substance, did the young lieutenant understand? Sex, literally, as a Eucharist: a body, a blood, a lasting emotion, a reason; therefore, a history . . . And if liberating a city like Cuzco, which reeked of prisons, jails, blood, and death, is permissible, then it's equally permissible to liberate sex, which also reeks of its own prisons . . .

"In other words, Lieutenant, the vow of chastity is renewable, and that's my law. This is a rebel cleric talking to you. You, on the other hand, don't have those limitations; instead, like a fool, you impose them on yourself. I've been watching you for days. You take nothing unless it's offered. Look, my dear lieutenant from Buenos Aires, let's make a deal. I'll swear to you, on the heads of my two hundred boys: I'll carry out your decrees, even if it costs us our balls. But you have to promise me to lose your virginity this very night. Don't blush now, Lieutenant. It's written all over your face, and it's easily visible from a long way off. What do you say: for me, the law;

for you, a woman. Or better put: for me, *your* law. For you, *my* woman. A rebel cleric guarantees it."

"Why do you do these things?" asked our rather flustered friend.

"Because you've become part of my madness, without even knowing it. And that's always pleasant."

[2]

A man should always sleep in the same position in which he was born. If he dies before he wakes, his life will end just as it began. Everything is a circle. It has no meaning if it doesn't end as it began. Baltasar, curled up for nine months inside his mother's womb, with his eyes closed and his knees touching his chin. Expecting that when everything ends it will begin again. A voice, known and unknown at the same time, was saying this in his ear. He'd always listened to that voice. And he was listening to it now. It was new and it was ancient.

When he opened his eyes, he saw women sitting on the floor. They were weaving. They were dyeing wool clothing. Then he went back to sleep. Perhaps he only closed his eyes. In any case, he dreamed. In his dream, his head separated from his body and went to visit his beloved Ofelia Salamanca. Where might she be now? Returning to Chile with her husband? Mourning the death of her child? Did everyone still think the child that had died in the fire was theirs? Unrecognizable because of the flames? Recognizable despite everything? And if so, not dead but only lost? Would Ofelia weep, "Where can my child be?" And Baltasar dreams: where can my Ofelia be?

The women weave in the midst of the smoke. They patiently dye the clothes. Baltasar tries to make out their faces. His eyes fail him. Or his imagination. Then his head escapes again, soaring, hopping, making funny noises, until it strikes the back of the marquis, Ofelia Salamanca's husband, as if the old aristocrat could not command his wife's sleeping body and Baltasar's head had come, despite the husband, to the marquis's back, summoned by Ofelia's ardent dream, Ofelia, who didn't even know Baltasar. The lieutenant woke up, in a panic, in pain, and the women came to him, calming him, lulling him, bringing him a steaming cup.

"Broth made from young condor fights madness and frees up your dreams."

He fell asleep disgusted by his own body. Later its fire fused in him without contaminating itself or losing its separateness. Without destroying him. Fire approached his body and joined itself to him without destroying him. The child in the cradle surrounded by twenty-five candles did not have such luck. The fire triumphed. It devoured the child. Yet this fire touched Baltasar, pierced and consumed him, but did not destroy him.

"We're afraid of fire. They burned us with fire. We have to create a fire that doesn't kill."

Then he saw a girl kneading cornmeal, preparing loaves in a corner. When he woke up, Baltasar Bustos saw that his pallet was surrounded by ashes, and in the ashes he clearly saw the tracks of an animal. He tried to get up. He couldn't. He was tied to the bed. He was tied to himself. Gray bandages held him to the bed, to himself, to his dream about ashes, and to the animal tracks. Yet he felt free. His tied-up, ash-covered body, caught in a heavy sleep, was at the same time the freest body on earth. It floated, but it was the earth's. But the earth was the air's. He enjoyed all the elements: the earth that pulled him down, the air that drew him up, the fire that excited without destroying him, the water that liquefied every inch of his skin without breaking it. Everything was possible. Everything coexisted. Only he and the girl making bread were alive, suspended, in the world. Barely did he unite all the elements when the world became palpable. And when he tried to envision those elements, he discovered a woman at his side who was not Ofelia Salamanca. She turned to face him. He turned his back to her. She invited him to clasp her around the waist.

She mounted him quickly. Her thighs were the fire. Her buttocks the earth. Her breasts the air. Her mouth the water. She burned without flame. She made him wish that the morning would never come. The idea that daytime life, the revolution, the Buenos Aires junta, the liberation of the slaves, the power of the warlord Ildefonso de las Muñecas, the distant hatred of those men with tall velvet hats, the nearby, resigned incomprehension of a people in rags, his father's warnings, the rancor of his sister, the astute glances of the gauchos, Buenos Aires, his friends Dorrego and me, Varela, all of it, would flee, evaporate when he touched the elements of creation in the kisses, caresses, the surrender of an Indian woman meant that the world and its frenzy were excluded, outside, behind, ahead, but not here, not now. The woman who loved him physically had the power to prolong the night.

"No one knows you and I are here together."

"*Acla cuna, Acla cuna*," people were shouting in the distance, outside, voices that could be birds calling; the cawing of crows, the screech of some bird of prey. "The chosen one, the chosen one."

She went back to kneading the cornmeal.

When he wakened, feverish and in the heaviness of a shout, the women were no longer there. The shack was freezing cold. All the fires had gone out. But the clothes dyed purple were scattered over the dirt floor. The man who helped him stand was an old mestizo. He wore a dirty shirt, a frayed tie, blue baize trousers, and hobnail boots. His hair was short, his beard long. He led Baltasar out of the shack and its cold ashes. They were standing in a narrow mountain lane. Baltasar recognized the mountains and smelled the muddy nearness of the lake. The old man led him gently. It was difficult for Baltasar to stay upright, and he leaned on the old mestizo and on the walls made of such smooth, perfectly aligned stones they seemed the labor of titans.

He'd been here a week, but he hadn't even noticed the most

remarkable thing in the place: the architecture, the stones—perfect polygons joined together as if in a magic brotherhood. The discarded, unused stones were called "tired stones," because they never attained the fraternal embrace of the other polygons.

But only the stones remained. There were no human beings in the streets; no Indians, no creole or Spanish officers, no top-hatted mine owners, no warlords in priestly robes. The micro-republic seemed empty.

"Is anyone left?" asked the astounded Baltasar.

The old man did not appear to hear.

"You wanted to bring these poor people to a mountain peak and show them a limitless empire. From the mountain, they saw an empire that had once been theirs. But it no longer is. They invited you to enter. You did."

"Damn it! I'm asking you if there is anyone left in this village!" Baltasar Bustos shouted, unable to contain himself. He felt different, speaking in that tone, he who never got angry, he who, when he had to take control of the gauchos, did so with a smile. "Don't you hear me, old man?"

"No, I don't hear you. Neither do the people from here."

"What I said was very clear. Slavery was over, the land will be divided, schools will be built . . ."

"The Indians didn't listen to you. For them, you're just one more arrogant *porteño*, the same as an arrogant Spaniard, distant, in the end indifferent and cruel. They don't see the difference. Words don't convince them. Not even when spoken on horseback."

"I ordered the priest to implement my edicts."

"Led by the warlord Ildefonso, they attacked the treasury at Oruro the moment they found out the Spaniards had abandoned the city and before the troops of the other warlord, Miguel Lanza, could arrive. These auxiliary armies exist for themselves, not to serve the Buenos Aires revolution. Fortunately, or unfortunately, it is they who have filled the void between the Crown and the republic. They are here. You merely come, promise things that are never done, and then go."

"The priest promised to obey the laws," said Baltasar, obsessed, bewildered.

"There will be time for laws. Eternity can't be changed in a day. Just think, is Father Ildefonso going to eliminate taxation and the *mita* while his ally, the Indian leader Pumacusi, thinking that he's helping him, is assassinating any priest who is not a follower of Ildefonso de las Muñecas? The most urgent item of business is to halt Pumacusi's excesses. That is, 'Friends like those make enemies superfluous.' "

The old man stopped in front of a building more luxurious than the others. It must be the town hall, Baltasar thought, trying to identify it as he emerged little by little from his long sleep. The old man—the vain old man—combed out his flowing beard, looking at his face in a windowpane.

"And you, old man, who are you?"

"My name is Simón Rodríguez."

"What do you do?"

"I teach this and that. My students never forget my teachings, but they do forget me. Woe is me!"

"And the women?" Baltasar Bustos went on asking questions, more to free himself from the old man's explanations, which said precious little to his fevered mind, than to increase his knowledge of a self-evident fact: Baltasar Bustos knew only one thing, and it was that in his long night, most certainly consisting of many negated days, he had ceased to be a virgin.

"They died, Lieutenant," said Simón Rodríguez, pausing along with Baltasar in sight of the turbid mountains, the agitated lake, and the empty plaza. "It's not possible to be an *Acla cuna* virgin in the service of the ancient gods and sleep with the first petty creole officer who turns up."

"I didn't ask . . ." Baltasar began idiotically, forgetting the exchange of promises with Ildefonso de las Muñecas and then only wanting to say, "I don't remember anything." He only wanted to alert himself to something he'd secretly felt when he'd pronounced the liberating edicts at Lake Titicaca, decrees written in the radical rhetoric and the spirit of Castelli but spoken to a people who perhaps had their own roads to liberty, not necessarily—Baltasar wrote in a letter sent both to Dorrego and to me—those we have piously devised:

> When, surrounded by the physical desolation of the plateau and looking into the unflinching faces of the Indians, I read our proclamations, I felt a terrible temptation, which perhaps was the only one the Devil himself could never resist. I felt the temptation to exercise power with impunity over the weak. I wanted to impose my laws, my customs, my fears, and my temptations on them, even though I knew that they do not have, for the time being, any means to answer me. I wanted to see myself at that moment, astride my horse, with my three-cornered hat in one hand and the proclamation in the other, transformed into a statue. That is, dead. And something worse, my friends. For a moment I felt mortally proud of my superiority, and at the same time in love with the inferiority of others. I knew of no other way to relieve my pride than through an immense tenderness and a huge shame as I dismounted to touch the heads of those who respected me merely for my tone of voice even though they understood not a word of what I'd read them.

But Simón Rodríguez went on talking. "She was supposed to grow old a virgin. It was her vow, and she broke it for you."

"Why?" Baltasar asked again furiously—without recognizing himself—before he wrote us the letter and before he found something of an answer in the very fact of asking why.

"You entered this place without knowing it. You spoke to

these people from a mountaintop. Now you must descend to the poor land of the Indians. It is land that has been subjugated by the laws of poverty and slavery. But it is also a land liberated by magic and dreams . . ."

"Where are you taking me?" asked Baltasar, whose intelligence informed him that here in this abandoned village on the shore of the lake, he had no alternative but to follow.

Simón Rodríguez, with a strength that was supernatural in a man his age, first clasped Baltasar's arms and then his shoulders, turning him to face the windowpane. Finally, he grasped the nape of the young Argentine military man's neck, forcing him to see himself in the window where just a few minutes earlier the old man had combed his beard.

Baltasar, examining himself, saw a different man. His mane of copper-colored curls had grown. The fat had gone from his face. His nose grew sharper by the moment. His mouth became firmer. His eyes, behind his glasses, revealed a rage and a desire where before they had only seemed good-natured. His beard and mustache had grown. With this face he could look on the world in a different way. He didn't say it. He merely asked himself again. He was no longer a virgin—a boy, as that strange priest de las Muñecas insisted on calling him. For whom had he been a virgin? Not for Ofelia Salamanca, whom he'd only seen and loved from a distance, three years ago. Did his tranquil passion to save himself for a woman have any other objective? Was there another, one who wasn't Ofelia or the Indian virgin who had violated her vows to give herself to him? What are we doing here on this earth? Jean-Jacques had asked himself. "I was brought to life, and I'm dying without having lived."

[3]

He would remember a trap door and some wooden steps in the cellar of the abandoned town hall. He would remember that at the bottom of the steps there was a sheer-rock precipice that fell away sharply to the bed of a river deep down. He would remember a trail, as wide as a mule's back, cut into the cheek of the mountain. He would remember the hand of the old mestizo in hobnail boots leading him along that vertiginous, narrow path. He would remember barely glimpsed vistas through the crags: snowcapped volcanoes and dead salt pits. He would remember a red lake veined with flamingo eggs. He would remember the swift flight of the *huallata*, the white turkey of the Andes marked with its black wound, scouring the lake for food. He would remember a forest of starlit clouds against the wall of the mountain, bearing the moisture of the forest and the river but refusing to yield it to the desert on the other side of the Andes. He would remember the noise of bells behind the forest of clouds and then the sight of terrified flocks of llamas blocking the path, spitting and chattering in their venomous tongue, accompanied by the *huallata*'s distant lament. Then a hailstorm scattered the llamas and the birds, but when Baltasar turned to make sure of what he'd seen, he found himself enclosed within a dark cave. He felt around, seeking the company of Simón Rodríguez; the old mestizo reached a hand out to him and said he should try to get used to what light there was. But barely did Baltasar move his hand when he felt six, eight, a dozen hands touching his own, taking it with joy, feeling it, running fingers over it, and all he felt were the hot hands of those creatures who were invisible to him but who screeched like those white turkeys, excited by the presence of their mates and by their eager search for food in the lake.

"They say you're cold, that your hands and feet give off no heat . . ."

Baltasar did not say to old Simón that the hands and feet of Indians always burned, something he found out that night, those nights, the time spent with the Indian woman, virgin like him, whose flame, unburning, was the natural protection of those born at an altitude of six thousand feet, who have more veins in their fingers and toes than other human beings. He would have wanted to end his journey right there—how long it had taken them to get wherever they were, he could not tell—and curl up like an animal to sleep with those warm-blooded people, protected forever by the heat of their extremities, the heat needed to sleep. But as he grew more accustomed to the darkness, he began to sense another zone of heat in the bodies around him: their eyes.

Hot hands, hot feet, and luminous eyes. But they had their eyes closed. They all moved as if the band of light that bound their closed eyelids was a substitute for vision, until a dozen or more of those simultaneously veiled and transparent eyes combined their rays in one single beam that enveloped and preceded Baltasar and Simón Rodríguez, guided them to the edge of a new abyss, this one within the cavern, as if the cave (was it really that?) replicated the external world, the world of the sun, in its internal darkness.

The bodies that were leading them stopped, surrounding the two outsiders. The light in their eyes blinded Baltasar and Simón at first; but as soon as the bodies turned toward the abyss, those eyes cast a stronger and stronger, whiter and whiter light on a vast but strangely near panorama that was very deep and at the same time one-dimensional. It was an immense globe, the color of silver but crystal, like a mirror. In the center of that space—globe, abyss, mirror?—there was a light. But that light was neither separate from the other lights in the cavern's amphitheater nor the simple sum or reflection of the lights in the eyes of the cave's inhabitants. Were they really underground? Hadn't they gone up, despite the descent through the trap door in the cellar of the town hall? Was he above or below?

This was light, pure and simple, with no fanfare, no cheering. It was more than the origin of light, although it resembled nothing so much as that—Baltasar and Simón, chagrined, stood still and touched hands, just to touch something familiar, flesh, warmth. It was light before light showed itself. It was the idea of light.

How did they discover that? How did Simón communicate it to Baltasar and Baltasar to the old mestizo without either of them opening his mouth? The two stared at the closed but bright eyes of their guides. Messages transmitted by light passed through those closed lids. There the two men could read and understand. But there was nothing written on the eyes, which were, in effect, blindfolded by light; there was only light. And the light said: I am the idea of light before light was ever seen.

Then all the eyes in the Inca cavern turned toward the outsiders and flooded the abyss with light. Peering over the edge, the old man and the young man saw an entire city slowly but clearly coming into view. A city made entirely of light. The buildings were the product of light, from the doors and windows to the high roofs of the towers; the clocks were made of light. The streets were grand, luminous paths; along the avenues sped rapid carriages of light: they seemed powered by light and heading toward the light; and on every corner, at every door, on every roof, the light produced incomprehensible messages, traced letters, signs, and figures, names quickly composed out of a dizzying number of points of light, in a frame that was like the very symbol of light. And within that frame, the rapid flashing of the luminous points spelled out a single name, repeating it in successive flashes until it was etched on the retinas of the two outsiders as if carved in stone. And that name was OFELIA SALAMANCA, OFELIA SALAMANCA, OFELIA SALAMANCA.

Baltasar held back a gesture of terror and tenderness, as if he expected another revelation: the letters faded, but within the same frame there appeared the face of the beloved, not a painting, not a reproduction, not a symbolic rendering, but she herself, her flesh, her eyes, the movement of her lips and neck; and as the figure shrank so as to be seen in its entirety, they saw that she was naked. She offered herself to Baltasar, to the spectator, to the world, complete in every forbidden detail, each soft and caressable surface, every feared, harsh, spidery secretion . . . Ofelia Salamanca was there; she moved, was seen, and now spoke. And what she said was true, because Baltasar had heard her say it:

"Don't send me flowers. I hate them. And think what you like about me."

She repeated these words several times; then her voice began to fade, along with her image. And Baltasar Bustos felt the vertigo of one who has seen what belongs to the realm of death, which he had just discovered slumbering in the middle of life.

"You have just seen," said Simón Rodríguez, when the lights in the basin went out, "what our Spanish ancestors searched for with such frenzy in the New World. I saved the vision of El Dorado for you. El Dorado, the city of gold of the Indian world."

But for Baltasar Bustos, listening to the old mestizo, there was no cry of rejection, but something worse, more insidious: a nausea like that of the loss of innocence, an affirmation as subtle as poison, something totally irrational, magic, which with a few seductive, ethereal images destroyed all the patient, rational structures of civilized man. Never in his life—Baltasar wrote us—until that moment had a repulsion and an affirmation, as diametrically opposed as they were complementary, united in him with such force. He was convinced that he'd reached the remotest past, the origin of all things, and that this magic origin of sorcery and illusion was not that of a perfect assimilation of man with nature but, again, an intolerable divorce, a separation that wounded him in the most certain of his enlightened convictions. He wanted to believe in the myth of origins, not as a myth but as the reality of the world reconciled with the individual. What had he seen here, what trick or what warning? Unity with nature is not necessarily the formula for happiness; do not go back to the origins, do not seek an impossible harmony, cherish all the differences you find on the road . . . Do not think that at the beginning we were happy. By the same token, don't think we'll be happy at the end.

"What you are seeing is not the past; perhaps it's the future," said old Rodríguez to calm him down. "This city is a harbinger, not of the magic you detest, Baltasar, but of the reason to come." But for Baltasar anything that wasn't reason was magic. "And if it wasn't magic but science, what would your reason say?" asked the old man, afraid, once more, that he'd shown too much to his new disciple, who, for that very reason, would hate his teacher and spend the rest of his days trying to forget this extraordinary vision that no one wanted to share, because it was disconcerting, because it put our own rational convictions into doubt.

This is how I answered Baltasar: You should put your certainties to the test, staring whatever negates them straight in the eye. I don't know if Dorrego answered him or what he would have said, but I could see he was more distressed than I, perhaps even more distressed than Baltasar himself.

"Don't let yourself be distracted from war and government," Dorrego told me from Buenos Aires. "Upper Peru, as everyone knows, is a land of witch doctors, hallucinations, and drugs. We'll have to put a stop to it someday."

"We've got to leave it all untouched," said Simón Rodríguez, using his arms to shield the weakened, almost lifeless body of the young Baltasar Bustos as he tried to lead him out of the city of light. "Swear you'll never send anyone here. To explore it would be to destroy it. Let it survive until the moment in which everyone understands it because the future itself leaves it behind."

But Baltasar could only ask: What have I seen? Have I really seen this, though I could not even touch it, or is it a dream? Where are we? He could only implore as Simón Rodríguez got him out of there, ignoring the tales passing through the luminous but now open eyes of the inhabitants of El Dorado. Yet those tales held the secret to the place, and it was to a feverish Baltasar as he clung to the back of a mule on the dizzying spiral descent from the mountain that Simón Rodríguez told the truth he himself had just grasped.

"Everything you imagine is true. Today we happened on one fantasy among many possible fantasies. We don't know if it's yours, if it goes before you, or if it is the prelude to the next one."

Baltasar did not seem to be listening and only muttered something, as if trying to forget what he was saying as he said it, rather than remember it.

That dreams are our real life

That the night is never over

That dreams overcome time

That the only sin is the separation of the sentient from the spiritual world

But Simón said no, no, no, that is not the lesson, the lesson is to accept that everything we imagine is true, that today we witnessed only one brief moment of that unending ribbon where truth is inscribed, and we do not know if what we saw is part of our imagination today, of an imagination that precedes us, or if it proclaims an imagination to come . . .

"I have experienced the vertigo of learning that something which is death's can exist in life," our younger brother, Baltasar, wrote us.

When we received his letter, Baltasar had recovered in a hospital in Cochabamba, where the disillusioned Simón Rodríguez had brought him. The old man went off, doubtless in search of newer, more receptive disciples. Baltasar, after writing us, waited for word from us. He said that, more than ever, he desired to take action in the real world and forget nightmares. What commission did we want to send him? He felt strong, was fully recovered, and he'd lost twenty pounds. Oh yes, and he reminded us that he'd been lost in one of the five thousand tunnels that connect Cuzco with the mines in Potosí, that it takes potatoes hours to cook there because of the altitude, that the lake is merely a track left by the retreating ice, that the lava of the volcanoes whistles as it flows downhill, that Upper Peru smells of the mercury transported in leather sacks to treat the silver, that I slept with a girl whose breasts sprouted between her legs, that I've seen the sun swimming beneath the world at dusk.

4

Upper Peru

[1]

His dappled stallion, who smelled until then of the sweat of
bare mountain horses, now joined a new herd that smelled of
gunpowder, horseshoes, and leather. The mountain horses,
without saddles or bridles, gradually slowed down until they
were left behind, as if amazed by that unfamiliar smell. Baltasar
Bustos's stallion was the only one to follow the charge, joining
the war horses.

Holding on to the animal's sweaty neck as best he could,
Baltasar Bustos felt his face slapped by its wild, coarse mane,
which snapped like a hundred small whips. He didn't dare grab
the forelock for fear of making the horse buck. But its furious
gallop, multiplied in emulation of the war charge of twenty or
thirty others, made the young officer's body slip back.

They picked him up at full gallop as if he were a sack, the
way leaves are blown away or something is snatched up by the
wind. He didn't know what was happening. All he understood
for certain was that the world of the imagination was behind
him and that he would forget it; he was now tossed into the
tumult called reality, which carried him along in its wake. Two

strong arms lifted him up on the run, draped him over the saddle, and pressed his face into the wool of the gaucho gear. A voice muttered barbarous obscenities. The voice was close but the words were blown away by the clamor of the fighting. Baltasar's head, hanging down, suffocated by the dust, saw the world upside down.

When he regained consciousness, it was night, and the noise had subsided. The first thing he saw was a pair of blue eyes, like two lights, that belonged to a bearded man sipping maté. The man never stopped looking at him. He was hairy, his black mop barely parted over his bushy brows, his beard and mustache covering his face right up to his cheekbones and hanging down to his chest. His skin, though, was as pale as wax. The complexion of a saint who's never seen the light outside the church; his blue eyes, which nevertheless illuminated it, were paler even than his skin. His hands, holding the maté gourd, negated his waxen pallor, not with color but with roughness. And despite everything, there was, in those fingers, a hint of piety, of blessing and sacrifice.

They stared at each other for a long time, as if the hirsute man did not want to take advantage of Baltasar's prostration to say something to which Baltasar would not be able to reply. Each gesture with which the man disturbed his basically immobile posture was, by contrast, dramatic, or even eloquent. His gaze, a slight movement, a shrug conspired to communicate command and dignity all at the same time. Finally, Baltasar was able to ask for a maté. Before uttering a word, he quickly summed up for himself what he understood now that he was back in reality. After observing his host for a few moments—where were they?—he listened to the man's first words:

"My name is Miguel Lanza. Where we are is the Inquisivi mud. The other man is Baltasar Cárdenas. Out in the hills we've got more than a hundred guerrillas and five hundred Indians."

Lanza lifted a burning rush out of the fire to show a dark

Indian standing behind him, who held out a maté to Baltasar
Bustos.

"The Indian and I have the same name," said Baltasar, smiling idiotically.

"We'll soon find out if you've got the same courage," said
Lanza.

"My danger is that I admire everything I'm not." This is
what Baltasar had thought and what he now felt empowered
to say.

"Like what?"

"Strength, realism, and cruelty. You might as well know it."

"You're the *porteño* who proclaimed twenty thousand free-
doms in the Ayopaya plaza with the priest Muñecas, isn't that
right?"

"That's right, and I assume my orders have been carried
out."

Lanza stared at him without changing expression. Then
laughter burst forth like a vein of silver from between his teeth:
his mouth opened; a guffaw exploded; tears of laughter rolled
down the short span between his blue eyes and his black beard
as if down a long-dry channel. Again, he picked up the burning
reed to light up Baltasar Cárdenas's dark face. The Indian was
not laughing. "Just look at him," said Lanza, choking on his
unfamiliar glee. "I'm dying of laughter, but he's not. I know
your proclamations are nothing but words, and they make me
laugh, but the Indian doesn't know that. He took them seriously. And he won't forgive you for them."

Baltasar Cárdenas took a step forward and, with the toe of
his spurred boot, shoved Baltasar Bustos back on his straw
mat.

"You owe your life to us," said the Indian in answer to
Baltasar's puzzled look. "Your Buenos Aires battalion scattered," Lanza explained. "You were left between the Spaniards
and us. If the Spaniards had taken you, you'd be dead right
now. So give thanks you ended up with us."

"Go on, give thanks," said the other Baltasar, who was just about to prod the officer from Buenos Aires one more time. But Lanza stopped him. "We're brothers in this calvary," he reminded both Baltasars, "so let our offenses be forgotten so we may abound in virtues."

"Tell me your reasons now, quickly, and I'll tell you mine," Miguel Lanza went on, suddenly serious. "So we can get this over with and understand each other."

Baltasar Bustos closed his eyes. A rivulet of blood ran through his lips, and he could say nothing more. Perhaps they would understand his silence, and the sleep that followed it, as an honorable reiteration of what he had managed to say earlier.

"I admire everything I'm not."

During the days following this night, Baltasar tried to recognize the physical characteristics of the camps where he stopped, but they moved constantly from place to place. He discovered that his cot was a stretcher and that Miguel Lanza's guerrilla group never stayed anywhere longer than forty hours. They were moving through unknown territory; but Lanza and the Indian leader, Cárdenas, seemed to know it well: the valleys, the plains they crossed as they expropriated crops, the passes, the crevasses and wrinkles in the mountains, and, suddenly, the rope bridges that led them down to the bottom of the jungle and the bottom of the bottom, the mud flats, the mud of the Inquisivi that the guerrilla leader had spoken of.

The landscape changed constantly; Lanza's guerrillas had to change their ways, too. What was permanent in this? When Baltasar saw Lanza again, at dawn, standing by a labyrinth of peaks that the night before had looked from a distance like a half-closed fan, he remembered Lanza's words: We're going to give you our reasons.

That wouldn't be the last time that Baltasar Bustos would hear Miguel Lanza tell his life story. His Indian namesake always stood behind Lanza and would interrupt him when he felt he was talking too much. For the other Baltasar, the Indian, speech was superfluous, an excessive effort. There were so many things waiting to be done that saying them was unnecessary. As he regained his strength, Baltasar the creole gradually took part in the labors of the mountain troops. They interrupt communications. They kidnap messengers. They collect rations and arms. They attack at night. By day they vanish (this morning they're standing before the fan of mountains, they've come back from fighting, they will have some bacon and maté before going to sleep). They attack again, then bury themselves in the hills, luring the royalist forces toward their lairs in the jungle, attacking the Spanish rear guard sometimes and the advance guard others; they harass the Spaniards' flanks, attacking their baggage again and again, their supplies, their mail, their gold, stopping to melt down church bells and make them into cannons, making powder and shot from the nitrates and the lead in the very mines which supplied Spain with the wealth it squandered and which now were the powder magazine of the independentist insurgents: first the war must be won, then justice and laws will come, Lanza repeated from time to time to Bustos in the midst of all this activity. Then he reminded Bustos:

"Whenever you *porteños* come here to the jungle and the mountains to implement the revolution, you make a mess of things. It may be that your *porteño* chiefs know more than our Indian chiefs, but savage troops, whether from Buenos Aires or from the Chaco, want women, money, and the pure enjoyment of violence. You, Baltasar Bustos, are the victim of your predecessors, who came here proclaiming liberty, equality, and fraternity, while their soldiers raped, robbed, and burned everything down. Just like ours. But we don't put on airs. We want independence for ourselves here and for America in general, and we know the price we'll have to pay. You don't seem to. You'd like a clean little war, but there is none to be had. The mestizos in Potosí rose up against the troops from Buenos

Aires and killed two hundred *porteños* then and there. What do you want us to think, my young friend? You people are either rogues or fools. I don't understand you anymore. The illustrious General Belgrano, the truest hero of the revolution, came up here and ordered the Potosí treasury blown up to cut off the source of Spanish power. Fortunately, your namesake the Indian Baltasar Cárdenas was there to cut the burning fuse, which was moving toward the powder barrels faster than a greyhound. What use would the Potosí treasures have been to anyone, blown all to shit by Belgrano's revolutionary zeal? The fabled Pueyrredón, who's president of Argentina now, was wiser: he ran off with all the Potosí gold he could find, a million pesos in gold and silver he removed from the same treasury house and loaded onto two hundred pack mules. So the rebel mestizos killed as many of his men as he had mules, just to settle accounts with him. See what I mean? Either you're all really stupid or really clever. We're better off governing ourselves! Long live the Republic of the Inquisivi!"

"Viva! Viva!" chorused his entire band, who seemed to listen to their chief even when he spoke in a low voice as he educated Baltasar Bustos, the most recent recruit to this incessant war in which no quarter was ever given and about which it was impossible to say "it started up again" because it never really died down. Viva Inquisivi and its leader, our General Miguel Lanza! Long live the creole Baltasar Bustos! Just like them, side by side with them, he attacked, retreated, pretended to be losing so as to catch the Spaniards off guard, robbed Pueyrredón and Belgrano's gold, stole letters and thought how much time it would have taken the ones he wrote his adored friends, Varela (me) and Dorrego, to reach Buenos Aires (if they ever reached Buenos Aires). We counted the days we lived without our younger brother, the brother we'd sent—severe comrades but convinced we were doing the right thing—to get experience, become a man, compare books to life, while we collected clocks. Baltasar was a man: he never hesitated to ford a swollen river, to drop a church bell from the tower down to the atrium to melt it down and make a copper cannon, to burn his face in the sun and his hands with the nitrates. It was that Baltasar Bustos who stole chickens, equipment, ammunition, who did everything but kill a man or take a woman whether she was willing or not. He became identical to all the others; he ate what they ate, slept when they slept. He was different only in that the others weren't living, killing, stealing, or risking their lives for a distant woman named Ofelia Salamanca.

He had avoided two things until now: fornication and murder.

And the guerrillas said that an angel protected the *porteño* cherub Baltasar, who though he never ceased moving and doing things for a single instant, never killed a fellow human being, not even the most detestable Spaniard, never took his pleasure with a woman, no matter how delectable or willing she might be.

Little by little, he came to compensate for these two sins of omission through his loyalty to the troops.

In secret, as he slept on the cot they gave him after they saw how weak, how creole, how much of a *porteño* he was— none of them knew he was born of the pampa—but also in public, speaking to the other Baltasar, who never said a word to him but at least listened, so he felt he wasn't going mad, talking to himself, he would say, to himself and to his name-sake: "I admire everything I'm not, you know. Strength, re-alism, and cruelty. My salvation, my silent brother, will be to become the best I can be. That's why I'm with you."

"It was an accident." The Indian's eyes reproached him.

"Now it's my wish," replied Baltasar the creole. "Here I am with you, and I'll stay with you because I want to. Either way, I'm serving the cause of independence."

That was his answer to the mystery, the dream, the nausea of El Dorado, that bewitched city where a man could see and hear the woman he loved without being able to touch her: once again, the torture of Tantalus, not in the veiled but immediate reality of a Buenos Aires bedroom, but in a ghostly, mediated evocation that took place inside a mountain of savage witchcraft.

We should mention that this was also his answer to the labors that we, his older brothers, Dorrego and Varela, imposed on our younger brother, comfortably, without running any of the risks to which we exposed our cadet. But where was the dividing line between our orders and young Baltasar's acceptance? The reply would come not from his distant comrades, Dorrego and I, but from his immediate superior, the chieftain Miguel Lanza.

"I simply want to become the best I can be. What should I do? Is that the way to become one with nature?"

The Indian did not give an answer; neither did the landslides caused by the rains, or the swollen rivers the guerrillas knew to avoid even as they lured the overladen royalists into the current to drown. Miguel Lanza's men had no uniforms, traveled light, and drew the Spaniards toward the most secret, most dangerous spots in South America, as if to say: Look, this proves the land is ours. You die here. We survive.

Through rationalizations like that, they stifled their own guilt: we are not formal soldiers, we don't show our faces in daylight, we fight without taking risks, we are nocturnal warriors who grow at night, like the jungle itself.

That was how the conquistadors had survived, and there was something of them in Miguel Lanza, not only because he looked like a seasoned soldier as well as a mystic baptized in blood but because of his life story, which Baltasar Bustos, little by little, over the course of the interminable guerrilla war with its infrequent rest periods, was able to extract from him. He was destitute. He had been left an orphan as a child and was brought up by the Franciscans in their seminary at La Paz. His older brother Gregorio brought banned books into the monastery. "He was like you, Baltasar the creole. He believed what he read. He believed in independence. On July 16, 1809, in La Paz, he joined those who proclaimed emancipation from Spain without hiding behind the mask of Fernando VII. That was the first time he told himself what you believe: the representatives of the people can declare the rights of the people, with or without a Spanish monarchy. The repression carried out by the viceroy Abascal was savage. If the royalists wouldn't stand for insurgence in the name of Ferdinand VII, what would they do to those who'd shit on the king? Well, what they did to my brother Gregorio: they hung him in the main square of La Paz. I always see in my mind's eye my dead brother's head—with that tongue of his that could speak so beautifully hanging down to his chest. What could that voice say now which had taught us younger brothers everything we knew? See how a life and a handful of ideas that belong only to you end up belonging to others, and tell me if what followed was just revenge on my part or the very reason why I'm rebelling."

"You certainly talk a lot," the Indian Baltasar would punctuate these conversations. But Miguel Lanza tenderly remembered his second older brother, Manuel Victorio, who followed the war of independence at the point where death cut off Gregorio's life. His struggle came to a head on the banks of the Totorani River in a hand-to-hand battle without firearms against a Spanish captain, Gabriel Antonio Castro. "They say that afternoon no other sounds were heard along the entire Totorani but the panting of the two warriors, famished, exhausted, covered with wounds, completely alone in their struggle. In the end, both fell dead in the waters of the twilit river. Despite a shared death, their destinies were different. The Spaniards cut off Manuel Victorio's head, stuck it on a pike, and brought it to La Paz, where it was exhibited as a warning to insurgents and rebels. I looked at it for a long time there, until it rotted and they took it down, until I was old enough to join my brothers' struggle. Now, creole Baltasar, you tell me whether this war of mine is one of vengeance, conviction, or the fatality of destiny."

Yes, Baltasar said to his namesake, the Indian caudillo; yes, he said to himself or to Lanza. Call it revenge, conviction, or fate, but it is your destiny. Baltasar understood then, and quickly wrote it down, so that Dorrego and I would receive his words someday, that just as Miguel Lanza spun a destiny for himself out of the entwined threads of liberty and fate, he, Baltasar Bustos, would create his own. How to admit, weeks, months after joining the guerrillas, that Miguel Lanza the orphan had a new brother, this time younger than he, Baltasar the creole, heir, without wanting it, to the lives of Gregorio and Manuel Victorio Lanza? Because Lanza, after telling him the personal reasons for his revolt, revealed the objective reasons for his military strategy as they stood over maps rolled out in the dust and held down by lanterns stolen from some hacienda or convent—because everything here was stolen, though Miguel Lanza explained: "All I do is circulate dormant capital. I am an agent of liberal economics."

The maps told another story, and as he looked them over, listening to Lanza and noting his reasons, Bustos, barely liberated by experience, began to feel he was a prisoner. The poles of the revolution in southern America, according to Lanza, were in viceregal Lima and revolutionary Buenos Aires. "We've been going at it now for six years: Lima can't beat Buenos Aires, and Buenos Aires can't beat Lima. The two powers cancel each other out. We're right between them: the guerrilla fighters of Upper Peru. Buenos Aires is a long way off. Colonial oppression is right at hand. We have to keep up the guerrilla war. The royalist forces are here, and so are we. You and yours, Bustos, should come, help out, give speeches. But don't lose sight of reality. There are three armies here. Your people from Buenos Aires don't know how to fight in the mountains. The royalist has to fight. We mountaineers are the only ones who have to fight and also know how to fight here."

If he, Baltasar Bustos, felt the need to talk about laws, injustice, and ideals, he should also note how guerrilla freedom worked—it was the very inhabitants of the place who made up the troop, they elected the chief, they disciplined themselves to serve the cause. The liberty he wanted for his great city was perhaps not the same as the liberty the Indians and mestizos of Upper Peru wanted. But if down there liberty became one with the law that proclaimed it, here, Lanza went on, liberty was inseparable from an equality that had never before been known in these lands.

"Maybe they'll never know it unless they use their strength to implement the law," replied our younger brother, Baltasar, following our advice: favor what contradicts you, to put your ideas to the test and strengthen them.

"They want to change their lives, not their laws," said Lanza, speaking like Bustos in the Café de Malcos.

"Maybe they won't get either thing and will go on living as always, in misery," concluded Baltasar, because events were piling up on him, stealing his words, adding him to the cryptic, disguised, enigmatic strength of Miguel Lanza. They were making their way along a road of lances crowned with severed heads, heads like Miguel Lanza's, all balanced in unnerving plasticity on the hollow reed lances with steel points knotted to them that the guerrillas carried on the steep paths taking them this time to the bare, windy peaks where there was no vegetation, not even enough to hang a rebel, before they tumbled down the slate slopes again to the tropical forests in the depths of the gorges, always with the intent of luring the Spaniards into an ambush, making them believe that they, the guerrillas, had been defeated. Thus, by slowly bleeding the royalist forces, they were devastating them, forcing them to commit acts of repression, to exterminate the villages from which the guerrillas, whom they called thieves, bandits, murderers, and mad dogs, came. Entire towns disappeared, and only the roads to them remained, until they, too, were devoured by nature, ever moving, ceaseless—overflowing rivers no one could harness, flooded lands, gangrenous forests with no one to prune them, snow-covered mountains, dying thickets, disappeared towns . . .

All of them fell during that year Baltasar Bustos spent with Miguel Lanza's band. Like the landscape around him, the towns, and the men he met there, he, too, changed. Father Ildefonso de las Muñecas fell in Larecaja, from whence he closed the road to Lima; Vicente Camargo fell on the way to Potosí, from whence the way to Buenos Aires was open. Padilla and his guerrilla wife—their last words were "This war is eternal!"—fell. The generous Warnes fell, and when he did, the sanctuary he offered in times of defeat closed up. Only Lanza refused to admit defeat.

One day he appeared in camp. His blue eyes were as black as his beard.

He said simply, "They've killed Baltasar Cárdenas, they've killed our brother."

The Indian's head was paraded around the plaza at Cochabamba and then thrown to the hogs. But Lanza did not leave off intercepting communications, capturing couriers, stockpiling food, gunpowder, lead, horses, feed, medicine, alcohol, and even women—although they were becoming a very scarce commodity. On the other hand, the horses' natural inclinations caused them to join the guerrillas' herd. Runaways, ownerless, they straggled into the micro-republic of Inquisivi from no one knew where. Their bodies gave off the steam of the jungle. This altitude wasn't the best place for them. What were they doing here?

"They're trying to tell us something," Baltasar, the only Baltasar left in the band, imagined.

"Don't say it," said Lanza, now with black eyes, as if the Indian Baltasar Cárdenas had given him his eyes when he died.

"But you don't even know what I'm going to say," exclaimed Baltasar, with exasperated logic.

"You're one of us. We end up reading each other's thoughts."

"They're inviting us to saddle up and go with them, far away, to abandon this land which we've crossed inch by inch and which we know perfectly well is hostile, dry, and not worth a shit?"

"That's it," said Miguel Lanza. "Don't even think it. This war's never going to end. It's our fate. To fight to the death. Never to leave here. And not to let anyone out once they get in."

Then he repeated, so there would be no doubt about his meaning, "It's very difficult to get here, so it should be impossible to get out."

He said it as if, despite their great friendship, he feared that a deserter—which is what anyone who walked out on Miguel Lanza alive would be—would tell down there in the cities, tell the *porteños* or the Spaniards, who Miguel Lanza was, how and where he lived, and what roads to take to get to him. Miguel Lanza's secret intention was known to them all; it was the unwritten law of the Inquisivi. We'll move around all the time, never stop, but never leave the perimeter of the mountains, the jungle, and the river. And all his soldiers should think the same thing. Without exception. Not even the little creole Baltasar.

Yet it was the arrival of the runaways that made this rule explicit. It was only then that Miguel Lanza stated categorically to Baltasar what Baltasar already knew and accepted day by day as part of his integration into the band of guerrillas and into the wild nature of Upper Peru. They would be together until the end. But the decision was his, Baltasar's. It was a pact he made with himself. Miguel Lanza made a serious mistake when he told him out loud, when the runaway horses came:

"He who becomes a member of my band never leaves it. Don't even think it, Baltasar. Neither you nor anyone else leaves here. We're all citizens of Miguel Lanza's Inquisivi until the final victory or death."

That night Baltasar Cárdenas's head was brought to camp, stolen by someone who supported the guerrillas. It was brought in by the squad assigned to lure the Spaniards into the Vallegrande sand pits and then to the jungle, where anyone who enters gets lost.

Someone had gouged out the Indian's eyes.

Baltasar Bustos glanced over at Miguel Lanza, whose black eyes were once blue, and he understood all.

That night, as he had on his first day, he fell asleep shaking with fever. He tried to write to Dorrego and me in Buenos Aires to ask if we had ever considered this matter of destiny; he, our younger brother, our young comrade, had just realized that, without his being aware of it, a year had passed in which he'd followed a destiny which he thought was his but which wasn't his, which was in fact the destiny Miguel Lanza sought to impose on him. The price was the reward we would understand better than anyone: to be brothers. He would expand his brotherhood at the cost of his personal liberty. Which is why he wrote to us, his real brothers: a minimal brotherhood made up of only three men. Baltasar Bustos wrote us to say he had no reason to live out the truncated destiny of another set of brothers: the Lanzas—Miguel, Gregorio, and Manuel Victorio.

He would admit he admired everything he wasn't. And he hoped his salvation lay in being the best he could be as circumstances unfolded and multiplied, pressuring him. He wanted to be the best he could be in this collision between what he proposed for himself and what others imposed on him.

He remembered the distant, feverish discussions in the Café de Malcos back when the revolution was imminent. Seeing himself with the aid of hindsight, Baltasar Bustos knew now that he had been less sure of his ideals than he was eager to impose them on others. Or eager to punish those who didn't share them. Baltasar's ideals mattered not at all to Miguel Lanza, but he did take seriously Baltasar's intention to impose them on others. Because, if Baltasar was right, wasn't Miguel

Lanza equally right when he confused the destiny of a single man with endless, repetitive, tedious war without quarter? And at the end of this calvary Lanza and his followers could only glimpse a claustrophobic paradise: to live within fixed boundaries, not to yield an inch of what they'd conquered with so much zeal and at such sacrifice, to convert the isolated, repetitive, besieged fatality of a land that wasn't worth shit into a supreme value of existence?

In that instant, Baltasar Bustos saw Miguel Lanza's destiny as that of one of the heroes of ancient Iberian Numantia, who chose to throw themselves on Roman swords rather than surrender or compromise the purity of their struggle.

That being the case, who was the real idealist? Miguel Lanza, locked within the circle of his struggle to the death? Or Baltasar Bustos, who proposed an ideal but who now also understood the struggle that ideal demanded? The bad thing for him that night was that he could not understand—he wrote to Dorrego and me—if the struggle compromised and postponed the ideal indefinitely or if the ideal, ultimately, was not worth it and deserved to be defeated by human reality, the hunger for action and movement that justified Miguel Lanza's life.

"Life, death. What a short distance and what a short span of time between them. Tell me now, my faithful friends Manuel Varela and Xavier Dorrego, have we made a mistake, was my father right, could we, through compromise, patience, and tenacity, have saved ourselves the spilling of this blood? Perhaps, if we hadn't taken up arms, we would have suffered only the exemplary holocaust of the meek. But there was no one more violent than those who today accuse us of violence toward them: our time-honored executioners, whispers the voice, creole like my own, of the deplorable, admirable madman Miguel Lanza, dictating my destiny to me tonight, a destiny identical to his so he won't be left alone now that his own brothers have been killed. And in understanding this I understand enough, Dorrego, Varela, to understand that my destiny will cease to be my own between Lanza and his guerrilla fighters, because my options will shrink to one only—not the struggle for independence but death in the name of an ideal; or a cloistered life so that Lanza won't be left brotherless, alone with this enemy nature.

"Another voice speaks to me, but secretly; it's the dead voice of the eyeless head of my namesake Baltasar Cárdenas.

"When the Spaniards fell into the trap Miguel Lanza prepared for them in Vallegrande, I was among the first to throw myself on them. I said goodbye to the angel of peace who protected me until then, and I gave myself to his dark comrade, the angel of death. I discovered they were twins. I joined in the hand-to-hand fighting that scattered us over the sandy ground, isolating us from each other, royalists and guerrillas; but during the exchange of saber cuts and dagger thrusts, I realized that if I was in fact going to kill an enemy, he couldn't be my equal, my fellow man, but a non-fellow man, my real enemy brother, not because he was fighting in the ranks of the Spaniards but because he was really different, other, Indian.

"My glasses were streaked with mud in that mortal Upper Peru spring, and wiping them clean with the sleeve of my coat, I sought out the coppery face, the features of this person who was weak, even if physically strong. Weak when confronted by my reasoning, my learning, my theories, my refinements, my ways . . . Weak because his time was not mine but that of the magic, spectral city Simón Rodríguez had shown me. He was other because he dreamed of other myths, which were not my myths, weak because he did not speak my language, different because he did not understand me . . . because in me he saw his enemy, the master, the overseer, the rapacious, irredeemable white man.

"I embraced him wholeheartedly, as if in killing him I was also loving him and he was suddenly the consummation of the two acts I refused to perform in the guerrilla fighting. Killing and fornicating. I looked at the glassy yellow eyes of the Indian fighting on the side of the Spaniards, and I did not let my partiality confuse me. I wasn't killing him for being a royalist but because he was Indian, weak, poor, different . . . I deprived him forever of his destiny without knowing if I could really (forever) make him part of mine . . .

"Embracing him, I sank my knife as deep as I could into his dark belly, his guts as hot as mine even if they were fed from a different kitchen. In these parts, it takes water a long time to boil—I thought absurdly as I killed him, hugging him around the neck, burying my knife in his stomach—and it takes hours to boil potatoes . . .

"I killed for the first time. It was over in a flash. And I felt the stupor of still being alive.

"I killed the Indian in a secluded spot. No one saw me commit the crime. I thought of Baltasar Cárdenas and the way the Spaniards made his death memorable. Tearing out his eyes and sticking his head up in the plaza.

"I wanted to make the death of this anonymous Indian soldier memorable, too. He was my first dead man.

"I quickly got undressed. I was completely naked in the mud and the rain, which had started up again and which washed away the blood and dirt of the battle.

"Then I undressed the dead Indian. I did it slowly. I put my clothes on him, carefully, without worrying that my dead man was small and my clothes were grotesquely big for him.

"Only when I saw him there, stretched out in the mud, washed clean, like me, by the rains, did I feel that I had done my duty by my first dead man and that I could kill from then on with a clear conscience, without thinking twice about it. He was my propitiatory victim, my memorable dead man.

"I put on the Indian's clothes, which are cut large and made of thick stuff to protect him from the cold nights of the uplands.

"And then I set about memorizing his face.

"But I could not etch his face into my mind. I saw his face as identical to all the other Indian faces. Identical one to the other. Indistinguishable to my urban, white eye.

"In that case, what face could I give this victim of mine to make it truly memorable? I had scarcely thought this when I stopped seeing the face of the dead Indian and saw my own as the face of a glorious warrior. It made me laugh. I tried to transpose the face of my victory on the battlefield onto the Indian soldier dressed in my clothes, lying at my feet. That, my friends, I could do. The mask of glory passed over without any difficulty from my face to his, covering it with a rictus of horror and violence. I didn't have to see myself in a mirror to know that now the Indian and I finally shared the same face.

"It was the face of violence.

"I fled the place as soon as I felt that both faces, mine and that of my victim, were changing once again. It was no longer glory. It wasn't even violence. Once the masks of war were gone, the face that united us was that of death.

"I had paid my debt to Miguel Lanza."

That night, Baltasar Bustos set aside the things he considered his—a leather document case, his glasses—and wrote out the pages I have quoted. Then he tucked the letters destined for Buenos Aires between his belt and his skin, and that night, while the troops were celebrating the victory of Vallegrande with drinking and song, he left Ayopaya and the dying fires of Miguel Lanza's camp. Leaving the same way he'd arrived, he stretched out over the ribs of one of the runaway horses and held on for dear life. He set this member of the fabulous wild herd loose in the hope the horse would find the road back to his home: the pampa, his father, Sabina, the gauchos . . .

[2]

José Antonio Bustos was laid out in the drawing room, the same place they'd held the wake for his wife, the Basque María Teresa Echegaray, ten years before. But while the wife had died as she'd lived—oblivious—her husband had announced to their son, Baltasar: "If you find me dead with a candle in my hand, it means I finally came around to your way of thinking. If you find me with my hands crossed over my chest, entwined in a scapulary, it means that I held on to my ideas and died fighting yours. Try to convince me."

Baltasar returned to the pampa too late and too early. Too late to convince José Antonio Bustos, who had died two days before. Too early to avoid the uncertainty that would accompany him from that day on. His father was laid out with his hands folded, his fingers wrapped around a scapulary and with a candle, like a white phallus, between his fists, clenched forever in rigor mortis.

His father was so fragile and wasted that to Baltasar he seemed about to fly away. And while the candle looked like a mast, the scapulary was an anchor more powerful than any wind. Actually, his father looked more like wax. Bustos the creole recalled Miguel Lanza and his saint's complexion. Now Bustos's father had acquired it as well, but at the price of death.

He questioned Sabina: what did he say, what was he thinking at the end, did he die in peace, did he remember me, did he leave me any final message?

"You think you're asking about him, but you're only thinking of yourself," said his sister, scowling in the way that made her ugly, making it impossible for Baltasar to see her as lovable despite her ugliness.

"You'd like to know, if you were me."

"The Prodigal Son," Sabina declared in staccato tones, grimacing hideously. "He said it was impossible to swim against the tide. He thought everything was a mirage, that everyone was deluded, and he was right. He died calm but uncertain, as you can see by the candle and the scapulary. He left the message for you I've just given you."

She seemed to hesitate for an instant, then added: "To me he said nothing and left no message."

"You're lying again. He loved you and was most tender with you. You were close to him. You spoke harshly to him, and he allowed it. You're saying these things to make me feel sorry for you and guilty about myself. Didn't someone bring a blond child to live with you here?"

Sabina shook her head. "No child, no father. And you've come back. You can no longer ask me to stay on here."

"Do as you please, sister."

The filial word turned bitter on his lips. He had just left so many brothers, dead, alive, or on the point of perishing; there were others he missed, Dorrego and me, Varela, whom he had not embraced for five years. And Sabina could only look at him in wonder, as if his words were those of a man who was not (or was no longer) standing before her. She spoke to her memory of Baltasar.

"You've changed. You're not the same."

"How so?"

"You're like them," she said, looking out toward the gauchos gathered in mourning around the house. They, too, were staring, with a wonder even more secret than Sabina's, at the prodigal son who returned looking like them, Don José Antonio's peons, once nomadic and now firmly rooted in place by the laws of the Buenos Aires revolution. It shouldn't be this way, said the eyes that followed him around the shops and stables; the son of the master shouldn't look like the master's peons, his mule skinners, his experts in tossing the *bolas*, his riders, his horse breakers, his cowpunchers, his blacksmiths, his bellows operators. He should always be the little gentleman; he should always be different from them. How many of José Antonio's bastards were there among the gauchos? One or a thousand: now Baltasar looked like all of them, no longer like himself.

Ever since Simón Rodríguez had raised him from the bed of *Acla cuna* and showed him his reflection in a windowpane in Ayopaya, Baltasar hadn't wanted to look at himself in mirrors. Usually, the guerrillas didn't carry them; he hoped nature would sculpt his features, using life's blows. The mountain, after all, did not look at itself in the mirror, nor did those overflowing rivers in the jungle. The condor never thought about itself; why should Baltasar? Only now, parted from the band of guerrillas, back home and concerned with a death in the family, and under the gaze of his old servants, did he feel the temptation to look at himself in the mirror. Again, he resisted that temptation. The looks the gauchos gave him were enough: he'd turned into them. He touched his long hair, his unshaven beard, his skin tanned to leather by the sun, and his lean cheeks. Only his metal-rimmed glasses betrayed the Baltasar of before. How could his eyes change? His old antagonisms about inequality could still creep in through those eyes. He looked like them, he wanted to prove it by strolling through the ranch as he did out in the wild, showing his recently acquired familiarity with nitrates and iron, with the products of cattle ranching—jerked beef, tallow, bristles, bones.

But he was different from the gauchos. Not one of those men felt, as Baltasar did on returning to his house, that he was still trapped by the land of the Indians, the royalist army, the separatist petty republics, and the enlightened hegemony of Buenos Aires. Not one of these gauchos shared this *political* and *moral* anguish; for them, these divisions did not exist. All they knew was the immediate division between mine and yours: if you give me enough of yours, I'll be satisfied with mine. During his ill-fated campaign in Upper Peru, didn't Castelli say that the people should make their own decisions, exercise self-control, develop their economic, political, and cultural potential, and think whatever they chose? Baltasar Bustos looked one last time at his father's crossed hands, entwined in the scapulary, stained by the candle, insensible to the scorching pain, and then looked at the puzzled faces of the gauchos, who hadn't expected the return of a master equal to them. It was then he remembered how infinitely far away the Indian world was, how infinitely far away the fantasy his reason fought against, and how close his namesake, the Indian leader. None of them thought as they *wished*. They all thought as they *believed*.

The idea devastated him; he lost all heart, and finally understood why Miguel Lanza laughed, the only time that rueful saint, that sleepless warrior, ever laughed, when he repeated the words of the emissary from the Buenos Aires revolution in Upper Peru: "In one day, we shall do the work of eternity!"

They were risible words. Was the burden Baltasar Bustos felt on his shoulders as he said that in his father's frozen ear also risible? "It's up to me to do, over the course of my entire life, the work of one day. The entire responsibility for the revolution for independence weighs on me and on each one of us."

The candle finally melted in the unfeeling hands of his dead father. The scapulary, however, remained, coiled like a sacred serpent. What would change, who would change it, how long would it take to change things? But was it worth it to change? All this came from so far off. He hadn't realized before, their origin was so remote, that the American cosmogonies preceded all of secular reasoning's feeble speculations; *écraser l'infâme* was in itself an infamy that called for its own destruction: it was a weak, rationalistic bulwark against the ancient tide of cycles governed by forces which were here before us and which will survive us . . . In El Dorado, he had seen the eyes of light that contemplated the origin of time and celebrated the birth of mankind. They did not remember the past; they were there always, without losing, because of it, either their immediate present or their most remote beginnings . . . How was it possible to stand next to them without losing our humanity but augmenting it thanks to everything we've been? Can we be at the same time all we have been and all we want to be?

His father did not answer his questions. But Baltasar was sure he was listening. Sabina had let the candle burn down.

She shrieked when the flame touched the flesh. He can't feel, said Baltasar. But she did feel: she felt the knives she wore, like scapularies, between her breasts, over her sex, between her thighs. He didn't have to see them to know they were there; he could smell them, near his sister and his father's cadaver, he could feel them piercing his own body with the same conviction his own fighting dagger had entered the Indian's body in the Vallegrande skirmish. In the same way he knew "I killed my racial enemy in battle," he also knew "My sister wears secret, warm, magical knives near her private parts"; just as he'd earlier found out "Miguel Lanza does not want me ever to escape from his troops, so that I can be his younger brother and not his dead brother." Having taken all this into himself, he now wanted to distance himself from it so that he could go forward to his own passion, the woman named Ofelia Salamanca.

He later wrote to his friends that perhaps it was his fate to return to his father's estate too late for some things, too soon for others. He was untimely. But they themselves had pointed out the opportunity to him. Ofelia Salamanca had left Chile and was now in Peru. There were, then, immediate and sensual reasons for being.

"Your friends sent you a note. They could not find the child. The woman's in Lima. That's that. Will you go?"

Baltasar said yes.

"Won't you take me with you?"

"No. I'm sorry."

"You're not, but it doesn't matter. You won't take me because you respect me. I expected nothing less of your love for me. You would never dishonor me. We'll leave that to the gauchos."

"Excuse me if I am distracted. I've always wanted to be open to what others think and want."

"You know I have nothing left to do here. I have no one to care for."

"There's the house. The gauchos. You just said it yourself."

"Am I the mistress?"

"If that's what you want, Sabina."

"I'm going to die of loneliness if I don't give myself to them."

"Do it. Now let's bury our father."

5

The City of the Kings

The drizzle falling on Lima during that summer of 1815 stopped when the Marquis de Cabra, venturing out onto his baroque balcony suspended over the small plaza of the Mercederian Nuns, said, to no one in particular—to the fractured cloud, to the invisible rain that chilled one's soul: "This city enervates us Spaniards. It depresses and demoralizes us. The good thing is that it has the same effect on the Peruvians."

He cackled like a hen over his own wit and closed the complicated lattices of the viceregal windows. His Indian valet had already helped him into his silver-trimmed dress coat, his starched linen shirt, his short silk trousers, his white stockings, and his black shoes with silver buckles. All he needed was his ivory-handled malacca stick.

"*Cholito!*" he said to his servant with imperious tenderness. He was just about to give the order, but the Indian boy already had the walking stick ready and handed it to his master, not as he should have—so the marquis could take it by the handle—but offering the middle of the stick, as if handing over a vanquished sword. This *cholito*, this little half-breed, must have seen quite a few defeated swords handed to the winners of duels over the course of his short life. They were part of the legend of Peru: every victory was negated by two defeats, so the arithmetic of failure was inevitable. Now what attracted the Marquis de Cabra's attention was something familiar: the ivory handle of his stick was a Medusa with a fixed, terrifying gaze and hard breasts that seemed to herald the stones set in the eyes.

It was a present from his wife, Ofelia Salamanca, and from being handled so much, the Medusa's facial features had lost some of their sharpness. For the same reason, the atrocious mythological figure had completely lost her ancient nipples. The marquis shook his head, and his recently powdered wig dropped a few snowflakes on the shoulders of the former President of the Royal Council of Chile. The brocade absorbed them, just as it absorbed the dandruff that fell from the thinning hair of the sixty-year-old man who this afternoon was walking out into a Lima divided, as always, by public and private rumors.

The rumors concerned the situation created by Waterloo and the exile of Bonaparte to Saint Helena. Ferdinand VII had been restored to his throne in Spain, and refused to swear allegiance to the liberal constitution of Cádiz which had made his restoration possible. The Inquisition had been reinstated, and the Spanish liberals were the object of a persecution that to some seemed incompatible with the liberals' defense of the homeland against the French invaders, during which time the idiot king lived in gilded exile in Bayonne. The important thing for Spain's American colonies was that, once and for all, the famous "Fernandine mask" had fallen. Now it was simply a matter of being either in favor of the restored Bourbon monarchy or against it. It was no longer possible to hedge. Spaniards against Spanish Americans. Simón Bolívar had done everyone the favor of giving a name to the conflict: *a fight to the death.*

The Marquis de Cabra preferred to prolong, just as he was doing at that very moment, to the rhythm of the coach, the public rumors in order to put off the private ones. During this enervating summer of unrealized rains—like a marriage left unconsummated night after night—he himself was the preferred object of Lima gossip. His entrance into the gardens of Viceroy Abascal, in this city where gardens proliferated as an escape from earthquakes, would, as the witty Chileans called it, keep the rumor mill churning at top speed.

The truth is that other things held the attention of the guests at the viceroy's soiree, first a game of blindman's buff that the young people who basked in the blessings of the Crown—the *jeunesse dorée*, as the Marquis de Cabra, always aware of the latest Paris fashions, called them—were enjoying, as they dashed and stumbled their way around the eighteenth-century viceregal garden, a pale imitation of the gardens of the Spanish palace at Aranjuez, themselves the palest reflection, finally, of Lenôtre's royal gardens.

"Goodness, with all these blindfolded figures in it, the garden looks like a courtroom," said the marquis, as usual to no one and to everyone. That allowed him to make ironic, snide comments no one could take amiss because they weren't directed at anyone in particular. Of course, anyone who so desired could apply them to himself.

The garden actually resembled nothing so much as beautiful, flapping laundry because the flutter of white cloth, gauze, silks, handkerchiefs, and parasols dominated the space: floating skirts, scarves, linen shirts, hoopskirts, frock coats the color of deerskin, tassels, fringes, silver braid, epaulets, and military sashes, but above all handkerchiefs, passed laughingly from one person to another, blindfolding them, handcuffing them, allowing the blindman only an instant, as white as a lightning flash, to locate his or her chosen prey. Two young priests had also joined the game, and their black habits provided the only contrast amid so much white. From his privileged distance, the marquis noted with approval the nervous blushes of the beautiful creole youngsters, who avidly cultivated fair complexions, blond gazes, and solar tresses. That explained the parasols in the hands of the girls, who wouldn't set them aside even when they were blindfolded. They would run charmingly, one hand holding the parasol, the other feeling for the ideal match promised by the luck of the game. On the other hand, the heat and the excitement of the game brought out dark blushes among the boys, as if the image of the pure white creole required total inactivity.

The newly arrived spectator smiled; either in the curtained bedroom of a lattice-windowed palace or in a dungeon, that's where these fine young gentlemen would finally take their rest; that was what the war of independence promised Lima's beautiful young people: renewed power or jail. *War to the death . . .* For the moment, far from the insane, incredible resistance of the bands of Upper Peru's guerrillas, far, even, from the perilous peace of Chile, Peru remained Spain's principal bastion in South America. But for how long?

It was like playing blindman's buff, said the roguish, amused marquis, introducing himself like some sort of minstrel into the circle of young people, striking coquettish poses, tossing away his three-cornered hat, nostalgic perhaps for the capes and broad-brimmed hats that Charles III had banned in a vain attempt to modernize the Spanish masses. As he walked, he scattered the perfume and powder of his eighteenth-century toilette among these fresh but perspiring young people, who had abandoned the classic wig in favor of long, romantic tresses that floated in the breeze . . . Even in Lima the generation gap began with hairstyles; it indicated—and this the Marquis de Cabra, of an understanding nature, wanted to believe—that it began in their heads. It was the era of heads. Isn't that exactly what Philip IV's minister had demanded? "Bring me heads!"

He could think no more because his own head collided with that of a blindfolded youth searching for his lady-love. He spun with more energy and zeal than anyone else, shaking his mane of bronzed curls, half opening his full, red lips, around which the pallor of his carefully shaped cheeks contrasted with the skin on his forehead and cheeks, which was dark, tanned by the sun. The white blindfold covered his eyes; and if his curly head cracked into the Marquis de Cabra's wig, it was as much because of the agitation of the young man as it was because of the old man's intrusion into the game.

The young man grabbed the old man's arms, felt the folds of his frock coat, and pulled off the blindfold just as the old man was rearranging his unsettled wig, which had slipped to one side of his head. Baltasar Bustos smothered a cry, muffled, almost animal-like, like that of a bull whose strength has been mocked, for what he actually imagined in the darkness demanded by the game was a nocturnal encounter with Ofelia Salamanca, an encounter of which this game of blindman's buff was but a foretaste, a preliminary ritual. He'd been assured she was in Lima; it was for her that he'd journeyed here from the pampa, through the desert and the mountains to Ayacucho and the Peruvian coast; for her he'd trimmed his beard and mustache, combed his hair, dabbed on perfume, and dressed in the clothes fashionable in the viceroyalty. It was for her he'd come looking, visiting the twilight parties of Lima, the final bastion of the Spanish empire in the Americas, seeking her because his friends had told him, "She is in the Americas, but no one has seen her." "She is in Lima, but she is with someone else." It was for her that he took part in blindman's buff, imagining that each woman he touched when he pulled the handkerchief off his eyes would be she, the woman he'd sighed for since that terrible night of the kidnapping and fire in Buenos Aires. And even before that: since he'd seen her in outline, naked, sitting before her mirror, powdering herself, a new mother, but with an incomparable waist and infinitely caressable buttocks, buttocks that would fit the hands of a man, the secret, strokable buttocks of Ofelia Salamanca, which drove Baltasar Bustos mad.

Instead, he was embracing his beloved's aged husband.

The Marquis de Cabra looked at him without knowing him. He'd never seen him before. Baltasar's vision ended; he took the handkerchief off his eyes and handed it in confusion, iron- ically, to Ofelia Salamanca's startled husband. The platonic lover struggled to put on his oval glasses, showing that he was blinder than any blindfolded man: his heavy breathing fogged the lenses.

The magic circle of the game dissolved, but courtesy was a more complicated game, and it took the players a few minutes to allow one another to pass, to invite one another to go first.

"After you. Please, go ahead."

"Certainly not."

"Come now, don't make me plead."

"Beauty before experience."

"It is more honorable to follow experience, not to precede it."

"I am at your service."

"I beg you, please."

"Your servant."

"I kiss your hand."

"Please do me this signal honor."

"I cannot allow it."

"But how can I repay your kindness?"

"After you, please."

"The person who precedes you has yet to be born, ma'am."

"I envy the carpet under your feet, ma'am."

"Your most humble servant."

"After you, I implore you."

These endless Lima courtesies obstructed all the doorways to the palace, but no sooner was everyone inside and partaking of warm punch and sugar concoctions, candied egg yolks and honey fritters prepared by the nuns of the order of St. Clare, than the two rumors—the public and the private—over- whelmed the elaborate rituals of courtesy.

It was, nevertheless, the presence of the Marquis de Cabra

that forged the perfect union of the street and the bedroom gossip, and it was he himself who broke the news when he announced, "My wife has departed Lima. Yes, yes, you haven't seen her for several weeks now and you've wondered why." (That was true. Baltasar had been told that she was in Lima but that she had not been seen; she was not, perhaps, the perfect wife but at least she was under wraps—ha, ha.) "Perhaps you've invented reasons." (They say she's following a gallant artillery captain transferred from the viceroyalty in Lima to the captaincy-general of Chile, for him the promotion was a demotion, having parted him from the sweet Ofelia; the sweet Ofelia? Just let me tell you what I heard . . .) "But the truth is that the marquise has had a terrible attack of nerves because of all this patriotic commotion, and her royalist faith cannot bear the spectacle of a defeated, humiliated Spain expelled from the very world she discovered and built." (They say she hasn't been able to come to terms with the death of her child in Buenos Aires; a most mysterious death, my most respected Doña Carmelita, because no one knows what happened, the story of a simple accident convinces no one: just think what sort of accident it had to have been to concentrate all the fires of Buenos Aires in that innocent cradle. There's something fishy here, I tell you, and we'll never learn the truth of what took place five years ago. Just look how it's livened up the gossip flying from Montevideo to Bogotá; long are these roads, late are the documents when they finally get here, and how lost the laws get, my dear Don Manuelito, but how gossip flies, if you please!) "The Spanish empire in America has lasted three hundred years, longer than any other empire in history," the Marquis de Cabra was saying, his three-cornered hat under his arm, "and a soul as sensitive as my wife could hardly be expected to bear the spectacle of its end." (Isn't the marquis speaking treason? How dare he predict the end of the Spanish empire in America? This Ofelia Salamanca must have done something terrible for the old gallant to expose himself in this way and in these times to suspicion of treason—the Inquisition in Lima was not asleep. Surely the Marquis de Cabra knows how many heretics and rebels the ecclesiastical arm has taken, to give them their just deserts.) "She is a descendant of the first conquistadors, a pure creole of the best lineage, and whenever my imagination flags, she's there to rekindle its flame with the memory of those incomparable deeds: five hundred men marching from Veracruz to Tenochtitlán after scuttling their ships to capture the great Moctezuma and conquer the Aztec empire; a similar number vanquishing the Inca Atahualpa in the space of one week; the conquest of the Andes, the Amazon, the Pacific; cities strung like a rosary of baroque pearls, from California to Tierra del Fuego; souls converted and saved: thousands, thousands, repaying with interest the loss of perverse lives in thrall to stubborn rebelliousness and idolatry." The Marquis de Cabra laughed, strolling through the crowded salons of the viceregal palace in Lima that afternoon of Baltasar Bustos's return to the world, a world that seemed even more unreal to him after his recent life on the pampa, in Ayopaya, and with Miguel Lanza's troops.

"The Marquise de Cabra, then, begs your pardon for not being present at this soiree, but you all know that there is no better way of calling attention to oneself than by calling attention to one's absence." The elfin marquis laughed again, inviting the animated but languid company (who were perhaps wise to mix one drop of Indian fatality with another of creole indolence) to turn away from the theme of Ofelia Salamanca, the wife of the Marquis de Cabra, which they did so as not to admit he was right, not to let him feel that he could read them so easily or manipulate them without mercy. In doing so, they left Baltasar Bustos alone, flustered, hungry for the truth, or at least for company.

The brilliant Lima gathering did not keep the young Argentine from looking at the stockings which a forty-year-old but still appetizing woman showed off with incredible sauciness by refusing to allow her skirts to conceal the novelty of her *bas*—as she called them—decorated from toes to knees with small, linked violet clocks that reminded our friend Baltasar about us, Varela and Dorrego, playing with our clocks in Buenos Aires, adjusting them as we adjusted our political lives, accommodating ourselves, when Posadas resigned, to Alvear's leadership, never daring to ask ourselves what we were doing there while our younger brother, Baltasar Bustos, the weakest of the three, the most physically awkward, the most intellectual as well, was exposing himself to the Spaniards way out in the mountains.

"The theme of our time is time!" announced the lady—who, at the back of her neck, wore feathers the color of the embroidered clocks—inviting the young creole gentlemen to play with words and ideas, responding to them herself in a way the ignorant colonial ladies—who soon found themselves bereft of their gallants, as attracted by the novelty as fireflies by a burning candle—could not.

"What a contretemps!"

"You, ma'am, can make time march backwards . . ."

"Or even better: such abundance of time . . ."

"Do my legs seem fat to you?"

"They seem to me a heralding of the face with which you confront time."

"Time, my friend, is ageless."

"But it does suffer evils, ma'am."

"I think I'm on time."

"And we here in Peru, alas, are always either too early or too late."

They all laughed, but Baltasar Bustos, looking at the lady's violet legs and her hoopskirt, allowed himself to be distracted by the black skirts of the two young priests who had been playing blindman's buff and who were now looking at him, waiting for him to raise his eyes. He forgot the provocative lady, whose days as a coquette were numbered (even Micaela

Villegas, the notorious Perrichole, the loosest woman in the colony, had just turned sixty—just think of that, your lordship), to look back at them as they smiled at him: one priest was very ugly, the other very handsome; their combined age wouldn't have added up to the violet lady's forty. They stared shamelessly at him, but only when they stopped and raised their tiny glasses of wine to toast each other did Baltasar become aware of the immense tenderness that joined them; the looks the two young priests exchanged indicated as well that the ugly one had the subservient function of pampering, worshipping, caring for, and attending the handsome one.

Baltasar Bustos stared at the skirts of the handsome priest for a while with no desire to ascertain the reaction of the other. He found himself so alone after the long Upper Peru campaign and the death of his father that he feared the attraction of that young cleric with fine features, dark hair, and waxy complexion—like that of Miguel Lanza, like his father's dead hands holding the candle, burning because of the cruelty, the rancor of Sabina, who was so eager to form with him a circle of two, like the one formed by the two priests—might obstruct his relationship with the devout priest with rough features, slightly prognathous, and, like Baltasar, myopic. When he raised his eyes to meet theirs, however, he found satisfaction, shared attraction, and an invitation. They guessed his hunger for company, his solitude; they did not imagine that behind his eyes was the desired figure of Ofelia Salamanca.

Other eyes attracted him, although they never paid him the slightest attention and instead made him feel he was an intruder, alien to the exclusive circle of these aristocratic creoles, who in the city of Lima, capital of capitals, only rivaled in Spanish America by Mexico City, reached not only their splendor but their purest essence. Those eyes belonged to the most beautiful woman—beyond any doubt—attending the afternoon party. She looked like the sunset, her dark beauty shone, and her outfit, which turned mourning into show, glittered, in part thanks to the gold thread subtly woven into her funereal gown. The gold did not obviate her grief but gave a feeling of luxury to death, no doubt the death of the husband of the young woman, whose true, fatal glow was in her skin and not in her clothing or jewels. In fact, she wore no jewelry. She needed none. Her beauty dazzled Baltasar, whose eyes were full of blood and gore, hills of slate and thickets.

Was she as beautiful as he saw her? The object of her gaze was a couple. Another couple, obviously married, her arm resting ever on his, as if to initiate, also for eternity, a solemn promenade that with each step would announce: we are a couple. He was saying to the dark woman: dare to break up this pair, I invite you to do it, come with us. The wife's face expressed marital fidelity so strongly that it almost contradicted itself to become the most subtle of invitations. That afternoon, Baltasar Bustos instinctively sought out the lady in mourning's solitude to accompany his own. He learned that the solitary woman would cease to be so in the company of the married man who said to her, secretly yet so publicly, "You are my possible lover. In the presence of my own wife, I invite you to be my actual lover. I can do no more to attract you to me."

"Luz María . . ."

The name escaped like a sigh or a threat from the shared voice of the married couple. "We are so sorry about what happened."

"It's all right: time works miracles."

They began to speak about Masses and novenas, a castrato began to sing a passage from Palestrina, and a very old lady, draped in veils and wearing more combs than she had hairs on her head, lectured Baltasar the way someone teaches a basic lesson: "The servants know. They are the only ones who know in a society like ours. The Quechuan nurses abandoned the Incan nobles to serve the Spaniards. Now they will abandon the Spaniards to serve creole patriots like you, callow boy."

She scratched the moles that marked the spot where the

hair missing from her skull once grew, and she giggled in pure joy, announcing that her head was still good for something: "And besides. Did you ever see this Ofelia Salamanca's silver service? Well, get her husband, the cuckold marquis, to invite you to dinner, and there you will see the fate of all the silver mined in these Indies of ours, lad, youth, boy, what to call you?" The crone cackled, dressed in transparent gauze and propped up by two Indian servants wearing Versaillesque frock coats and cotton wigs. The old lady flapped her arms: "Get moving, you shitty *cholitos*, help me, don't stop, no one deserves more than a minute of my conversation, I have so little time."

Baltasar sought out the stockings embroidered with clocks, but perhaps their owner had been invited to withdraw. On the other hand, these scenes were like sideshows—mere sleight-of-hand by these mountebanks, whispered a familiar voice that reached Baltasar Bustos. Incredulous, he spun around to see the tall, slightly stooped figure of his old mentor Julián Ríos, the Jesuit who had put aside his cassock and had taught half the pampa the local flora and fauna, and the local languages—all in the hope of discovering, he said, remembering the childhood of Baltasar and Sabina Bustos, a universal imagination, even if it was an imagination nurtured in the soil; roots, said the old Jesuit, smiling and adding with a glint from his silver-framed glasses, "*Mais mes racines sont plutôt rabelaiesiennes, dit la corneille quand elle boît l'eau de la fontaine . . .*"

Baltasar laughed, squeezing Ríos's arm and listening as the old man gently led the young one to the other end of the viceregal party: "Everything else is a sideshow, to use circus jargon—I didn't say Circe's barroom, now—no: the main show is always the Marquis de Cabra himself."

Who, in fact, was holding court. Because—Julián Ríos pointed out—the rug has been swept clean of gossip by edict of the marquis himself, who was the first to mention the rumor about his wife, his life, his strife, rhymed Father Ríos irrepressibly. The marquis was talking now in an endless flow:

"Modern revolution is divided evenly between those enemy brothers, Rousseau and Voltaire. The Genevan wanted the people to act. The other wanted them to be led. But it takes a long time for the people to become educated and to act prudently, so they have to be guided at first—thence Voltaire wins the match, he can never lose it. What did that old cynic say?"

"That the light of reason falls by degrees," quoted Julián Ríos. "The lowest level of society needs the example of its superiors. Forty thousand wise men: that's more or less what we need."

"Forty thousand wise men!" said the old marquis, sighing. "Include me among them. The first thing I'll do is keep the people from ever taking my place or instructing me. All modern revolution does is create a new elite. Why? The old elite was more elegant and practiced in the very thing the new elite is going to do: mete out injustice."

"To transfer property from a minute group of landowners to four million electors in one year does not seem so elitist to me, your lordship. There has never been a redistribution of wealth as large or as swift in all of recorded history."

"Bah." The marquis did not even look at the tutor. "Revolutions of interests end up costing more than revolutions of ideals. All the Jacobin terror in France seems less painful to me than the elitist injustice of the North American revolution. Some revolution, gentlemen—a revolution that not only leaves slavery intact but actually consecrates it."

"Are we less racist than they?" asked Ríos.

"What is to be done, Mr., Mr.—" said the Marquis haughtily, not finding the proper title for the tutor. "I mean, what is to be done when the people of color themselves come to the courts here in Lima, in Barranquilla, or in La Guaira, requesting written proof that they are white? How many venal judges have stared into the scorched face of a man whose father and grandfather were black and whose mother and grandmother were Indian, and stated: 'He may be considered white'? Our courts are flooded with requests for certification of whiteness, Mr., Mr.—"

"Father Rivers," the tutor supplied, smiling.

"Ah, a perfidious son of Albion . . ."

"No, your Lordship, merely a poor albino dazzled with admiration at your wisdom."

"That's what I like to hear. Rivers should flow. Or, better yet, run."

"Having the runs is something that happens all too frequently in these parts, sir. But the way you say my name makes me think of *reverse*, so perhaps you would prefer me to step back."

"I was merely commenting on the irony of the blacks submitting legal petitions so as not to be termed 'poor black' or 'poor mulatto.' "

"We are all cooperating, your lordship. White families in Lima, Caracas, and Panama are also initiating legal actions to keep any family members from marrying people of color."

"In sum, then, Mr. Reverse, I'm right to declare here, before all of you, that my only virtue has been the proper administration of injustice and that, personally, I would rather die than cease to be unjust."

A chorus of laughter followed these lapidary witticisms of the Marquis de Cabra, a device by which he dissipated not only the attention initially focused on his wife's *affaires* but also whatever attention was being paid to the poor castrato performing Palestrina. In any case, he certainly hushed the comment of the old Jesuit: "Privilege is like the robe of Nessus; when you tear it off, you also tear off the flesh under it."

The marquis spun around like a wasp and spoke like a whip: "Go ahead and wage your war of independence. Disillusionment will soon follow. And, I assure you, I am not making idle pronouncements. I am predicting the most concrete things. A stagnant economy, without the protection of Spain and incapable of competing in world markets. A society of privilege; the mere act of casting out the Spaniards will not make the creoles less unjust, cruel, or greedy. And dictatorship after dictatorship will be necessary to bridge the gap between the country as constituted by law and the country as reality. You will be left to the mercy of the elements, my dear patriots. You will wrench off the roof of tradition. But you do not know how to survive in the new, open air. The modern age, which for an Englishman, Father Rivers, is a breeze, will be a hurricane for a Peruvian. We who speak Spanish were not born for it."

"We shall make our own modernity, and it will be unlike that of the English or the French, your lordship," said young Baltasar, imagining a French roof over the head of his sister, Sabina, to protect her, after being abandoned by Spain, from the cruel elements she so feared.

The marquis stared at him curiously, as if the old man's intelligence would never dare to reject a possible relationship, association, or contiguity, no matter how arbitrary it might seem at first glance.

"Father Rivers"—the marquis smiled—"your young disciple—that is what he is, isn't that so?—knows that all waters ultimately flow into each other. Am I right?"

"Rivers do flow," said the tutor.

"Rivers roll, servants serve, priests pray—or is it prey?—but castrati, fortunately, do not castrate. Yet young men with sunburned faces and newly shorn beards pique my curiosity. Do they flow, serve, pray, prey, or castrate?"

"None of those things, your lordship," said Baltasar. "At times, they merely desire."

"Just so long as they don't covet that which belongs to others," said the old man in acid tones. "In this country, the wise practice is to stick a finger up the ass of every miner as he leaves his work, to see that he isn't stealing the gold."

"Good heavens, your lordship! Not even I allow myself such obscenities," cackled the balding old woman bristling with combs, "in spite of the fact that I'm older and that Viceroy Abascal isn't listening to what I say."

That very personage was standing behind Cabra with his solemn, Visigoth face. The marquis bowed. Everyone awaited the words of the viceroy, Don Fernando de Abascal, Marquis de Concordia, who no doubt hoped to cancel any discussion of independence or loyalty to the Crown—the only fashionable topics, since no others lent themselves so well to animated conversation—with a few words more lapidary than any the others might utter. He imagined himself captivating his audience with his eyes, which were like those of an offended codfish:

"The Americans were born to be slaves, destined by nature to vegetate in obscurity and melancholy."

He said it out of obligation, to give offense, because he thought that under the present circumstances his obligation was to offend and that his greatest offense would be to overlook any arguments the others might propose. He was the viceroy, but not even the viceroy and his attributes could dampen— now was the time to prove it—the imagination and humor of the Marquis de Cabra, who sought thus to suggest that, more than Abascal, the man who should be viceroy was he who was speaking: Cabra himself.

He looked straight at Baltasar Bustos and commented that his tanned complexion and pale chin indicated many months in the open air and sun and a beard until recently unshaven. Baltasar nodded. This fellow looked like no one else: was he a soldier? But none of the officers present showed such a contrast, such roughness. "What campaigns were you in, Mr., Mr.—"

"Bustos. Baltasar Bustos."

"And a classical bust it is. Am I right, Father Rivers?"

"Quite right. This Balshazar seems ready for his feast."

"But it was Nebuchadnezzar who saw the writing on the wall."

"From which we should all take warning: the end is near, gentlemen."

Cabra glanced mockingly at the viceroy, who from offended codfish had metamorphosed into a satisfied mollusk. He had spoken, and nothing else mattered.

"So, Baltasar Bustos."

The marquis said he did not know if this Baltasar was a loyalist or an insurgent, but he was a creole, that much was obvious. And an officer, although on which side was *not* obvious, added Cabra with the mildest hint of menace in his voice. But he was an officer and a creole, so he would no doubt do what all of them did, which was to take an Indian, like this boy in livery and cotton wig attending the most excellent widow of the Marquis de Z———, who was Viceroy of Peru, and tell him, just as the Marquis de Cabra was telling him now, grabbing him roughly, you half-breed shit, that's right, half-breed shit a thousand times, I won't stick my finger up your ass to see if you steal my gold, half-breed, but if I were this creole officer—patriot? rebel? loyal to the king? who knows, who cares?—he would say to you, half-breed shit, sweep out the barracks, make my bed, wash the floor, disinfect the lavatories, carry in wood, pour me a glass of water, don't move a muscle if I give you a kick in the ass, don't let so much as a sigh escape your lips if I slap your face, don't you dare raise your head if I order you, you half-breed shit, to look down at my feet, because your soul, assuming you have one, you poor devil, doesn't even reach as high as my feet."

The marquis, more upset even than he thought, paused and took a deep breath, saying that a creole would say all that to this half-breed shit he'd grabbed by the neck. He would say it even if he was a patriot, because, before being a patriot, he was creole shit. Why didn't little Master Bustos do what the marquis was inviting him to do, when one day, sooner or later, he would have to do it to prove *who was in charge here.*

Cabra held out the servant of the widow of the Marquis de Z—— as if he were some exotic trophy. The bald old lady shook the tortoiseshell daggers jutting out of her head and protested, Miguelito is so good, so faithful, she would allow no one, not even the most distinguished President of the Court of Visitation, to . . .

Cabra spun ferociously on his heel to face the crone, she who had ordered Perrichole publicly flogged for bragging that she was the Viceroy de Amat's concubine, and, worse still, for thinking that the sins of prostitution could be expiated by publicly, not secretly, walking barefoot behind the carriage of the Blessed Sacrament, without adding scandal to scandal and publicity to virtue; she who witnessed and rejoiced in the drawing and quartering of the rebel Indian Tupac Amaru, the pretender to the title of last Inca, who in the name of the oppressed rose up in arms to turn the poor of Peru into Indian kings—was she now going to defend this half-breed shit in her service from a beating?

"Oh, but your lordship, that Tupac Amaru forced the governor of Cuzco to drink molten gold from the mines and die horribly. Miguelito the *cholo*, on the other hand, is neither a whore nor a rebel, but one of God's true souls," said the old crone, her voice racked with phlegm.

Laughter broke out, but Cabra did not release the bewigged *cholo.* He waited for silence, to proclaim that from that day forward, to prevent the fall of the Spanish empire in America, he, Leocadio Cabra, marquis of the same, quondam President of the Royal Council of Chile, would consider himself dead— after all, a man like himself could hardly survive the death of his world—and would celebrate, right here, in the City of the Kings, his own funeral, with pomp and splendor, presided over by the Viceroy Don Fernando de Abascal, Marquis de Concordia (who looked bewildered as he tried to understand these antinomian ideas for which he had no ready answer—how to term this mad marquis: "slave," "obscure," "abject"?). His excellency was not to take this anticipation of death as an impious or *cocasse* act, like the premature funeral of the heretic Voltaire or the rebel Fray Servando Teresa de Mier, the liberal Mexican in Cádiz, but rather as an act of devotion and profound piety, like the burial-in-advance of His Majesty Charles V in the monastery at Yuste, amid solemn hymns and ecclesiastical panegyrics. Therefore: the burial-in-advance of the Marquis de Cabra would be not (God save us!) a Voltairean joke or a sublime foreshadowing of our common destiny incarnate in the most catholic of monarchs, but a bitter commentary on the times. (The lady banished from the presence of the viceroy gazed at her stockings with their tiny clocks; the tutor Julián Ríos let the marquis rattle on.) "When Simón Bolívar enters this city from the north and José de San Martín from the south, something I also predict today, all of you will say that I am dead and buried, knowing full well that in my place will be this half-breed shit, the servant of the widow of the Marquis de Z———. I hereby condemn him to die young, in my place, so that the world will think I am dead and leave me in peace, leave me in peace, leave me in peace, alone and old and forgotten and abandoned and cuckolded by my sweet Ofelia," said the raving-mad Marquis de Cabra, tossing with a sportsman's skill (unless it was pure luck) his wig, which landed on the old lady's bald head bristling with combs. And with that the marquis withdrew, dragging his feet, sobbing, as the strains of the minuet being played by the *cholo* musicians in cotton wigs and red frock coats metamorphosed, in Baltasar Bustos's ear, into a melancholy, remote mountain air, a melody of irremediable farewells, carrying with it the din of arms, of age-old llamas and new horses, the trembling of the earth and the storms in the heavens, its ever so sad *quena* pipes, the only voice of the uplands, silencing both.

But not now. A great rush of candelabras being extinguished,

rustling tablecloths, and clinking china accompanied the merry
farewells of the young people arranging to meet that night and
the following nights: Let's go to the Bodegones Café. We'll
see each other in the theater. Don't miss Paca Rodríguez—
you've never seen as charming an Andalusian; a shame she
loves her husband, Bufo Rodríguez. Careful, a year's gone by
and no one talks about anything but the murder of the most
famous actress before this Paca, María Moreno, killed by her
rejected lover, a certain Cebada, whose passionate jealousy
was pardoned by everyone in Lima except our host of the
evening. Lower your voice, Juan Francisco, don't be disre-
spectful to our illustrious viceroy who ordered him garrotted
like a common criminal, doubtless because the viceroy himself
desired the actress María Moreno and paid no heed to the
warnings scrawled on every wall in Lima: *Abascal, Abascal, if
you hang Cebada, you're sure to fall!* Fall, Matilde, fall? Just look
at him, as fresh as a head of lettuce. Don't talk about lettuce,
it makes me hungry. Everyone to the café and then to the
theater!

[2]

Baltasar Bustos embraced the old Jesuit tutor and asked him
to wrap him in his cape. Julián Ríos, no doubt because of the
adverse feelings inspired in him by the Bourbons' decision to
expel the Society, insisted stubbornly on dressing in the style
banned by Charles III: wide-brimmed hat and cape. More than
hiding Baltasar, the cape helped protect him: the sage tutor
recognized the need of this boy, who was not only going out
into the world but going out into a radically new world, who
was painfully breaking away from a past he deemed abominable
but which was his own. Would the South American patriots
ever understand that without that past they would never be
what they so desired: paradigms of modernity? Novelty for its
own sake is an anachronism: it races toward its inevitable old

age and death. A past renewed is the only guarantee of modernity: that was Father Ríos's lesson for his young Argentine disciple, who that night seemed so helpless. As helpless as the entire continent.

An enlightened cleric like Julián Ríos could not escape his own contradiction; therefore he could understand it in others. His contradiction was both to approve and to condemn the riots that led to the burning down of Esquilache's mansion in Madrid when the decree to expel the Jesuits was published and the people laid at the feet of the Bourbon court all the evils unleashed in the absence of the Society of Jesus. The Esquilache riot had its touches of comedy, but for Ríos they only confirmed, in his own soul, the conflict between maintaining order through pragmatic, evolving solutions and transforming everything through violence, risking thereby a fall back to a level lower than the one that promoted the revolt but also taking the opportunity to achieve things that otherwise would never be realized.

These thoughts vexed the tutor as he led Baltasar, invisible under his cape, out of the viceregal palace. One part of him was asking (and so he said to Bustos): "Where are you staying? You must rest. Let me take you to your lodgings; we'll talk there. I'm concerned about your future. What are you going to do? Why don't you go back home and take care of your own? There is no other politics than that of the soil; all politics is local, but I don't know anything about you, about what you've been doing since you were a boy." The other half of him pulled him toward the palace occupied by the Marquis de Cabra in the plaza of the Mercedarian church. But first they took a long, roundabout walk to the other side of the river, so as to converse at some ease.

Leading Baltasar Bustos through the night streets of this always dangerous, secret city fashioned of the incompatible clays of arrogance and resentment, which made it fierce in its capacity to humiliate the weak and do violence to the powerful,

Julián Ríos allowed himself the observation that all a thief of the kind that abounds in this capital of social extremes would need would be a jug of water and a spoon to open a hole in Lima's mud walls. Lima: improvident, with no long-range projects to concentrate the will of its citizens; a city wasting itself in waiting all day, yet again, for a rain which was always threatened but never came, because a real tropical storm would melt away this city with no stone structures all the way to the Avenue of the Discalced Carmelites, from which the Amancoes hills could be seen.

"Someday a huge rainstorm is going to come down," Ríos said to his pupil. But, given the circumstances, Baltasar seemed even more depressed than the Marquis de Cabra himself. There appeared to be one cause in both cases: Ofelia Salamanca.

"How are you? Have you traveled? I haven't seen you since you were a boy!" said the tutor to his disciple as they stood by the tiny convent of St. Liberata.

They stopped in the plaza crowded with mules and drovers arriving from the mountains or setting out for the desert. The fresh scent of mint, coriander, parsley, and verbena prevailed with difficulty over the thick smells of wet wool, hides fresh from the slaughterhouse, spurs that still stank of the mine, steaming excrement, and the long urination of beasts of burden. Baltasar, his strong hands, longing for mercy, on his old teacher's shoulders, told Ríos the story of his life since they'd last seen each other: his reading Rousseau, his incandescent faith in the May revolution, his private decision not to join the rebellion without first returning home, to his own tradition, and to the confrontation with what he was and where he came from: and then, the campaign of Upper Peru.

"With these hands, I have killed. And don't say, *C'est la guerre*, Father."

"As for me, I no longer have a personal history. My history has no meaning outside History. How sad. But the world has made us this way."

"No one could erase the sign of the priesthood from you, not even God. Could you hear my confession?"

"I could. I could even tell you your confession. Don't think it's my pride speaking when I say that. Put simply: in my order each individual is something more than himself."

"The first man I killed was an Indian. After that, it didn't matter that I went on killing. I was a good guerrilla. Lanza is a brave man. I don't blame him for anything. Only that one action was blameworthy. The first. It was bound to happen. I killed someone, and that someone was an Indian."

"You know that we Jesuits armed the Guaranís in Paraguay. Thanks to those weapons, no one crossed into Indian territory: not the viceroys, not the traffickers in alcohol, not even the slavers. The Indians stopped using money, the land belonged to the community, the work day was six hours, everyone prospered, and no one was unjust. Does it sound like utopia to you? It wasn't. The thirty-three settlements we created, from the Paraná to the Río Negro and from Belém to Paysandú, were only possible because of a political and military act: Philip IV's decision to give the Guaranís weapons. If that hadn't happened, those Indians, like all the others, would have been exterminated by alcohol, forced labor, the *mita*, and disease. An armed utopia! No money, but lots of firearms. But all you need is one musket for utopia to cease being utopia. The seed of all evil is justifying the death of a fellow man."

"Was it a community?"

Ríos said it was, but Baltasar that night would not have set out for utopia or any other community without stopping first for this frank conversation with a person he respected. The solitude of his time on the pampa, culminating in the death of José Antonio Bustos and the final break with his sister, Sabina; the solitude of the months spent with the guerrillas in the Inquisivi, where brotherhood was nipped by Miguel Lanza's "to-the-last-man" decision: we all may die here, but no one leaves. The solitude of distance and time—five years already! without seeing Dorrego and Varela and feeling that they lived in the mad, loving, tight fraternity of the Café de Malcos. All that was not compensated for by a soiree in viceregal Lima, a tacitly perverse invitation from two young priests, or the sovereign indifference of a beautiful, brilliant dark woman who succumbed to the temptation of a man who certainly did not deserve her. And, finally, the absence of Ofelia Salamanca embittered him, as did the ugly rumor surrounding that absence: adultery, prejudice, cruelty, ostentatious frivolity.

"I've had the feeling that I was totally alone during these past years," Baltasar said later to Ríos. "Now I've just lost myself in other people. I don't feel free either way, alone or in company. I need society or I wouldn't miss it. But when I'm in society, I feel sick. I find scenes like the one we witnessed tonight repugnant."

"That's because you want to change society," said Julián Ríos. "But such desires are very costly. You will only feel free when the society you want to change is so perfect it no longer needs you."

Baltasar Bustos asked if he had any other options but to fight for the impossible or to conform to what already existed. Ríos begged him to offer now what he said he was seeking and what he was sharing with his Buenos Aires friends: a bit of sincerity. For whose sake were they going through all these difficulties? Who was the individual channel of all this anguish?

Now, walking quickly among weeping willows arranged without symmetry, in a night whose fogs had lifted and whose Pacific stars adorned the only beautiful sky in Lima, which is the sky veiled to the light of day, Baltasar Bustos told the tutor what had taken place on the night of May 24–25 in Buenos Aires. The youth's shame mounted as the tutor's laughter grew louder, and Baltasar, incredulous, fell physically into his own trap: his body, his words, his energetic pace now that he'd lost so much weight in the campaign with Lanza were, in that moment, the worst trap, because they left him no gestures, no convincing corporeal responses to that laugh, which could not be injurious, coming from whom it came, but which, despite everything, was just that: there was a slap in each guffaw, a sting in every smile.

"You poor naïve fool! You did not burn down the Buenos Aires court building, Baltasar. It was the mob. That night they decided to destroy the colonial archives, the registers of racial discrimination, the property exclusions—everything, my dear Baltasar, that this colony's chain of paper signifies. And remember, it has enslaved as much with words as with branding irons. Baltasar, you did not kill that child. Your thirty candles wouldn't have been enough to honor a saint!"

"Twenty-five," said Baltasar. "She was twenty-five then, she must be thirty now . . ."

"She lived right over there," said Ríos, turning to point out the palace from where they had stopped, alongside the fountain in the Mercedarians' plaza, amazed at the hustle and bustle—unusual at eleven o'clock in the evening—in the entranceways, doors, and windows of the house occupied by the Marquis de Cabra, former President of the Royal Council of Chile, and his vanished wife. Torches were seen in window after window, mules and carts were stopped outside the coachhouse door, trunks emerged, black drapes were carried in, a procession of puzzled acolytes paused as they searched for their pastor; the Blessed Sacrament was brought in, carried with proper solemnity; veiled women began to gather, tiny in their flat slippers, enveloped in capes and scarves.

"The doors of the house are wide open, Balta . . ."

In her bedroom, Ofelia Salamanca had left a box of powder and a silver scraper she used to cleanse her tongue. Also two popular books by Samuel Tissot, one on the disorders that afflict literary and sedentary people and their cure (walks, cinnamon, and fennel tea), the other, simply titled *Onanism and Madness*. She had also left behind the red, the blood-colored ribbon he'd watched her put around her neck from the balcony that May night in Buenos Aires. The thin line of blood symbolic of the guillotine. Baltasar discreetly slipped the ribbon into his pocket. He looked with distaste at the double bed and was overcome by a pounding wave of jealousy, imagining Ofelia in the arms of her husband, the marquis, who, wrapped in a shroud, was carried, in a perfectly synchronized ceremony, to the same bed from which Baltasar Bustos, no matter how he tried, could not banish the image of the erotic couple. Ofelia Salamanca, her legs spread, astride the skeleton of her husband Cabra, the old goat; the she-goat rubbing the mons Veneris he'd been imagining for five years as bulging yet deep, hairy yet prepubescent, the hidden, monastic sex of Ofelia Salamanca, invisible one moment and fleshy the next, protruding, visible from any angle, reproduced with febrile symmetry behind and in front of the thighs of the desired woman. Possessed by Cabra and how many others?

Baltasar Bustos and Julián Ríos were pushed into a corner of the bedroom when the servants carrying candles entered along with the hired mourners, the acolytes, the curious, the disconcerted priests, and especially the principal actor: Don Leocadio, Marquis de Cabra, who was laid out, wrapped in his shroud, paler than Miguel Lanza, in the same bed where he had enjoyed the love of his wife, Ofelia. Was he really dead? Was he pretending? Did he have an attack after the painful scene at Viceroy Abascal's party? Baltasar did not want to find out. He approached the marquis's funereal head and whispered into the dead or alive Marquis de Cabra's ear, "I love your wife. I burned your son to death, and you will have no other, dead or alive, because in the past five years you've lost your virility and are nothing but a senile scarecrow. I will follow your wife to the ends of the world and force her to love me in the name of justice, because she must love a man who is passionately in love with her and would do anything for her."

It did not matter to him that, either to simulate death or because he really was dead, the Marquis de Cabra's ears were sealed with wax. But two crystallized tears, as hard as silver, had added another furrow to the wrinkled cheeks of the former President of the Royal Council of Chile.

[3]

I need only a few sheets of paper to end this chapter. One of them is the Marquis de Cabra's will, worthy of mention for two reasons. The first is that in it he offers a substantial lifetime annuity to the *cholo* who will every day stand at the corner of Pilón del Molino Quebrado and allow himself to be kicked by any passing creole. The sagacious husband of Ofelia Salamanca explains that he is guided in this bequest by a desire to alleviate the frustration of all Peruvians bereft of slaves.

The second, more bitter bequest is an uncalled-for, counterproductive, impracticable command. The Marquis de Cabra orders the colonial aristocracy to pillage itself so that the rebels will find nothing.

But where are those rebels in this year of 1815? All sorts of news reaches Buenos Aires, most of it depressing. Bolívar is in exile in Jamaica, and instead of raising armies, he writes letters complaining about our perennially infantile nations, their incapacity to govern themselves, and the distance between our liberal institutions and our customs and character. In the south, Belgrano's expedition to Upper Peru has failed, and only the resistance of caudillos like Miguel Lanza has prevented the total restoration of colonial rule. Right here in Buenos Aires, Alvear's directorate has fallen, and the estate owners, merchants, and priests have seized power, persecuting the liberals, confiscating their property, and sentencing them to exile or to death. The saddest news comes at year's end from Mexico: the rebel priest Morelos has been captured, tried, and sentenced. His severed head is like a black moon clapped onto a lance in San Cristóbal Ecatepec.

Dorrego and I, Varela, get along as best we can, hoping for better times, keeping our eyes open, and reading the letters of our friend Baltasar. Sometimes we write back, but since we don't really know where he is, we send our letters to the estate of his dead father. Let's hope they reach him. We learned that Lanza sentenced him to death for desertion; we fix our clocks, and on afternoons when the pampa wind blows, we stand in front of maps of the continent and trace the imaginary movements of nonexistent armies: campaigns that are always dangerous but ultimately triumphant, waged by ideal, phantasmagorical, South American armies . . .

In this way, Dorrego and I, Varela, transform History into the presence of an absence. Is that another name for ideal perfection?

6

The Army of the Andes

[1]

"His name is Baltasar Bustos, his family owns an estate—reasonable people, but half savage, like all ranch owners." "If at least his father were a merchant." "Is he a good marriage prospect?" "But he fought alongside the mountain rebels in Upper Peru—when did he become a royalist?" "When Miguel Lanza put a price on his head for deserting." "He says that he's in love, that he came here looking for the woman." "That's not important, but the news he brings from Inquisivi and Jujuy is." "He's very open; we know everything about him." "He doesn't hide anything from us." "He knows we'll crush the rebellion, so he's doing us a favor." "He certainly doesn't look like a guerrilla." "Your excellency shouldn't judge by appearances." "Plump, perfumed, dressed in silks, nearsighted . . ."

He strolled the salons of Santiago de Chile just as he'd strolled those of Lima, but he did not cut the same figure. Rather, he conformed to the description recorded above by the authorities of the captaincy-general of Chile. What a fuss this Baltasar Bustos made about his search for Ofelia Salamanca, now the widow of the Marquis de Cabra, who had died of bile and apoplexy in Lima! Who had died, it should be noted, in bed. Of course, no one knows if he died before or after his rehearsed death. Was he already dead when they laid him in his wife's bed? Or did he die there, transforming the rehearsal into reality and the attempt at playfulness into God's punishment?

The marquis fully deserved it. He left behind in Chile so many bad memories of his cruelty and injustice—which he carried out, it must be noted, with a smile and a joke on his lips! But his wife, Ofelia Salamanca, is no longer here; people say she went north, fleeing from the imminent fall of Chile, so ill defended, she said before departing, by the most pusillanimous captain-general in three centuries, Francisco Casimiro Marcó del Pont, who sought to compensate for his lack of military prowess by investing excessive energy in repression, passing judgment on the loyalty of all creoles without exception, expropriating their properties, burning their houses, and occasionally exiling them to the Island of Juan Fernández.

While none of that made up for Marcó del Pont's stupidity on the battlefield, it did succeed in making Spanish rule the object of general hatred and threw the inhabitants of Santiago and Valparaíso into a state of total hysteria. It was from that that Ofelia Salamanca had fled. She was fed up with suspicion, fear, sudden changes! Now this nearsighted, fat fellow was looking for her, and just by chance he came from Jujuy, Upper Peru, and Mendoza, and had friends in the rebel officer corps in Argentina, who, though they protected him from Lanza's death sentence, had no confidence in him.

In any case, the sword of Damocles is hanging over his head; obviously, he's not meant for war; he says that Lanza conscripted him; he seems as edgy as everyone else; he only wants to find the widow of the Marquis de Cabra and ease his anxiety with exasperated waves of his handkerchief, nervous twitches of his head, as if he were expecting bad news or a worse blow at any moment. He complains about not finding his usual lotions in Chile; this country is the end of the world! He wonders what he's doing here, if he's not looking for Ofelia Salamanca, until someone suggests he form a club for those whose hearts have been broken by the Chilean beauty, stubborn enemy of independence and the rebels, about whom it is said, but perhaps it's nothing but pure gossip, that it was she who personally plunged a dagger into the back of the insurgent Colonel Martín Echagüe to keep him from taking part in the battle of Rancagua, a rebel defeat that forced the vanquished leaders O'Higgins and Carrera to flee to Mendoza on the other side of the Andes. Whence comes to us this confused, edgy, beardless youngster to tell us that a rebel attack is imminent, that San Martín has deployed armies of more than twenty thousand men in mobile units north and south along the Argentine Andes in preparation for a general assault on Chile, from Aconcagua to Valdivia.

Santiago de Chile lived in terror at the outset of the summer of 1816, and precisely for that reason its forty thousand inhabitants decided to enjoy themselves until they died and to spend every cent they had. But the rumor mill, as in Lima, worked to its full capacity in the continuous, simultaneous parties with which royalist society, more and more depleted, sought to exorcise its fear of an insurgent victory, and sought in vain for possible allies among the creoles, whom Marcó del Pont's repressive violence had delivered over to the patriots. They clandestinely circulated Father Camilo Henríquez's newspaper, *Dawn of Chile*, which contained news that should have been assumed to be false since it came from the mutinous enemy, unless the rebels were deluding themselves. The purpose of the social gatherings in the Chilean capital, during those months of oppressive heat and of peaches peeled a second before they rotted, was to gather information, air all rumors, place wagers on the future of the colony, and listen to anyone who had the merest particle of information.

"The rebels are mad," Baltasar Bustos would say, strolling contemptuously through the Chilean soirees with a tiny glass of white wine in his hand. "They've gone all-out in deploying troops for a general attack along an *eeeenormous* front; they're going to cut all of you to bits, so get a good night's sleep. Me? I'm harmless, just looking for a certain woman."

Those listening to this fop—as the English court, adorned at the time by Beau Brummel, would no doubt have called him—wondered if a myopic, soft dandy who proclaimed his passion so publicly could really love the woman he said he was pursuing. No, he couldn't possibly love her so much if he was so vocal in mentioning her. Perhaps it was just the sickness of the age: tiring passionately, being oneself only by being one's romantic passion, which was certainly sufficient, if painful, for the interior hero invented by the likes of Rousseau and Chateaubriand.

"All I ask of the world is that it grant me a point of departure: the woman I love," said Bustos, between the sighs of the Chilean girls, the most beautiful in America. But he would quickly disillusion them with a mannered gesture and a clarification: "But I don't want you to think I desire a companion. Not in the slightest. I only need—can you chaste damsels listening to me understand?—a love object. An *object* for my love."

They turned their backs on him. Perhaps that young, handsome priest looking so intently at Baltasar understood him. Approaching him, the priest said that Baltasar's words made him think there was something more in them than it seemed from their apparent frivolity. Unrequited love is the most intense of all.

"So you, too, have read St. John Chrysostom," said Baltasar, remembering a violent May night in Buenos Aires. "But now"—he sighed—"our secret passions no longer matter. Order itself is in danger. I have lived with these guerrilla criminals. I know what they're capable of doing, to women, to priests like you . . . We've got to hang them before they hang us."

"Dandy," blurted out the priest, slapping Baltasar across the face.

"Oh! I saw you from a distance in Lima, I know who you are, so be careful," replied Bustos.

A third young man, a royalist officer, whose high, embroidered collar pinched his cheeks painfully and eclipsed his thick, reddish, carefully cultivated sideburns, pulled them apart. The young lieutenant said this was no time for provoking arguments and making people more nervous. The priest put himself in serious danger by defending the rebels, even if he did so out of Christian charity. Bustos should try to restrain himself, however understandable it might be for a man with a price on his head to be on edge. But the Inquisivi rebels had not yet reached Santiago. He could relax. No, Baltasar replied, they hadn't, but San Martín had. "The army he's gathered in Argentina is going to attack us from all sides, there won't be enough supplies . . ."

The lieutenant with the sideburns ordered him to be quiet. He was sowing confusion and raising tensions. San Martín would attack from the south, where crossing the mountains was easier. Who would risk crossing the highest peaks? No one had ever marched an army through the Aconcagua Valley. It's almost four miles up! In fact, San Martín himself had had a great meeting with the Pechuenche chiefs to get permission to pass through their flatlands. He would surprise us Spaniards at Planchón and give the Indians back their freedom.

"Forces sufficient to stop any rebel invasion are already marching to Planchón," said the cocky lieutenant, hooking one thumb over his wide belt while with his other hand he caressed the soft fingers of his snow-white parade gloves.

"Do you actually believe one word of what those lying Indians tell you?" Baltasar Bustos laughed.

"Everything suggests they've betrayed San Martín," said Lieutenant Sideburns.

"Just as they would betray us royalists," insisted Baltasar, playing on the expectations of the small group gathering to listen to them. "No one knows what to think anymore!"

"We should really beware of illuminati priests besotted with French readings," added the young priest, as if to erase, then and there, any bad impression he might have made and to confuse the discussion even more. "We have the power of confession, and we have influence on the conscience of the military, the bureaucrats, the housewives . . . I know that disloyal priests abound in Chile, and that they never leave off their labor of undermining everything."

"Those divisive priests have split my family, fathers against sons," said a sallow little captain as he arranged his cream-colored shirt front with a gesture that belied his rancor. "And that I can never forgive them."

"I know nothing about that," said the red-haired lieutenant energetically. "All I know is that there isn't a single mountain pass where we don't have troops ready to repel San Martín, no matter where in the Andes he turns up."

"Do you know that your beloved Ofelia murdered Captain Echagüe in bed, while they were fornicating?" the young priest said to Baltasar in a mysterious, seductive, cruel tone, but loud enough that the summer girls, the eternal little mistresses of Santiago society, could hear him with scandalized delight.

[2]

Baltasar cut such a comic, blind, addled-witted figure at the parties of the waning Chilean colony that it shouldn't have surprised him that people took more notice of him than he of them. The soirees followed on each other like a series of prolonged farewells extending from the salons of the Royal Council to the elegant country houses east of the city, through the baroque of the carved ceiling panels, the wrought-iron work, and the huge portals of Velasco House in the center of the city.

To honor the memory of Ofelia Salamanca, Baltasar made a big show of haunting the chambers of the Royal Council, like a soul in torment; that was where the deceased Marquis de Cabra had presided before being sent to Buenos Aires. It was a new building, just finished in 1808, with twenty cast-iron windows on the second floor, wrought-iron balconies on the third, and a sequence of patios and galleries that reminded our hero (which is what you are, Baltasar) of the spacious River Plate Superior Court where his life was determined for all time.

This Santiago building owed its existence to a governor who arrived firmly committed to implanting the culture of the Enlightenment in Spain's most remote southern colony. Luis Muñoz de Guzmán took Charles III's ideas of modernization seriously and disembarked at the port of Valparaíso bearing musical instruments, baroque-music scores, perhaps some forbidden books, and no doubt the plays that soon began to be put on in those same patios and salons, under the patronage of his wife, Doña Luisa de Esterripa.

Nothing on this summer afternoon would have kept Baltasar Bustos from the performance taking place in one of the mansions—after all, it was nothing less than Jean-Jacques Rousseau's *The Discovery of America*—except that at that same hour, on every afternoon since he arrived in Santiago, Baltasar Bustos would step out on the balcony of the house where he was staying, a house that belonged to an old friend of his father's, a Spaniard who'd made his fortune in the New World and left all his property to go back to Spain. From that vantage point, he would observe a vision in the neighboring garden.

At around five in the afternoon, a girl would appear among the olive and almond trees. Dressed all in white, she seemed to float in a private cloud of soft cottons and gauze bodices.

Baltasar would wait for the appearance of this phantom: she was always punctual and always distant, like a new star, half sun, half moon, displaying herself to him alone, offering herself to him in the tender orbit of a satellite around a true star— him. As she approached, this delightful girl would spin among the almond trees; coming closer and closer, she would twirl on her always bare feet in a dance that Baltasar wanted to think was dedicated to him—after all, there were no other spectators but the sun and the moon, which at that uncertain hour coexist in the Andean sky.

Only once, Baltasar looked at the two of them, the sun and moon present at five o'clock in the afternoon over a garden of wise and serene plants. They could not compete with her; she was both of them at once, and many other things as well.

A fine sun, as hot and caressing as the familiar hand of a mother who knows she is taken for granted and resigns herself to not being especially loved; but also an evil sun about to execute the day by hurling it into an irreversible conflagration from which it would never rise: the sun was the stepmother of time.

And a bad moon, which appeared now as if to seal the day's fate with a silver lock, white moon drained of life, pale moon with a vampire's face, bloodless moon hungry for offal and bloody discharges; but a good moon too, the bed of the day reposing in white sheets, the final bath that washes off the day's grime and sinks us into the amorous re-creation of time which is sleep.

Baltasar Bustos would watch all that from his balcony, afternoon after afternoon, until he came to distinguish a face, the unusual face of the moon, unexpected, individual, marked by eyebrows that in another woman would have been repulsive, joined together with no break, like a second sex about to devour her black eyes, her haughty nose, her red lips, and her expression of disdain, sweet disdain that began to madden Baltasar and to distance him from his obsession with Ofelia Salamanca.

Each afternoon, for a week now, this most beautiful girl—
she could be no more than eighteen—came closer and closer
until she disappeared through the series of arches of the house
next door. Perhaps she had seen him, because she teased him
coquettishly, appearing and then hiding behind the columns
in the long aisles before she disappeared until the next day.

But this afternoon she was not there.

Baltasar felt a burning desire to jump over the wall, embrace
her and kiss first her red lips and then her provocative eyebrows, like velvet, joined like a divine scourge, the promise
of lust and terror. She was sun and moon, and this afternoon
she was missing.

Only this afternoon. Why? What could have interrupted a
rite he by now considered sacred, indispensable to his romantic
life—once again he realized it and said it when he described
this episode to us; his amorous emotions depended on distance, on absence, on the intensity of the desire manifested
to a woman he could not touch, saw from afar, who now, just
like Ofelia Salamanca, had disappeared without keeping the
appointment, not with him, but with the sun and the moon.

Then Baltasar Bustos took his hat, ran out of the house, ran
without noticing the ten blocks that separated him from the
Red House in whose grand patio Rousseau's short tragedy was
being performed, ran along the Calle del Rey, burst through
the grand doorway, and saw her dancing in the middle of the
patio surrounded by a chorus, by Indians and Spaniards, she
herself acting the role of an allegorical Spanish maiden who
sang and recited at the same time: Let us row, let us cross the
seas, our pleasures will have their time, because to discover
new worlds is to offer new flowers to love . . .

She raised her arms, and the gauze of her bodice revealed
two fresh cherries, kissable, doing a short and merry quadrille
on the girl's bosom.

"It isn't Jean-Jacques's best effort," said the handsome priest
to Baltasar as the public applauded and the actors bowed and
thanked them. "I prefer *Narcissus, or He Who Loves Himself,*

where Rousseau has the audacity to begin the dialogue with two women talking about a man, the brother of one of them, who, because of the refinement and affectation of his clothes, is a kind of woman disguised in man's clothing. Yet his feminine appearance, instead of being a disguise, restores him to his natural state."

"Are you telling me that this marvelous girl is really a man in disguise?" said Baltasar, instantly assuming his own vapid, cruel affectation.

"No"—the priest laughed—"her name is Gabriela Cóo, and her father's job, an endless, labyrinthine task, is to sell off the Jesuits' rural properties in Chile for the benefit of the Crown. His daughter is no less emancipated than Rousseau himself, so she works at acting, avidly reading the authors of the age, and communing with nature. Allow me to introduce you, Bustos."

"Are you telling me that all these afternoons she's merely been rehearsing a part?" asked Baltasar, plainly disillusioned.

"Pardon me?"

He accepted the invitation to meet her socially, but only under the condition that no one ever find out that each afternoon at five, for as long as he had to live in Chile, he would see her appear, vaporous and infinitely desirable, in the garden next door to his own house. He was afraid that she might already have met him at one of the myriad Santiago gatherings and that she would despise him, as did the other girls, who were, besides, fully aware of his obsession for the vanished Marquise de Cabra. He was just about to reject the introduction and to propose, since both of them were Rousseau enthusiasts, a purely epistolary relationship, like the one in the novel causing a furor throughout the New World, from Mexico to Buenos Aires: *La Nouvelle Héloïse*.

But three things happened, three foreseeable yet unexpected things. Myopic and foppish, chubby and not very attractive, Baltasar launched into one of an infinite number of dinner conversations with the lady next to him at table. Their dialogue was well under way when Baltasar realized he was acting a romantic part he'd learned perfectly and would recite at these functions. But this role was, at the same time, perfectly authentic, because everything he said corresponded to an intimate conviction, even if its verbal expression was not especially felicitous. This divorce was, simultaneously, the matrimony of his words. He'd repeated them again and again with a mixture of apathy and passion ever since his visit to Lima, searching for Ofelia Salamanca and insinuating that, sentenced to death by the ferocious guerrilla leader Miguel Lanza, he had to place his sympathies with the Crown; after all, the insurgents would deny him any protection whatever.

He could not alter his discourse that night; it was authentic and false at the same time. But he addressed it to her, since he had discovered halfway through dinner that he was speaking to Gabriela Cóo. He gave a face to that face, eyebrows to that visage, a perfume to that body, and now he could not stop the flow of his words, careening like a cart down a mountainside. And each time she answered him in a polite but cutting, intelligent, firm, even amused way, was she laughing at him, as almost all these Chilean girls did who were too beautiful and intelligent to take him seriously? And wasn't that exactly what he most desired: to be left free to pursue his true passion, the search for Ofelia?

"Whenever I come near to a woman like you, I feel the desire to avenge my pain and my sin on you."

"You don't say."

"Only you can kill the passion in me."

"It would be a pleasure."

"I mean: do me the favor of hastening my calvary."

"To whom are you speaking, Mr. Bustos?"

"I tell you that my soul only wants to recover or die, milady."

"But I only know how to cure, not to kill."

"Try to be another woman, and I will not try to seduce you," said Baltasar, lowering his voice.

"I want neither to be someone else nor to be seduced by

you," she replied in the same low tone, before laughing out loud. "Be more reasonable, Mr. Bustos."

The second thing that happened was that each afternoon at five she reappeared, far off in her garden. She approached little by little, as if suggesting that she would come closer, allowing herself to be desired, allowing him to make her more and more his own, first in his eyes and his desire and someday perhaps through real possession. The movements of the dance, the increasing languors, the increasing nakedness of that svelte, almost infantile body governed by a mask whose will was a mouth as red as a wound and brows as black as a whip, spelled out her name, Gabriela, Gabriela Cóo, desired, desirable, promising, promised, confident she would not deceive her lover, if he wanted to be her lover, if he gave himself to her, distant and nubile in her garden, as he had given himself to Ofelia Salamanca, distant and widowed, a mother who had given birth twice to the same child, given birth, that is, to life and to death, a woman burdened by suffering and rumors and probable cruelties and imagined betrayals. Gabriela Cóo's dancing body was asking him to choose but did not say to him, "I am better than the other"; it merely said, "I am different, and you must accept me as I am."

It had to be that way, Baltasar said to himself every afternoon, because she was no longer rehearsing Rousseau's play, which was put on just once in the patio of the grand Portuguese-style mansion on Calle del Rey. No longer. Now the performance was for him alone.

She was his little mistress—he decided to give her that name, just as we called him our little brother.

One afternoon, the little brother and the little mistress met without having fixed a time. He jumped over the low wall separating the two properties just as she was coming out of the entrance to her house. Neither yielded, but both gave all. She explained to him that her behavior the other night had not been the infantile act of a spoiled girl trying to entertain in polite society. She really did want to be an actress, she believed in independence—not only political but personal, too. The two went together, at least that is what she believed. Here in Chile, in other parts of the New World, even in Europe, she would pursue her career. She loved words, said Gabriela Cóo; each word had its own life and required the same care as a newborn child. When she opened her mouth, as she did the other night, and repeated a word—love, pleasure, world, sea—she had to take charge of that word like a mother, like a shepherdess, like a lover, yes, even like a little mistress, convinced that, without her, without her mouth, her tongue, the word would smash against a wall of silence and die forsaken.

But to take charge of words that weren't her own, the words of Rousseau, Ruiz de Alarcón, or Sophocles, she had to prepare herself for a long time. She would give nothing to a man unless he first gave her words. For her, love was a vocation as strong as the theater, but words also sustained love. All this was very difficult, even a little sad—Gabriela Cóo put her arm around Baltasar and patted his curls—because her work was pure shadow, fleeting, left no mark: only the words, poor things, that preceded it were left, and would be, even without her. In order to give meaning to her life of spectral voices, what else could Gabriela think except that, thanks to her mouth, the words had not died but had actually gained a modicum of life, body, dignity, who knows what else?

She felt for Baltasar's nape under his curly hair and asked if he understood her. He said he did; he knew she understood him equally well. She knew he loved her and why he acted and spoke that way at the Santiago dinners he frequented and why they would be parting soon.

"Tell me it's not because of that other woman." Gabriela Cóo thus made her only faux pas, explicable in any case, and he forgave her but decided at that moment to separate her from his life, to give her the freedom she needed, and to give himself to the slavery his obsession with Ofelia entailed until he consummated his passion. At the moment, he could see no other way to be faithful to this adorable girl, Gabriela, Gabriela Cóo, my love, my adored little love, delightful Gabriela; we shall never truly know our own hearts, Little Mistress.

He so desired the only kiss he and Gabriela exchanged, his vision of that act was so intense, so red were the girl's lips when they joined his, their mouths parting and their tongues joining and separating only to tickle their palates and count their avid, cruel, and tender teeth, that from it there emerged another mouth, another kiss, a kiss that stole theirs away, banished it, took it from them and turned it into the kiss, the mouth, the voice of Ofelia Salamanca.

And that was the third thing that happened.

He promised himself not to think about Gabriela until he could be hers alone.

[3]

Facing Santiago, but separated from it by the rampart of the Andes, Mendoza—capital of the Argentine province of Cuyo—was the revolutionary center of the Americas. The sweetness of its valley of vines and cherry trees, the eternal springtime of its warm breezes and its snow-capped backdrop, its lands given over to golden pear trees and fertile earth, was all negated. Mendoza was given over to the extremes of cold calculation and infernal din because of the activities of the Army of the Andes that was forming, in spite of all apathy and against all obstacles.

At the beginning, there was nothing; San Martín set about turning that nothing into war supplies. He ordered contributions, extorted money from everyone, pestered President Pueyrredón to distraction, exhorted the ladies of Mendoza to donate their jewels at the municipal council, proscribed luxury, and cut officers' salaries in half. From the back of a horse no taller than the liberating general himself, sitting bolt upright, barely thirty-seven years old but already showing an incipient maturity that did not wholly extinguish the veiled glint in his eyes or the stubborn determination in his mouth, he proclaimed:

"Cuyo must sweat money for the liberation of America; from this day forward, each one of us must stand guard over his own life."

The Supreme Director of the Junta of Buenos Aires, Pueyrredón, was not willing to be second to San Martín either in will or in zeal in a feat which in Buenos Aires was being compared with those of Hannibal, Caesar, and Napoleon: "From Buenos Aires we send you dispatch cases, uniforms, shirts. We send you two thousand replacement sabers and two hundred field tents. We send you, in a small box, the only two bugles we could find. And that's enough," wrote Pueyrredón. "We send the World. We send the Flesh. We send the Devil. I don't have the remotest idea how I'm going to worm my way out of the contracts I've signed to pay for all of it. Damn it! Don't ask me for another thing!"

Cuyo did sweat, Mendoza dried up, and even the church bells and vineyards were squeezed to get blunderbusses and harquebuses, carbines and sabers, daggers and tridents, the pistols, and the yataghans, those fearsome Turkish-style swords with silver hilts.

Already Major De la Plaza is at work, quartermaster in charge of supplies and arms; Alvarez Condarco, the Tucumán chemist, mixes nitrates to make different kinds of gunpowder. In his armory, Brother Luis de Beltrán tucks his cassock up on his waist as he casts cannon and bombs, while his neighbor, Tejada, sweats over his vats, dyeing cloth blue to make new uniforms. Right down to the humblest artisan, everyone contributes something to the campaign, even if it's a lance cut from a reed; the poorest mule skinner turns over his animals, just as the doctors deliver their medicines to the hospital founded by Dr. Zapata. And if donations don't come willingly, then San Martín's men forcibly tear blankets and sheets off the beds, occupied or empty, of those living nearby. "There is no house that cannot give up an old sheet," shout these pirates of liberty, proclaiming themselves beggars rather than thieves. "When all else fails, we all have to beg."

But all the hustle and bustle, the clanging, the singing and dancing, the hammers smashing red-hot iron, the neighs, and the banging are like a vast silence when, at dusk on that January day, three horsemen enter General José de San Martín's camp in Mendoza. Three horsemen hurtling down the mountains who cannot rein in their mounts, who spur them on to run, jump, and dodge obstacles around the armories, the supply sheds, the shops, and the mills, until the three sweating, tense chargers meld in the corral and stables with the three thousand horses, the seven thousand mules, and the myriad cows that constitute the marching stock of the Army of the Andes.

The three friends dismount, laughing and shouting, embracing, congratulating one another for being friends, for being alive, for having arrived, for bringing news, and above all for their manly comradeship, the friendship of their twenty-five years, the success of having crossed the Andes on horseback from Santiago—so swiftly that they are their own messengers:

The priest Francisco Arias, handsome and devout, twenty years of age, given to fervent readings and to those sensualities he deems worthy of his all-embracing faith and his noble intelligence.

Lieutenant Juan de Echagüe, valiant and dashing with his reddish *favoris* that show to equal advantage combed for a ball or tangled with dust.

And the young hero Baltasar Bustos, hopelessly myopic but willfully plump—losing, because of a diet of honey fritters, creams, egg-yolk sweets, and powder cakes, the physical hardness won in the Inquisivi campaign, obeying the order to return to his natural state, fat and smooth; losing the pride of his svelte virility to serve the cause to which the three of them have pledged themselves, even if they have to dance with that ugliest of partners: deceit.

"Arias and Bustos will join with Echagüe in Chile. The country is on edge. Despite the Rancagua defeat, the spirit of rebellion has not been vanquished. The captain-general is both an incompetent and a savage. Santiago is the center of all this edginess. Mix with everyone. Make friends with everyone. Spread false rumors. Contradict one another. Confuse anyone who wants the Spaniards to win. Seduce anyone who can serve our cause. Don't leave a single truth unquestioned, create a universe of doubt, confusion, contradiction, false news, rumors . . . And don't think you're heroes. You are just part of an army of spies and counterspies scattered all over Chile. Spread misinformation but learn the truth for us. Find out the number and position of their troops, supplies, their movements, their plans. But, above all, make them believe we're going to attack from all sides, all along the line from Mount Aconcagua to Valdivia."

That is what General San Martín asked the three of them to do and that is what they accomplished. Now Baltasar wanted to eat steak and not vol-au-vent, Echagüe felt avenged for the death of his uncle (which took place, rumor had it, in the arms of Ofelia Salamanca, widow of the cuckold marquis), and Father Arias was looking at his two friends with his beautiful, languid, enigmatic eyes, which seduced both men and women, making everyone feel that this young priest could do whatever he wished—it was obvious that God Himself had so deemed it, and had incarnated His divine will in this delicate, strong, tender being ever ready to forgive but also disposed to anger, this youthful herald of Jehovah and Christ.

They walked arm in arm, at a distance from the stables where they'd dismounted, but always accompanied by the diminutive population of the encampment, whose habitual noises began to fill the afternoon once more after the galloping interruption of the friends. Geese, chickens, pigs, ducks. The honking, cackling, and squealing magically drowned out the hammers, bellows, and neighing. Arias looked at Bustos and Echagüe. If only it was true that Baltasar had invented—it was a stroke of genius—the pretext of the beautiful Ofelia to justify his passing through Chile; if only he did not know her or love her. If only Echagüe had never believed that his comrade loved the woman who had killed his uncle. If only this marvel of life, the union of the three young friends, who were not divided by anything, could last, glitter as long as possible, before the inevitable splits triumphed. When his friends asked him what he was doing, Arias said he was praying in his own fashion, using a word, *ojalá*—God willing—whose origin was the purest Arabic. Then they ate and drank together, told jokes, reminisced about family and lady friends, remembered childhood pranks, loved each other like brothers.

"That woman loved you," Echagüe said to Bustos.

"Which woman?" Baltasar asked, distressed.

But Echagüe and Arias exchanged a glance and were silent. They had sworn never to mention Gabriela Cóo.

[4]

The three of them reported to General San Martín with their lungs cleansed by the air of Mendoza, the most tree-filled city in the world, a city sweet because it is protected by a roof of leaves woven together like the fingers of a huge circle of inseparable lovers.

The priest was all in black, with his long cassock; his eyes, too, were an ecclesiastical color.

The lieutenant carried his leather morion with its gold bars and wore a blue tunic whose buttons were stamped with the arms of Argentina.

Baltasar Bustos placed his glasses in their leather case and put his blue cloth cap with its single gold bar under his arm.

It was a trio of proud friends looking into the face of a hero, wondering at which point the personal fate of each of them— Echagüe, Arias, Bustos—would change or be changed by events, war, or other men—San Martín, for instance. But vanity, wrote Rousseau, measures nature according to our weaknesses, making us believe that the qualities we don't possess are mere chimeras.

In the salon, bare except for a table strewn with maps, portfolios, magnifying glasses, inkwells, and document seals, the general stated outright that the plan for liberating South America hinged on the conquest of the viceroyalty that governed the rest: Peru. But to take Peru it was first necessary to invade Chile. A sustained long-term action could not be expected from the micro-republics in Upper Peru. They would do what they had always done: carry out raids to distract Lima's troops and resources.

Everything was ready. He congratulated the three of them for fulfilling their task of undermining things in Chile. Marcó del Pont was thoroughly confused about where the patriots would launch their attack. He was confident Echagüe had taken advantage of the return trip to carry out orders. The young lieutenant replied in the affirmative: he'd memorized the entire route, down to the last stone, without needing to take notes. Baltasar and Father Francisco looked at Juan and then at San Martín. They knew the secret; there was no need to swear them to silence. But an Indian leaning on a lance at the entrance to the Mendoza map room stared at them with far-off melancholy. Had he been listening? Of course. Had he understood? Yes; no; yes. "I've lived with them. I know they understand everything," said Baltasar when San Martín ordered the Indian to withdraw. But only by torturing Echagüe could anyone get the secret out of him, said Father Arias.

"In Peru we called them shitty *cholos*," Bustos said to Arias in a sudden fit of rage.

"Don't worry. They call each other worse."

"That doesn't solve the problem of justice," insisted Bustos, somewhat irritated by the young priest's cynical realism. "Are we going to free ourselves from the Spaniards just so we creoles can take their place, always above the *cholo* and the Indian?"

Echagüe laughed. "Don't think about that now, Balta. Concentrate on glory."

He hummed *"le jour de gloire est arrivé,"* blushed, and regained his composure. "Excuse me, General. I forgot where I was. It's just that the three of us are such close friends."

"I, too, am concerned about justice," said San Martín. "And wherever we go, we are going to establish free trade, suppress the Inquisition, abolish slavery, and prohibit torture. But you all saw what happened to Castelli and Belgrano in Upper Peru. They proclaimed the ideals of the Enlightenment to Indians who didn't understand them and to the creoles, who didn't want a permanent revolution. Neither theories nor individuals suffice to achieve justice. We must create permanent institutions. First, of course, we have to achieve independence. Then our headaches will really begin."

"You create laws, General. You must believe in them from the start," said the impetuous Baltasar, happy to be back in the ranks of the patriots, more and more certain of his ability to combine the dreams and the realities of the revolution.

"We are very legalistic." San Martín smiled. "We like balance, legal symmetry, because it masks the confusion of our ill-formed societies. We are delighted by hierarchy, protection through dogma, everything we've inherited from the Church and from Spain. We forget that beneath the cupolas of certainty and the columns of law there is a dream full of rocks, vermin, and quicksand that will put the equilibrium of the temple of the republic in danger."

"We need an iron will, a man who can save us," said a smiling Echagüe, his eternal glove in his hand.

"My young friends." San Martín returned them a bitter

smile. "I don't know if we are going to be victorious or if we're going to be cut to ribbons once and for all up in the mountains. That's why I'm telling you here and now that even if we win, we will have been defeated if we hand power over to the sword-wielding arm, the successful military man."

"But if it's a matter of saving the nation," insisted Echagüe.

"The nation will be saved by all its citizens, not by a military leader."

"In wartime you don't think that way."

"But in peacetime I do, Lieutenant Echagüe. If we don't create institutions, if we don't achieve unity among Americans, we will rapidly go from squabbles to fratricidal warfare. I swear to you that I will kill Spaniards but not Argentines. Never. My saber will never leave its sheath for political reasons."

"General, please pardon me for having spoken. I don't claim to speak for my friends, who . . ."

"He's just as fiery as his uncle."

"Don Martín Echagüe would be proud of my actions. I hope I will always be proud of yours, sir."

"Then never ask me or anyone else to be the executioner of my fellow citizens. A soldier can come to power with only that intention in mind. Beware of civilians as well," he said to Bustos, and, curiously enough, to Father Francisco Arias. "Let no one propel you to power so that you will kill in the name of the military. Let no one bring you to the crossroads of power in order to kill or be killed."

He laughed at the solemn silence of the young men and asked them to excuse the perorations of a man about to turn forty who only wanted to do his duty and then retire to some corner of the world to live like a man, in peace and with respect. "Would anyone believe, if I retire to my farm here in Mendoza, that I'm not a false Cincinnatus but a real Sulla waiting to take control of things? Damn!"

Everyone laughed, and he accused them of provoking this discussion about a hypothetical future because of the obvious, omnipresent fact—the American will to win independence: they had seen it, that will was all around them, nothing like it had ever before been seen in the Americas. It was the moment not to weep over the approaching storm clouds but to follow this sun, this will that manifested itself all around them—young men, patriots, Americans. Who could say, after these campaigns, that an Argentine, a Chilean, a Peruvian did not know how to organize or govern himself? The proof was right outside the door!

And outside the door, fresh recruits were being given uniforms, which they put on right out in the open after stripping themselves to the skin for a few seconds. Father Francisco Arias came over to help them dress; many did not know how to put the uniform on properly, button the tunic, adjust the belt, and cross the leather strap over their chests. He waved to the other two to come and help. Baltasar held Juan back.

"Don't. You are going to feel bad the day you can no longer be a comrade to those who are not your equals. Only the war unites us. Society will divide us."

The next morning, with the troops assembled in front of the Franciscan convent, San Martín put at the head of the column the Commander and declared Patroness of the Army of the Andes, Our Lady of Mount Carmel. At the center of that figure decked out like a doll, as triangular as the beloved sex of a woman, Baltasar replaced the face veiled in the white of maternal virginity with the visage of Ofelia Salamanca, smiling at him as if he were everything—the owner of the plaything, the lover of the woman, the son of the mother.

[5]

Echagüe gave General San Martín a detailed description of the Los Patos route, the one the bulk of the troops, commanded by Bernardo O'Higgins, would take. South of them, Colonel Las Heras would advance along the shorter Uspallata road with the artillery. Several smaller columns would spread north and south of these two to confirm the impression that the army was attacking Chile along a wide front, from Mount Aconcagua to Valdivia. They would thus divert the royalist forces, which were already demoralized by the campaign of rumors spread by San Martín like a fan of deception from La Rioja and the pass at Comecaballos to San Juan and the Pismanta route, down to the south, through the passes of Portillo and Planchón, where the Puechuenche Indians had already betrayed the patriots. Regular infantrymen and members of the militia, grenadiers, and lancers from the Province of Buenos Aires set out, following the routes of this great invasion, unprecedented in the New World. Of the 5,423 men in the army, only 4,000 were combatants. The rest made up the supply columns: grain wagons, cattle, sappers, bakers, lantern bearers, water wagons, and a carriage laden with dispatches and maps, pulled by six horses—all of which climbed to an altitude almost four miles above sea level, where they stared into the face of the Andes, which dominated those who sought to dominate them. These first men, the Adams of independence, their feet resting on an earth of volcanic ruins and extinct glaciers, contemplated the brown face and snowy crown of this dead god. Dead or not, he always seemed about to renew an interrupted catastrophe, latent in a nature which on the morning of San Martín's crossing to Chile trembled with the memories of devastated worlds and the promises of worlds to come, worlds these men, San Martín's five thousand, would never see.

Would they see, instead, the fratricidal war prophesied by the general, the new countries in ruins, destroyed by their own offspring? During the ascent to this highest temple of the Andes, Baltasar Bustos sought out the eyes of his friends Echagüe and Arias as well as those of José de San Martín himself. Occupied as they were in the effort to scale the heights, to give orders, exulting at the grandiose spectacle, inebriated perhaps with the will to triumph in battle and the will to arms of this incomparable army, did they have time, as Baltasar did, to look into their hearts and think about the moment in which rhetoric would be split from action? A sublime moment, and no one should spoil it. Let those who had the privilege of being Americans and of being on the roof of America in the company of the liberator of America exult in it in the name of the generations to come.

They slept. They drank from their canteens. Some even had themselves shaved by an impromptu barber so the Spaniards wouldn't think the army was made up of savage gauchos from the pampa. The nights were freezing, and they were grateful for the blankets stolen from the good people of Mendoza. The cannons passed in single file, and the Indians carried the gear. In the rear guard could be heard the lowing of the cattle bent down under the load of the supplies. Some men collapsed, fainting, vomiting, suffering from altitude sickness. No guitars were heard on that heroic night, although someone did sing a *vidalita*, a sad Argentine love song. San Martín dreamed he had stilts and could cross the mountains in one stride.

They started the ascent on January 18 and on February 2 began the descent; on the fourth, they encountered a royalist detachment in a mountain pass called Achupallas, one hundred soldiers of the king who couldn't stand up to the bare-saber charge of Juan Echagüe. From that moment on, the army's two columns raced from the Aconcagua to Chile's central valley. On February 12, by moonlight, they were all running downhill toward a clash with Marcó del Pont's royalist troops at Chacabuco. It was by moonlight that the three friends, Baltasar, Francisco, and Juan, looked at each other for the last time, unable to shake hands, unable to embrace, unable even to say another word to each other. O'Higgins's orders were: overwhelm the enemy, surround him; he's stationed himself right in the center, so we can do it—make a circle of death. The cavalry began the attack with O'Higgins along Cuesta Nueva, the Spaniards' right flank. This gave Soler time to come in later and destroy what remained of the enemy's left-flank rear guard. The three friends were among the first to attack on the left, and this was a war of saber against saber, hand-to-hand combat amid the clash of cavalry, closely followed by the infantry, who carried their sabers in their teeth so they could climb on one another's shoulders to get over the tree-trunk roadblocks erected by the enemy. The horses leapt over the parapets. The brave Juan Echagüe fell as he made a jump, and Baltasar saw his friend's head battered. In another charge, a musket ball stained the handsome Father Arias's black cassock with his own red blood. Baltasar charged, his glasses fogged, their metal frame wrapped tightly around his irritated, burning ears. He tried to leave his heart a blank, to keep the pain from encrusting itself there; yet, with his saber, he inscribed in his mind an involuntary act of thanksgiving that it was not he who had fallen. Baltasar Bustos wrote a testament like a lightning flash in which he left to himself the memory of the dead: he inherited his fallen friends. The death of a young soldier, handsomer and braver than the rest. The death of a young priest, handsomer and more pious than the rest. Baltasar Bustos bequeathed himself their lives, giving thanks for not being as handsome, brave, or pious as they. He was alive and could live for his enigma, Tantalus's passion, fleeting and untouchable. Death on the battlefield determined him, in that instant, to wring all he could out of his own life before perishing like his friends. Perhaps, as well, to hasten the moment that would reunite him with them.

The night of the battle of Chacabuco, San Martín's bugler blew so hard they say his brains flew out his ears.

[6]

Standing before the bodies of Father Arias and Captain Echagüe in the steepleless cathedral of the Chilean capital, which the liberating troops entered on February 14, General San Martín said to Baltasar Bustos:

"We lost only twelve men. A pity these two had to be among them."

"How many did the enemy lose?" asked Baltasar without looking at San Martín; he was grieving over the loss of his two friends and over the general's words, as if his pain extended to the Liberator's heart, which he had thought frozen.

"Five hundred. Chacabuco cost them Chile and Peru. They are no longer colonies of Spain."

Baltasar was tempted to say "What I lost is greater than two countries," but San Martín told him to take a good look at the faces of his dead friends, because soon he would see not the faces of friends dead in a just cause and in the glory of the battle for independence but the faces of brothers killed in fratricidal wars for power. Baltasar asked if that was as absolutely certain as San Martín's words led him to believe, words that reminded him of those uttered by a pessimist very different from San Martín, a Spanish council president. San Martín interrupted him: "We joined together to beat the Spaniards. We saw that if we were divided they would beat us. All I ask, Bustos, my friend, is that you realize this and that you be aware of the danger of a lack of unity. That lack of unity may well be our undoing; we have to create institutions where there are none. That takes time, clear thinking, and clean hands. We may think that laws, because they are separate from reality, make reality unreal. It isn't so. We are going to be divided by reality and by law, by the will to federation against the will to centralized power. We've gone out on the pampa and now we're left without a roof over our heads. But that's no reason to stop breathing free air and to stay indoors forever. All I ask is that you realize what the risks are. No, I am not a fatalist. But I don't want to be blind, either. See things as I see them, Bustos, my friend. Decide to be, along with me, a real citizen and renounce forever, as I do now before your dead friends, the possibility of being king, emperor, or devil."

"With my friends, I could have founded a world," said Baltasar Bustos, his head bent low.

"And without them . . ." San Martín began.

"I can only live out a passion."

The general did not understand what the young fellow was saying. He rested his hand on Baltasar's shoulder and said, "They were heroes." Then he promoted Baltasar to captain on the spot.

Baltasar stayed behind, alone, with the bodies of Francisco Arias and Juan Echagüe. Were they really heroes? Was José de San Martín himself a hero, the closest thing to a living hero Baltasar would ever know? In the funereal gloom of the cathedral, unbroken even by the baroque glitter scattered there by its architects, who besides being Jesuits were Bavarians, Baltasar saw in his mind's eye the Liberator, his friends, Miguel Lanza and the Indian Baltasar Cárdenas, Father Ildefonso de las Muñecas, all the warriors he'd met: he saw them without cavalry, without a battlefield, without infantry. Perhaps that was what José de San Martín held in his most secret soul: the vision of a world without heroes, in which men like himself, and also men like Lanza and Cárdenas, the young Father Arias and Captain Echagüe, his friends, would no longer be possible, because there would be no more saber battles, no more hand-to-hand fighting, no more code of honor, only fratricide, battles won against brothers, not against enemies; foreseeable, programmed wars in which death would be determined and accomplished at a distance. Dirty wars in which the victims would be the weak. The hero—he turned to look at the square shoulders of General José de San Martín in his dress uniform, solemnly walking toward the exit, speckled by the diffuse light of the cupolas—would then be like the god of the mountains, a dying god. Then he imagined the pathos of a San Martín grown old, firmly resolved never to stain his sword killing Argentine citizens, preaching through example, refusing to be "the vigorous arm," no matter how annoying the bickering of the "intractable, the apathetic, and the savage." At the apex of victory, San Martín refused to celebrate with romantic exuberance. His occasional solemnness was excused by the excessively stoic, Castilian severity of this son of Palencian parents. If he was going to avoid the temptation of dictatorship, it would not be to avoid responsibility for Argentina but to say to Argentina that everyone should behave as he did. Everyone should be responsible. From this day forward, each one of us must stand guard over his own life. Someone had to say it, and not from the abyss of the failures to come, but here and now, at the high noon of triumph, and triumphing over the passion for victory.

When he understood this, Baltasar Bustos felt a desire to run to the last hero and embrace him. But that would have been just one more celebration, a denial of the seriousness of the dying god. He wouldn't insult him with recriminations or with praise. It was better that Baltasar remain with his comrades, hold on to this tenderness, these hopes, these jokes, this intimacy he would never again know.

The general understood and wished him a good voyage.

One sunny February morning, Baltasar boarded a schooner, the *Araucana*, sailing from Valparaíso to Panama. It passed Lord Cochrane's flotilla, preparing for the attack on Lima. As he sailed by, Baltasar named the ships of the small fleet in a kind of farewell-to-arms: the forty-six-gun frigate *Lautaro*, the brig *Galvarino*, armed with incendiary rockets, the schooner *Moctezuma*, the man-of-war *San Martín*, and the transport ships and attack launches.

In Santiago he'd been told: "The woman you seek is in Caracas. But don't expect anything good from her."

For him, the war was over; only passion remained.

But in Santiago he did not want to look for Gabriela Cóo.

7

Harlequin House

Traveling with the Irish sailors between Callao and Panama, Baltasar Bustos recovered the slim figure he had during his days in Upper Peru; with only a Panama hat (bought in Guayaquil) for cover, he insisted on crossing the emerald forest between the two seas, between Pedro Miguel and Portobelo. The Indians of San Blas, whose faces marked with blue scars were a wounded parallel to the immutable colossi of Barriles, guided him among clay statues in the shape of men standing on each other's shoulders. The waters of the Panamanian lagoons reflected nothing, so intense was the sun that blinded the men during the day. And at night he could make out the lights of Portobelo, where a second schooner, on the other side of the isthmus, waited to take him to Maracaibo, the ancient fortress of the Spanish Main, besieged from time to time by the arms and later by the fame of Drake and Cavendish. But now, in more recent memory, Maracaibo's renown was associated with the pirate Laurent de Graff, who never attacked the Venezuelan harbor unless accompanied by a private orchestra of violinists and drummers; and the French captain

Montauban, who would appear on its briny streets only in a sedan chair carried by stevedores and preceded, even at midday, by a procession of torchbearers.

The fame of the ancient English, French, and Dutch pirates was nothing compared with that which ran before our hero, Baltasar Bustos, in his celebrated search for Ofelia Salamanca throughout the American continent. The trails of the alpaca and the mule were slow, the jungles thick, the mountain ranges arid and impassable, the seas of the buccaneers bloody, and the ravines deep, but news traveled faster than any Indian messenger or Irish schooner: a fellow of unimpressive aspect, plump, long-haired, myopic, has been in pursuit of the beautiful Chilean Ofelia Salamanca, from the estuary of the Plata to the gulf of Maracaibo. They say he's never seen her, much less touched her, but his passion compensates for everything and, despite his physical weakness, stirs him to fight, saber in hand, for the independence of America, side by side with the fearsome guerrillas of Miguel Lanza in the mud of the Inquisivi, with the legendary Father Ildefonso de las Muñecas at the head of the Indian hordes of the Ayopaya, with José de San Martín himself in the heroic crossing of the Andes.

Some hero! Baltasar Bustos said to himself when in the fetid port of Buenaventura he heard the first song about his love, transformed into a *cumbia* and danced, amid long, black plantains that resembled the phalluses of extinct giants, by immense black women, their heads decked out in red-checked handkerchiefs tied in fours. The multiple skirts the women wore did not impede them from communicating exactly what was there below or from moving their hips rhythmically, regularly, delightfully, and slowly. Some hero! Baltasar repeated to himself in Panama, listening to the story of his frustrated romance transformed into a *tamborito* and danced by creole girls as white as cream, wrapped in immense skirts that turned their bodies, like those of milky spiders, into fans. Some hero—who had to struggle to resist the temptation of shortbread and powder cakes that dissolve on your lips, prickly pears, and caramelized custard apples in those dancing ports between a scorching Pacific, free of the frozen waters of Baron von Humboldt's current, and a lulling Caribbean, separated only by Panama's pinched waist, the sash worn by the dancing and singing black girls: Here comes Baltasar Bustos, looking for Ofelia Salamanca, from the pampa to the lowlands! Some hero! Who would recognize him, not plump as the song had him, but once again thin, his stomach muscles hardened by days before the mast with the Irish sailors, who made their hours of work into a happy game and their hours of drunkenness and rest (which were one and the same) into nostalgic sobbing: Baltasar Bustos, chestnut-hued, his hair honey-colored, his beard and mustache blond—reborn, resembling the prickly pear he resisted the temptation to eat, his thighs taut, his bare legs covered with golden down, his chest hairless and damp with sweat, and the long hair in his armpits intimating the most salacious secrets. This was not the Baltasar of the *cumbia* or the *tamborito*—or, for that matter, of the merengue (here his mouth watered because he automatically thought of meringue).

His fame preceded him, but no one recognized him. He threw the last sign of his legendary identity—his round glasses with the silver frames—into the sea as he left the mouth of the Guayas River, where he heard his first satiric Andean song, a *zamba* that had come all the way from Lake Titicaca to Mount Chimborazo, if not dragged along by a dying condor, then hissed out by an irate llama.

This was his fate: people idolized him and wanted him to triumph both in war and in love. Even the blacks, who were kept away from the gangplank of the schooner in Maracaibo by shouts of "Evil race!" bawled out by exasperated royalist officers—even they peered out from among the sacks of cacao, whiter and certainly less damned than they. These blacks, despised by the Spaniards and the creoles, were the defeated troops of another revolt, "the insurrection of the other species," which very soon recognized the reality of the wars of independence: everyone wanted freedom for themselves, but no one wanted equality for the blacks, who unleashed their rage against every white man in Venezuela—Spaniard, creole, Simón Bolívar himself (who condemned the black explosion at Guatire as the work of an inhuman and atrocious people who fed on the blood and property of the patriots). Baltasar Bustos now saw the embers of rage in their yellow eyes and sweaty bodies, which the Spaniards kept back, so his baggage and that of the Irish sailors with whom he blended could be unloaded. He walked on ground that seemed to him unstable, under a sky he saw suspended, all of it, like certain clouds we stare at for a long time in the calmest summers, hoping they'll move so that we can, too: how can we move if the world has stopped dead in its tracks?

The revolution was winning in the south under San Martín; in the north, Bolívar's early victories had been wiped out by the Spanish reconquest led by the ferocious General Morillo. The revolution in the north was sustained only by the tenacity of Simón Bolívar, exiled first in Jamaica and now back in his southern base at Angostura, his redoubt and refuge after his defeat by Morillo in the battle of the Semen, which took place almost at the same time San Martín was winning the battle of Chacabuco, with Bustos at his side. Those battles were followed by the defeat of the great rebel plainsman Páez in the battle of Cojedes. Semen and Cojedes, two battles that bottled up the patriots south of the Orinoco, and two comic words— the first for obvious reasons, the second because it recalled a euphemistic creole verb for "fornication"—which were savored by Baltasar Bustos as a good omen about his amatory fortunes in this Venezuela which Ofelia Salamanca had already reached, ahead of him as always and wildly enthusiastic about the implacable royalist brutality of Morillo.

"She passed through Guayaquil, heading for Buenaventura."

"She disembarked in Panama, crossed the Isthmus."

"She took ship in Cartagena for Maracaibo. The Spaniards are strong there, so she can toast their victories, the bitch."

An ailing port of brothels and shops, the latter empty because Maracaibo was under constant siege by the rebel forces, the former overflowing with all the refuse tossed up by a war which had been going on for eight years, during which time the armies of the king fought the patriots over harvests and cattle, while slaves fled burned-out haciendas and masters doggedly clung to slavery with or without independence. The peasants had no land, the townspeople had no towns to return to, the artisans had no work, the widows and orphans flooded into the royalist port out of which chocolate, in ever diminishing quantities, was exported. As always, our bitter supper sent out all of its desserts to the world.

Baltasar Bustos tossed his glasses into the Guayas River. They hadn't helped him find Ofelia Salamanca. Now, with no guide but his passion, he would traverse plains and mountains, rivers and forests until he wore out the legend and made it into reality. For an entire year, while Bolívar conquered New Granada and royalist power spent itself because it had to be constantly on guard, Venezuela lived in suspense, waiting for the decisive battle between the Liberator and the royalists, between Páez and his lancers and Morillo and his Spanish regulars. But in Maracaibo's brothels, bars, hospitals, docks, and warehouses—and no longer in the salons, as he had in Lima and Santiago—Baltasar Bustos sought out news of his beloved that would justify, when the two met, the songs that were being sung right there—and not at nonexistent creole balls—by whores, mule drivers, children, stevedores, and nuns from the first-aid station: the ballad of Baltasar and Ofelia.

Did she know them? Did she know those lyrics, some funny, some silly, most dirty? Was she what the songs said: an Amazon with one breast cut off, the better to use her bow and arrow, who came from a country exclusively of women, who left it once a year to become pregnant and who killed all male children? The way those ballads described him was also not true. Obsessed, he walked every street and alley in the tropical port, hoping to glean accurate information and hearing only inaccurate songs, wearing himself out in the unrelenting humidity, eating bad food, in perpetual danger of fever.

A pair of eyes followed him as he became a familiar though unidentifiable figure. This man was not the one from the song. But the eyes that followed him had seen him like this before, as he was now, just as he had been when he returned from the Upper Peru campaign, thin and hard. From a bay window, the eyes watched him through shutter slats and black veils. This woman had always appeared enveloped in dark cloth, but now her dresses of gloomy, mournful black were no longer reflected in the glitter of drizzly Lima nights.

She sent a sharp little black boy dressed as a harlequin to bring him to her. Thus it was that Baltasar entered the Harlequin House in Maracaibo for the first time. Fame had kept him away; the whorehouse was as famous as the legend of Ofelia and Baltasar, and he was afraid of being recognized there. Fame is shared and recognized everywhere. Bustos was right. He was recognized, but not when he came in, not by the company of the bordello nymphs, women of all colors and tastes, whom Baltasar imagined, as he strolled among these odalisques with naked bellies, as all tied to nature by their wide or deep, wrinkled or pristine navels, nearer to or farther from the separating scissors, but all those navels sighing with a life of their own, as if a whore were a whore simply to prolong the splendid idleness and the sinless sensualities, suspended in nothingness, of prenatal life. Undulating whores: lewd blacks from Puerto Cabello, lank Indians from Guayana, repentant mestizas from Arauca, cynical creole girls from Caracas, the French from Martinique with their fans, a Chinese with a breast between her legs, bovine Dutch from Curaçao, distracted English tarts from Barbados who pretended not to be there at all. Baltasar Bustos, led by the black harlequin, smelled their mustard and urine, incense and skunk, conger eel and sandalwood, guava and Campeche wood, tea and wet sand, sheep; all these humors gathered in the grand salon decorated in the style of Napoleon I, with ottomans, plaster sphinxes, fixed lights, and stopped clocks, the grand salon of the most famous brothel in a port famous for piracy, plunder, and slavery, now besieged by the patriots of an empire, Spain's, that believed itself installed there for all eternity.

The harlequin and Baltasar finally reached their destination, and Baltasar stood as if before a conquered queen, conquered by herself. The greedy eyes of the prostitutes followed him until the doors closed behind him. The woman in black lost no time: she said she'd been expecting him to turn up, even though she knew that he did not want to find within the brothel what he was looking for outside. He was involved in other things—she was told everything—because out there he could not expect to find this Ofelia Salamanca. But here he did, correct? No, he shook his head, not here, either; I've almost lost all hope of ever finding her. At this stage in the game, Baltasar, would you prefer never to find her, to go on searching forever because that justifies your life, this rhythm that makes you crazy and makes all of us women crazy when we sing and dance it? Not even a Chinese girl with three breasts? Our dearest?

"Don't betray me. I recognized you from the party in Lima."

She swore not to say who Baltasar was. And she knew how to keep a secret. He did want to know how she had come to this house from the salons of the viceroyalty, did he not? Baltasar said nothing. She thanked him for his discretion but promised him: "When you come back, I'll tell you everything."

But now, she added quickly, with an expression of mourning that seemed to be the very face of evening, which glittered between her flesh and her dark robes, giving light to death, he had to go on to Mérida and from there go up to the mountains, to Páramo, the cold barren plain, and then, at Pico del Aguila, turn around and come back here.

"Will I find her there?"

"I cannot guarantee it. You will find her legend, in any case."

"That I already know. It's sung, along with my own."

"About that woman you desire, no one knows the truth."

"Then how will I know it?"

"I think by looking for her, even if you don't find her."

"Did you meet her in Lima, Luz María?"

"Never say that name again. I am not that person any longer."

[2]

These words intensified Baltasar's hunger. Without his glasses, he did not see well, but his other senses—smell, especially, and hearing—were more intense than ever. As he set out on his new journey, he felt unable to distinguish what he managed to see from what he smelled, heard, and, ultimately, what he dreamed. In Upper Peru, he'd once said he was afraid to admire everything he wasn't, simply for that reason. But now a swift concatenation of songs—would songs always be the fastest means of communication in this vast, sprawling continent?— offered Baltasar Bustos the image of a man who was and was not himself: physically he was not that man, although in his soul, the moving mirror of the times he was living, he was. The passion commemorated in the songs was real; who knows if the story of a hero who used war to compensate for his mournful lack of love was, as well. But no melody—Peruvian waltz, *cueca, cumbia, vidalita*—told the truth he'd communi- cated to two fathers, his own and the Jesuit tutor Julián Ríos, and to two friends, Dorrego and me, Varela. Of course, we were so far away, so involved with our clocks and our Buenos Aires politics—governments fell, warlords from the provinces invaded, anarchy took over our dreams—that we didn't even remember the legend of our friend Baltasar and the beautiful Ofelia. Two other friends, whose life and death filled us with envy and zeal, the priest Arias and Lieutenant Echagüe, died without knowing Baltasar's secret: the kidnapping and substituting of the two babies. That provided some relief to our battered pride. We had started to become Argentines without realizing it.

But we did realize that in seeking Ofelia Salamanca, Baltasar Bustos was seeking not only to satisfy a passion but also to receive a pardon.

And now, climbing by mule from the deep valleys and through the narrow passes of the Mérida mountains to the crenellated retaining walls of the foothills of the Andes, he asked forgiveness for one last time. Forgive me, Ofelia Salamanca, for what I did to your child.

And what about the black baby? Wasn't Baltasar going to ask forgiveness—out of politeness—for what he did to him? No. Perhaps the black mother, publicly flogged for daring to have a child though she had syphilis, had suffered all the child himself deserved to suffer. But in this search for Ofelia, Baltasar was satisfying another passion besides the romantic one attributed to him: the spiritual passion of seeking Ofelia to fall on his knees before her and ask forgiveness. Forgive me for having kidnapped your child.

Between Tabay and Mucurumba, the landscape of the Andes shed its cover, showing itself naked, grayish-brown, cracked, abrupt, and before it the young reader of Rousseau insisted on imagining a man in nature who was spontaneously good, who was alienated by society, and masked by an evil that had nothing at all to do with nature: evil comes from elsewhere, not from us. He lost this article of Romantic faith, as if it were a cold griddle cake, when an old man sitting on a sack of potatoes in the town of Mucuchíes told him that, yes, the treacherous Ofelia Salamanca had passed through, and at that very house you see there, the one painted red and pink, she had asked a royalist colonel not to kill an armed patriot who had barricaded himself in it, not expecting to get out alive, but with "his honor intact." The colonel agreed. The patriot threw his weapons out that white-framed window right there. Then she went in, took off her clothes, and showed herself naked to the patriot. She didn't say a word. The entire town was in suspense, waiting to see what would happen. Everything could be seen through the open windows. She was naked and said nothing. But she allowed the patriot to look at her, at all of her. Then she ordered him out and herself told the firing squad to shoot.

What had all the girls seen, the ones with round faces, with apple cheeks, who tied their hats on with scarves to keep the mountain wind from blowing them away? What did all the old men sitting along the principal streets of all these Andean towns think? Those old men never died. They'd been here for a thousand years. The same length of time as the red *yaraguá* grass, the rich cattle pasture that managed to survive on this bald mountain—old cattle, as well. In the towns farther up, only old men and children were left, old men with silvery wrinkles and girls with long hair. What had they seen, what had they heard said about Ofelia Salamanca? They say she had a rebel captain killed while he was shitting at the gates of La Guaira. She waited until that moment, just to humiliate him. In Valencia, on the other hand, she forced a royalist general to turn himself in and die with a rope around his neck, on his knees, to beg forgiveness for his sins.

Ofelia Salamanca: just as the yellow-flowered frailejon survives the cold of the highlands to dot the mountainsides like calligraphy, stories about Ofelia Salamanca dot this Santo Domingo mountain range. And just as the frailejon's flowers form a candelabrum that rises above the fleshy shrub, that's how she rose here, hunting down patriots until there were none left and she'd be without victims. Right here in this wasteland town, where the buzzards fly ceaselessly, that woman lacking a breast and good sense, said this to the rebel commander besieging the forts along the Orinoco:

"If you beat the royalists, you can take me prisoner and kill me."

"And if the Spaniards beat us?"

"You and I will make love."

"A delightful opportunity, you Spaniard-loving slut. I won't miss it, you can bet on it."

"But there's one condition. You mustn't allow yourself to lose just to make love to me. Because then I'll kill you. Agreed?"

He did let himself be beaten just to make love to her—as the mountain bards would sing it—and so he died in her arms, a dagger in his back.

What did all these men know who died in her arms, at her order, when they saw her naked, when they let themselves be conquered by her? Who was this creole Penthesilea?

In the desolate nature of the high Venezuelan wastes, Baltasar Bustos listened but did not find a joyful reciprocity in his solitary, self-sufficient soul, that would unite the individual with things, or promise with actuality. On the contrary, Ofelia's human acts obviated any possibility of reconciliation, rendering diabolical the very business of nature, from which the beautiful and cruel Chilean lady seemed to emanate and in which she found both her justification and her reflection. His faith in a possible reconciliation between man and nature was also shattered at that moment; we are burdened with too many sins, he whispered into the ear of the wasteland, to the old man and the young girl. Any reconciliation would be forced; we have no other choice but to go on hurting each other, and nothing will hurt us more than capricious passions, authoritarian disdain, power exercised without restraint: Ofelia Salamanca.

He saw the woman's face in the frozen, sterile, immensely beautiful mountains: he reached, protected by his Panama hat, the crest of the bird of prey, the back of the dead camel, the Eagle's Beak, which had the shape of a necklace lost there, as if carelessly, by Ofelia Salamanca, this incomprehensible woman, this endless enigma, who had finally worn out her romantic lover; he was thankful that the fierce yellow flower invaded this pure nakedness only between July and August, quickly abandoning the mountains to their clean, undecorated solitude. A baroque woman, of obscene sumptuousness, whose dazzling excretions and lugubrious rewards were seeking to revive something inert: in that instant, Baltasar believed he'd finally expunged her from his heart and exiled her from his mind.

But the void she left was immense. He descended bit by bit, convinced that he'd found the woman transformed into eternal stone, occasional flower, the stone sterile, the flower poisonous; and he again sought spontaneous delight in the diffuse sweetness of the reborn landscape of the valleys, the hooves of the sheep, the thatched roofs of the houses, and the fields of green carnations like lemon groves.

But all these Spanish flowers in the Venezuelan Andes—carnations, roses, and geraniums—could not fill the void left by Ofelia. The war could; trotting near the shadow of the extended eaves of the village houses, Baltasar accepted that his life, which he once imagined unique, without fissures—nature and history reconciled in his person—was forever sundered, and, as those inevitable song books already had it, all that was left to him was to bounce from war to war, from south to north and from north to south, to carry out his legendary destiny, which had already been mapped out in popular song . . . He would stop at sunrise to partake of delicious mountain cheese, Andean bread, and pineapple wine, but not even those details of life escaped the fate already dictated in the song. Chewing, he thought about Homer, the Cid, Shakespeare: their epic dramas were written before they were lived. Achilles and Ximena, Helen, and Richard the hunchback in real life had done nothing but follow the poet's scenic instructions and act out what had already been set down. We call this inversion of metaphor "history," the naïve belief that, first, things happen and then they are written. That was an illusion, but he no longer fooled himself.

At that very moment, as an old woman was serving him a plate of griddle cakes in an inn by the side of the Macurumba road, it occurred to Baltasar Bustos to ask her about the war. To which she replied, "What war?"

Baltasar laughed and ate. At times, in these isolated towns, people don't find out about anything—or they find out very late, only when the bard gives his version of events. But in Mucuchíes, hours later, he found the same old man sitting on the same sack of potatoes and asked him the same question—"How's the war going?"—and received the same reply—"What war? What are you talking about?" The news was all over town instantly. The children took the opportunity to have some fun and tease. They made a circle around him, singing, "What war? What war?" and when he broke out of the magic circle of children and asked their elders who Simón Bolívar, Antonio Páez, and José Antonio Sucre were, they all said the same thing: "We don't know them. Are they from around here? Has anyone heard of them? Ask the old man who plays the violin in El Tabay."

He was a man with a square head, sculpted by saber wounds until it looked like a block of wood. Baltasar found him inland, far from the road, in a vast, run-down house. To get to it, Baltasar had to climb over the skeletons of cows. The old man was on his shady terrace, sitting on the skull of a cow, just as José Antonio Bustos sat on his pampa ranch when Baltasar was a child. This old man played the violin; he did nothing else, except to contemplate a black man about thirty years of age, naked from the waist up and covered by filthy, tattered canvas trousers.

When Bustos approached on his mule, the squared-off, dark old man stopped playing, wiped his moist mustache with his hand, and stared with eyes overcome by the glare. The sun baked the cow bones and invited one's sight to become white as well, like the light. Baltasar understood, as never before, the need for shade; that is what he said, by way of greeting, to the old man; he didn't bother to greet the black—there was always a black or an Indian, silent, leaning on the doorposts. Justice turned into sun and white bones in his head; he'd come in search of the war and asked the old man, "Where? What is happening?"

"I know nothing," said the old man. "Eusebio here might have some news."

The black did not stop talking; that is, Baltasar realized that he'd been talking all the while, but in a very low voice. And now he spoke more loudly, repeating, "Thank you, master. Because of you I am not a thief. Thank you, master. Because of you I am not a fugitive. Thank you, General, for allowing me to be here on your estate."

"You'd like to be on the loose, killing and robbing," said a woman who'd appeared from the half-light in the house, wiping her hands on an apron. "And you, what do you want?" she said, looking at Baltasar.

"I'm a soldier," it occurred to Baltasar to say. "How can I join the nearest battalion?"

The woman stared at him in total incomprehension, the old man with pity, the black with a grin. They seemed, one with his violin, the other with his gratitude, the woman with her rage, as if suspended in time, as if absent.

"Bolívar," Bustos recited the magic names of the heroes, "San Martín . . ." as if they were amulets.

There was a long silence, then the old man stopped playing and spoke, "He said, 'Comrades, the revolution has no money, but it does have land. Look as far as you please, from the sea at Maracaibo to the jungle of Guayana, from Eagle Peak to the mouths of the Orinoco, and what you see is land. There is land. The Spaniards took it away from the Indians. Now we're taking it away from the Spaniards. Take your land,' he said to me, 'not today but tomorrow, when we win the war. Here is a voucher; there's another for your orderly, an ignorant black.' I cashed in the voucher, as did all the generals, but here you have this boy. He's an ignorant black. He didn't know how to cash anything. The war's over. Eusebio doesn't know how to exercise his rights."

"I'd be a thief if you didn't protect me," said the black.

"These people know nothing about papers. They only want to survive," said the dark, squared-off old man. "We own everything, but we finish nothing."

"Go on." The woman laughed, a sixtyish creole who must have been pretty a long time ago. "You're almost black yourself; don't be afraid of appearances. But I am, old man. I'm here on this cattle ranch you were given as payment for your service, ready to serve you as a maid as long as I don't have to know what's going on out there. For sure, the blacks have taken control of Caracas."

"Because for you everything's bad." The old man hugged the violin to his chest.

"I got tired of watching you fight. Thank your lucky stars. This is better than nothing," said the woman before leaving, her back turned to them.

No sooner had she gone than the old man shut his eyes, furrowed his brow, and summoned Baltasar with his hand. "Come closer," he said, "so she can't hear us. But I know the truth. I know what's happened. Bolívar was betrayed. They turned on him, just as my wife turned her back on us a moment ago, they sent him off to die alone, but that is our destiny. They ran San Martín out. They surrounded him with spies so he couldn't live in peace. They finished him off by forcing him into exile."

"Who? The Spaniards?" said Baltasar, trying to follow the old man's strange tale.

"No, the creole military men, us."

"Mulatto," said the young man, laughing. "You're a mulatto, old man."

"I am, hiding here because I don't want to be a part of the ingratitude or of the crimes committed against my brothers," said the old man with astonishing strength, and his wife reappeared, asking, "What are you saying? Still talking your foolishness, still telling what is going to happen? What a mania, for God's sake! Who ever gave you the idea you were a prophet, you old fool?"

"I'm not. I only tell what already happened," said the old man. He began to play his violin. "What happened a long time ago."

Over the course of his slow return to Mérida, and from there to the sea, Baltasar Bustos found no evidence of war; no one knew anything about the old battles, and not a soul remembered the heroes. Sometimes they would say yes, the battle's going to take place tomorrow, but later they would mention names that meant nothing to him—Boyacá, Pichincha, Junín—and when he asked for details, no one could tell him where those places were or give him dates; they could only say in a monotonous voice: "One more battle and the fatherland will be saved."

He entered a burned-out city where he walked in ashes up to his ankles. He was told that the ashes would be there forever, that nothing could get rid of them. Later, he returned to the violin-playing general's ranch. The woman had died. That afternoon they were burying her. The black had gone off to the mountains. He had fled. He would go down to the plains. He would fire his rifle. He would fight forever. Here he would have gone insane. The old man was left alone, and Baltasar felt that the solitude was giving him back his old spirit. The old man told more and more stories, about wars against the French, against the Yankees, military coups, torture, exile, an interminable history of failures and unrealized dreams, all postponed, all frustrated, pure hope; nothing ever ends and perhaps it's better that way, because here, when anything ends, it ends badly.

Here and there, Baltasar Bustos found forgotten iron wheels of cannons, and during the day he would cool his brow on them and at night use them to keep his hands warm. He lost all sense of time. Perhaps in Venezuela they'd lost it as well, resigned to frustration and to things done only halfway. One day, in a cemetery filled with tombs painted thousands of different colors, he happened on the old violinist-general leading a rickety funeral cortege, obviously made up of paid mourners, recruited by that same old hero whom Simón Bolívar had rewarded with land instead of money—exactly what the Cid did with his Castilian warriors. Who had died? Who else—the general looked at him with compassion—but Eusebio the rebel black? Baltasar made the Sign of the Cross before the coffin borne by four laborers.

"Don't worry," said the general. "My little Chebo isn't in there. Rebels are always buried far away in unknown land, at night and with no name on the grave. So that no one ever knows if they're alive or dead! The box is empty."

"Only one more crime and the fatherland will be saved." Baltasar paraphrased the last sentence he'd heard the general utter.

"Of course I'm burying him here with his name, next to the mother who was ashamed of him, damn it. But what shame, what fear, what shitty prohibitions!" exclaimed the old man.

[3]

He was afraid of turning into a Robinson Crusoe of the mountains, so one day he set out to return to Maracaibo. He left behind the frigid wasteland and the mountains dotted with frailejon; when he reached the valleys, the tall, slender trees with bearded limbs, tropical moss that hangs like perennially gray hair from the ever renewed head of a trunk filled with young sap, bade him farewell.

He left behind a lost battalion. He would never find it or name its heroes. He felt he was leaving a different time, and his passage through the high, bleak plateau reminded him vaguely of another brief period, which his memory did not want to register, which escaped the norms of his philosophic reason. But in those days his reason had been stronger; now everything conspired, or so he thought, to weaken it, and the time he spent in this bleak region seemed thus more comprehensible, more acceptable, than that other time on that other mountain. The key word, though, was *time*, and all he had to do was enter Maracaibo on a steamy morning, consult the front page of a Caracas newspaper sold in the port, corroborate the date with a pharmacist, who charged for the use of the calendar in his almanac, and he must accept that a period of time which in his experience was very long, which in his memory spanned three whole months, had been barely two weeks. Two weeks between his leaving Maracaibo and his return.

The woman in perpetual mourning was waiting for him in Harlequin House. She invited him to move in. He was like her, no one else was; both of them came from the creole south, were acquainted with the viceregal salons, knew how to eat properly, and he (she supposed) would step aside for a lady. No, it was not for what he was thinking. That gallant gentleman from Lima who one night, in the presence of his wife, silently invited her to be his lover knew what he was doing. Recently widowed, she was hungry for sex, but sex with imagination. The sagacious and perverse Peruvian understood that and knew she could not resist his daring to court her right under his wife's nose. It was as if he were taking away her mourning and anticipating his wife's widowhood. Yes, that aristocrat from Lima certainly had imagination. He also had syphilis and scorned the woman dressed in black for falling so easily and accepting the tainted love the gentleman could not offer his own wife. A widow, she told him, is totally useless. There are no aristocrats crueler or more arrogant than those of Peru, the widow concluded. They are the Florentines of the New World.

"Why, then, did you come to Maracaibo?"

"A Chinese doctor in Lima told me that the sea air in these parts spontaneously cures venereal disease."

"You don't disgust me," Baltasar said surprisingly—as if another voice had said it for him—surprised that a voice that was not his own would express itself thus. Yet he recognized it as his own—only, before, it had been asleep, hiding.

She laughed. "Go on, if that's what you want. The girls will let you have it for nothing. My sex, Baltasar, is a sewer."

"And your doctor, Lutecia, is a rogue and a charlatan."

Both of them liked the name, the name of permanent mourning of the woman from Lima. Day and night would find Baltasar in the bordello of the harlequins, where, by simple arithmetic, he realized he'd become a desirable man. Perhaps some of the girls approached him because Lutecia had explained the situation of the young, exhausted hero; but though he paid none of them, they all sought him out, because—as they began to whisper in his ear—he was handsome, because he was rich, because he was smooth, because of his distant, unseeing eyes, because of the way he treated women, all women, like high-born ladies. "You make me feel like a duchess," the English girl told him; *"Personne ne m'a traitée comme toi,"* the French girl told him; the sullen Indians said nothing but were as grateful as the chattering blacks, who did say, "With you we feel different. You relieve us of centuries of insults and kicks, damn it."

No one knew that he was giving to them, the harem of the Harlequin, what he had been saving for one alone, his sullied Columbine. He wanted to expunge her from his mind, just as the old general on the Tabay cattle ranch imagining disasters to come had expelled in anticipation all Liberators from their freshly minted nations. Still, he did not cease being loyal to Ofelia Salamanca, and a creole girl from Caracas, with heavy-lidded eyes and an olive-colored body, said to him, "It's possible to be loyal without having to be faithful."

He covered her face with kisses. He wished he could cover Ofelia Salamanca's face with kisses, too, but without her knowing it. At least in this instance, reality and desire were one: the creole girl melted in her orgasm because she was really in love. It no longer mattered what the night might bring. But Baltasar lived first (and he lived fully) only to present himself later before Ofelia after having lived with other women what he wanted to live with her: a night of endless kisses on the beloved's face, and she would never know.

"Listen, if you treat us like ladies, do you treat your lady like a whore?" asked the Cartesian inmate of the Harlequin.

He always thought (this was his greatest mental loyalty) that the best there was in him could emerge from his admiration for everything he wasn't. He had summarized his destiny in this idea. It was another way of thinking that, by being exposed to the danger of this admiration, he would ultimately be the best he could reasonably be. He patiently explained all this to Lutecia when at dawn, which was the end of the workday, the two of them were eating papayas with lemon and scented guavas in the madam's rooms, protected by the shutters from Maracaibo's nascent heat.

"These times have seen many men who are less convinced of their ideas than they are eager to impose them on others," he said to the woman from Lima. She listened to him talk and repeated, mysteriously, something he'd told her many years before: "Or to punish them for not having those ideas. You're right."

He told Lutecia, the former Luz María of the Lima salons, everything he knew about himself except for the kidnapping of Ofelia Salamanca's child. She replied that there is always something not known or left unsaid, simply because there hasn't yet been a correspondence between the deed and the word. We keep things in reserve without knowing it, to say or do them when the occasion presents itself. They've always been there, but we didn't know it and are surprised.

"I'm listening to voices inside me that I never listened to before," Baltasar said to her.

"Do you see what I mean? Don't silence them, no matter what."

One night the pale English girl began to vomit blood, and Baltasar, unwittingly transformed into the most gentlemanly pimp of the oldest profession, carried her himself, in his arms, to the Maracaibo hospital.

That yellow barracks, crowned with shrubs that refused to die, hadn't been painted in eight years. Why bother? The mass of wounded Spanish soldiers was so great, there was such doubt about the triumph of either side, the feeling that this was an interminable war was so strong, that to worry about the façade seemed at best a frivolity, at worst an act of cynicism. The Ursuline nuns with their headdresses that made them look like captive seagulls managed to find a bed for the duchess, as the nominative Baltasar dubbed her. For Baltasar, knowing names, giving them, devising pseudonyms, was part of a radical game that began when he read Plato under the tutelage of his pampa mentor Julián Ríos, who said: "It is important to note that our fascination with our own names gave rise to the first treatise of literary criticism, Plato's *Cratylus*. Remember, Baltasar, in that dialogue Socrates finds room for every theory of names. Some say the name is intrinsic to the thing. Some contradict that, saying that names are purely conventional. Socrates says names are mere approximations of things, a rough guess. And in that way names name philosophy itself, and love as well, and all human activities: a mere approximation."

"An *approach*," repeated Baltasar in English, holding the English girl's cold hand. Was this, given the fact that she was English, a good sign—the colder, the more full of life? It wasn't; she died a few hours later in Baltasar's arms, begging him to repeat the word *approach*. Approach to what? To death, to her lost home, to the unknown love of the poor foreign courtesan? He never found out. He stayed with her, holding her for a long while. Even after he was asked to leave her, he clung to the fair, pale body with its thin, matchstick limbs. It was hard for him to let go. A voice had told him: "Take charge of her. Until the end. She has no one else in the world. The day she's buried, there will be no one to accompany the body. Only you will know for certain that she died." He remembered the funeral and the nameless grave of Eusebio, the black son of the dark-skinned old general in Tabay, and did not want the English girl's tombstone to be without a name. Since he invented names, what name would he give to this woman, who had no identification papers? In the face of death, his imagination flagged. Perhaps, simply, the Duchess. The Duchess of Malfi. A literary homage. Webster. Elizabeth Webster. By naming her, he created her. But he was only obeying the voice that exhorted: "Take care of her."

He was afraid that if he listened to that voice he would cease to be master of his own destiny. The experiences of a short life told him, however—as he wandered through the hospital's long gallery, where the sick, mostly soldiers, were laid out on their cots—that his destiny was a chorus of voices, his own and others. Nothing more.

Every night, the Spanish officers would noisily burst into Lutecia's brothel—she herself had begun to use the name—and Baltasar would listen from afar to their shouts, confidences, and explosions of camaraderie. He never went out to them. They disgusted him and had nothing to do with his happy, free dealings with the madam from Lima. He would visit the girls in the afternoon, when all of them, without exception, were still virgins. They would talk a great deal about the officers, sometimes making observations that would otherwise pass unnoticed. The French logician, who had seen action even before Waterloo, insisted that women were a mere pretext, something to excite these handsome men who had degrees from European academies, for whom machismo was an essential part of their military calling and their national identity. But class identifications were even more important. They were the peacocks and, at times, the stud horses of the Maracaibo whores, but she, the French tart, noticed how they looked at each other, how they liked to catch each other in the women's beds, how their desire was stronger for each other than it was for the women. Bah, she didn't rule out the possibility that in Spain they would prefer the women of their own class to the men of the same class, but in this port of fevers and pubic lice, *allez-y*. Men and women all agreed: they wanted Spanish pricks.

One of the officers, so thin he was almost invisible from the front, because he was all profile—long nose, languid eyes, mustache combed upward, hair as highly polished as the leather of his cavalry boots, used his entire body to sniff around. He was like a greyhound. His nose would turn red, and he would cease being pure profile because of an unusual, exotic smell. His regiment was constantly in and out of Maracaibo, deeply engaged in a war to the death with Páez and Bolívar, but he always put up at Harlequin House. He prided himself on having gone to bed with all the girls except the English whore. He was afraid of "perfidious Albion," especially between the sheets, and was paralyzed with terror when he learned she'd died. He was sure, he said, that if she'd died on him in bed, she would have dragged him to the bottom of the sea, the paradise of the English.

One night he smelled something unusual. Feigning joviality, he approached, talking about August nights in Madrid, when wearing a uniform was a foretaste of hell, and suddenly pulled back the curtain of the lavatory where Baltasar Bustos, in turn, was pretending to wash his face in a basin, although in fact he was spying on the Spanish officers.

Their eyes met, and Baltasar wondered where he'd seen those eyes before, in what skirmish, viceregal salon, or crossroad between La Paz and Lake Titicaca. Where? The same question was as obvious in the royalist officer's eyes. Each knew that he would probably never recall their first meeting, or even if it had actually taken place.

Páez's plainsmen, advancing from the south, besieged Maracaibo. Food began to run out. The hospitals were filled with the wounded. War to the death desolated Venezuela. Black fugitives would arrive, thinking they could blend into the anonymity of the port, but irrevocably assumed to be rebels, they were caught and executed by the royalists as quickly as by the insurgents. No one knew who was going to be hanged or why: for being a royalist, for being rich, for being black, for being a rebel . . .

Baltasar Bustos would accompany the girls who became ill with typhus or appendicitis, or who just had ticks, to the Maracaibo hospital. Many never returned. Others returned because of the calomel cure. But after a while Baltasar needed no pretext to walk into the sanatorium. He suffered and was horrified by the suffering of all. Nothing was more terrible than watching amputations in which the only anesthetic given the soldiers was a glass of brandy and a napkin to bite. Baltasar would stand at their side, holding their hands, knowing they needed something warmer than a piece of cloth or a glass. And he felt how hard they held on to him, as if holding on to life. He immersed himself in the hospital world. He felt his place was there, not despite the fact that the wounded were his eternal enemies, but precisely because of it: the Spaniards, the murderers of Francisco Arias and Juan Echagüe, those who had corrupted (who could doubt it?) Ofelia Salamanca.

Among all the cases, one moved him deeply. A man whose face had been blown off. There was a hole of raw flesh between his eyebrows and his mouth. And he still lived. His brain wasn't gone. He had a life somewhere beyond the hideous wound, in a marvelous and melancholy corner of his head. He would move his hands, which were as thin as the rest of his body. A pair of cavalry boots stood upright, beautifully polished, at the foot of his cot.

Baltasar held that officer's hands. He was as sure that he recognized him now as he had been unsure in Harlequin House. No, he didn't remember where they'd first seen each other. The war had been waged for eight years and it ranged through an area three times larger than the lands in which

Caesar or Napoleon had fought their campaigns. But he did remember where they'd last seen each other: when a curtain was pulled back in a bordello a few weeks before.

This had to be the same man. And even if he wasn't, the remote possibility that he was the same man of narrow profile, shiny pomade, and sniffing nose, flirtatious, self-satisfied, so remote from the mere idea of being disfigured as he strolled around the house, recalling Madrid summers and sniffing with his nervous nose, now gone forever—that was enough for Baltasar to say to himself and to him: "I know who you are. I recognize you. Don't worry. You won't die without anyone's knowing who you are. Trust me. I'll be near you. I won't abandon you. I'll put a name on your tombstone."

When the Spanish officer died, Baltasar returned to Harlequin House weeping and told Lutecia what had happened. She caressed his head of copper-colored curls and said: "I was waiting for this moment, or for one like it, to free you from this place."

"I am free. I love you. You are my best friend. I don't want to lose you, I've already lost . . ."

"Take this note. It's from Ofelia Salamanca. She wants you to join her in Mexico. She's waiting with Father Quintana in Veracruz. Here are the directions and a map. Hurry, Baltasar. Oh yes, I bought you a pair of glasses. Start using them again. You have to read this letter carefully. Don't start hallucinating. You have to see things clearly."

8

Veracruz

[1]

The Virgin of Guadalupe had no time to spread her arms in imitation of her son on the cross before receiving the blast.

She stood there with her hands clasped in prayer, with her eyes lowered and sweet, until the bullets pierced her eyes and mouth, and then her blue mantle and her warm, maternal feet.

The stars were reduced to dust, the horns of the moon shattered into a thousand pieces, the scandalized cherubs fled.

The commander of the fort of San Juan de Ulúa repeated the order, take aim, fire, as if a single barrage wasn't sufficient for the independentist Virgin, as if the effigy venerated by the poor and the agitators who carried her image in their scapularies and on their insurgent flags deserved to be executed twice a day.

The priest Hidalgo in Guanajuato, the priest Morelos in Michoacán, and now the priest Quintana here in Veracruz had all thrown themselves into the revolt with the banner of the Virgin of Guadalupe raised on high. And though they were ultimately captured and beheaded—except for that damned Quintana, who was still running around loose—she, the Virgin, could be shot at will, whenever there was no rebel leader to take her place.

Baltasar Bustos watched this ceremony of the shooting of the Virgin when he reached Veracruz from Maracaibo, and he concluded that he'd reached the strangest land in the Americas.

The revolutionary decade was coming to a close, and if in South America San Martín, Bolívar, Sucre, and O'Higgins had beaten the Spaniards and there had been no chance for retaliation, in Mexico the sacrifice of the poor parish priests, who led the only uprising of the Indians and the peasants armed with clubs and picks, had left independence to the dubious outcome of an agreement among warriors. On the one side, there were the weary professional soldiers of the Spanish Army, representatives of the reactionaries restored after the Congress of Vienna and the return to the throne of Ferdinand VII, more stupid and ultramontane than ever. On the other were the nervous (and enervated) creole officers, led by Agustín de Iturbide, who could no longer pretend (not even to fool themselves) to support Ferdinand or Carlota. All the same, the creole military men promised to protect the interests of the upper classes and keep the damned races—Indians, blacks, mestizos, *zambos, cambujos*, quadroons, and other racial mixtures—from taking over the government.

So the Virgin of Guadalupe was shot to death once more on the morning of Baltasar Bustos's arrival at Veracruz, and through the perforated eyes of the Mother of God passed the rays of a tropical, leaden sun. Baltasar Bustos was entering Mexico: it was the final phase of his campaign of love and war. It had now been ten years since he'd kidnapped the white baby and put the black one in its place in Buenos Aires; but only two months had gone by since the quondam Luz María, Lutecia, the madam of Harlequin House, had handed him that ever so simple and direct note written in Veracruz:

Come instantly.
Ofelia.

Baltasar had brought something more than this note with him
from Maracaibo: he was entering Mexico with the documents
of a Spanish officer, as thin and nervous as a greyhound, whose
face had been blown off and who had died in Baltasar's arms.

He was entering Veracruz in search, first, as Lutecia had
instructed him, of the priest Quintana. And entering Veracruz
was like walking into a blazing oven.

Barely had Baltasar presented his papers to the port commander, Captain Carlos Saura, Fifth Grenadier Regiment of
the Virgin of Covadonga, than he took off his royalist officer's
coat and used it to cover a wretched dead man in Customs
House Street, an indigent, the other wretched creatures
around him said, for whom there was no money for a funeral.

"No one wants to bury them free, neither the priests nor
the government."

[2]

"You're looking for Father Quintana? Well, let's see you find
him!" the toothless man in Orizaba said, laughing, when Baltasar Bustos came within sight of that rainy city close to the
volcano, a city occupied by the insurgent forces of the priest
Anselmo Quintana for no other reason—according to the malicious gossips of Veracruz—than to destroy the Spaniards'
tobacco supplies, or—according to the kindhearted gossips of
the same port—to dress his troops in the excellent fabric produced in Orizaba, or—according to the cynics—because the
rich Spaniards had hidden their property in the convents and
this priest, they knew for a fact, had no respect for nuns; he'd
certainly had, with one nun or another, one or another of his
many bastards. After all, the principal purpose of this campaign
was to frighten the Spaniards and then enter the richest and

most devout city to sack it before running off with the loot
and mounting the next campaign.

"My God, when will there be peace!" said the creole ladies,
fanning themselves before the parish church of Veracruz.

"We've put all our faith in Iturbide and the royalist creole
officers," said another lady to Baltasar Bustos.

"Let the war be over, even if the Spaniards go. But, for
God's sake, don't let the Indians and the blacks take over
everything, like that excommunicated, heretical priest Quintana, who's taken the city of Orizaba. All the decent people
have come to the port, fleeing from the outrages perpetrated
by that damned priest," said a coffee grower from Cempoala,
standing at the entrance to the License Office. This man, named
Menchaca, had come to investigate tax exemptions, so he could
export his sacks of coffee. "Around here, they say the Indians
did the work of the conquest, because without them the Aztecs
would have dined on Cortez and his five hundred Spaniards.
Now it's up to us creoles to bring about independence, just
so the Indians don't take their revenge."

"Are you asking who this parish priest Quintana is?" the
gentlemen playing billiards and smoking in the bars near the
docks and the lethargic sea asked Baltasar rhetorically. "A
dangerous man. A womanizer. He's got a ton of kids. He laughs
out loud at the edicts of the Inquisition, which excommunicate
him. He used to be a parish priest right here near La Antigua.
Of course we know him. He liked to bathe naked in the Cha-
chalacas River with his flock. He's immoral. He would bet on
fighting cocks. Do you know why he became a rebel, Captain
Saura? Because in 1804 the consolidation law legislated by the
Bourbons took away his privileges as a member of the lesser
clergy. He lost those privileges, especially the exemption from
civil justice. That's the reason. And now they've assumed the
privilege of sacking every hacienda they find in their path. Just
like Hidalgo, Morelos, and Matamoros. This is a land of rebel
priests, who take advantage of religion to fool the asses and
behave like pirates."

"He's a show-off. He wears fancy cassocks. He covers his head with a red cap, as if he were a cardinal."

"He's the heir of Hidalgo and Morelos," said a young lawyer, slapping Baltasar's face with a glove as the tiles of an interrupted domino game poured over the floor of the entrance. "He's our last hope to keep criminals and scoundrels like you, Captain, from exploiting Mexico one second longer. Death to Iturbide! Death to the creoles! Hurrah for Father Quintana and the equality of the races!"

Baltasar Bustos had to agree to a duel with the petty lawyer from Veracruz at six o'clock the next morning on the road to Boca del Río, but that same evening he left on horseback for Orizaba, traveling uphill all the way. Two dawns later, in sight of the misty town where the tropics have hung the veils of an eternal Lent, he had no difficulty entering the town occupied by the famous priest Quintana, the last defender, or so everyone said, of an egalitarian revolution in North America. A few added that it would not be long before this revolution was betrayed by Iturbide and the creole military men.

In any case, this revolution could hardly be expected to triumph, and it would quite properly be the last, Baltasar wrote to us, his friends in Buenos Aires, if it was so careless as to allow anyone at all to ride into the camp of General Quintana and ask for him without being stopped by a single guard or even asked for a password. Why?

"Because Father Quintana says that if someone's out to get him not even the Pope himself could protect him." The toothless man from Orizaba who said that to him stared at Baltasar—blue flannel trousers, linen shirt, calico jacket, Panama hat, and the horse that Menchaca the coffee grower had given him just because he liked him—as if to imply that a rich little creole like him, turned out in such clothes and with gold-rimmed glasses, posed no threat to the priest Quintana. And once in the wolf's mouth, how long would this little gentleman with a straight nose, tangled sideburns, and honey-colored curls last if he tried any mischief?

"Just as night and the mountains, which are our real safe-guard, protect our army, the priest Quintana says, 'He who seeks me will find me.' Try it, young fellow," the boy encouraged Baltasar. "Find Anselmo Quintana on your own; there are standing orders never to point him out."

Veracruz roads are impassable in summer. The rain never ends, but all that water seems to originate in Orizaba and then flow back to it. Baltasar forded the rivers when the roads disappeared under mudslides. Before starting out for the day, he breakfasted on pineapple and mangoes still warm from the sun. But in Orizaba everything smelled of damp earth, and the fruits—oranges, strawberries, quinces, and sloes—boiled in immense caldrons to be made into preserves.

The rebels' weapons, compared with what he'd seen of José de San Martín's in Valparaíso and to the arms shipments that passed through Maracaibo, were not impressive. A few rifles, many lances, and even primitive slings. As if to make up for the paucity of artillery, there was an overabundance of archives. Mountains of paper at the entrance to the old tobacco warehouses, where military headquarters had been established. Sheets upon sheets, until they competed with the jealous mountain, the Orizaba peak the Indians called Citlaltepetl, Mountain of the Star. And running like mice around these huge parchment cheeses were secretaries and lawyers, scribes busily writing proclamations, agents and propagandists of all kinds. In greater numbers than the soldiers of the rebel army itself.

Baltasar Bustos had seen enough of the revolution in Spanish America to be able to tell who these people were without anyone's having to point them out. They were there to offer testimony about deeds, convince the incredulous, give the lie to the malicious, draw up laws, and elucidate constitutions. The star of this legal mountain was eloquence—easy, abundant, solemn, and seductive all at the same time: a rhetorical volcano. And while they were ambitious, these independence lawyers were not cynical. Dorrego and I, Varela, endlessly fixing our clocks in Buenos Aires, often said that in the case of the revolution for independence Pascal's bet about the existence of God was absolutely pointless: believing in God is a bet you cannot lose. If God exists, I win. If He doesn't, it doesn't matter.

In our revolutions (especially in one as fragile and harried as that of the priest Quintana along Mexico's Gulf Coast), if the independence movement failed, the insurgents would be shot. What was necessary, Xavier Dorrego told me, when he invited me to the estate he'd acquired on the road to San Isidro to admire his most recently acquired clock, was a faith comparable to that of the other Anselm, the saint who argued that if God is the greatest thing we can imagine, the nonexistence of God is impossible, because hardly have we negated God than we find His place taken by the greatest thing we can imagine, which is to say, God. But I, rather more of a Jacobin than our friend Dorrego, preferred to be satisfied with Tertulian's formula as a basis for belief in God: it's true because it's absurd.

Both arguments—Anselm's and Tertulian's—were necessary, we said in the anarchy of the Year XX in Argentina, for us to go on believing in the merits of independence. We could hardly imagine our third citizen of the Café de Malcos, our younger brother, Baltasar Bustos, ready to risk his life (and his faith?) in the first line of the last revolution, the Mexican revolution, and finding himself surrounded, as if through the worst gypsy curse, by lawyers, theologians of law, church fathers of the incipient nation, all of them excited, as if winning the war depended on paper and as if only that which was written could be real in our new nations and as if what was real were a mere mirage, to be disdained to the degree to which it did not adhere to the written ideal.

"The Law is the greatest thing imaginable."

"That's true because it's absurd."

Drones, pen pushers, and intriguers: he saw himself in them

and saw us, or perhaps men like me, Manuel Varela, an impenitent printer confident he could change the world by throwing words at it, and men like Xavier Dorrego, a rich creole convinced that an enlightened elite could, if guided by reason, save these poor nations destroyed first by tyranny, then by anarchy, and always by the simple, crushing fact of the ignorance of the majority. But weren't all of us also the bearers of the slim, provincial culture of our time, autodidacts instructed by censored books introduced into the Americas among the ornaments and sacred vessels of humble priests who did not pay duties, whose property was not searched, privileges the modernizing law of the Bourbons had prohibited?

Weren't we—Balta, Dorrego, and I, Varela, not forgetting the already deceased Echagüe and Arias—the patient kneaders of a civilization that was not yet bread and thus had nothing to distribute?

These thoughts were like a bridge that united us, here in the Río de la Plata, with our younger brother in the Gulf of Mexico.

But it wasn't among us or those who looked like us that Baltasar would find the person he sought.

The camp followers came and went with baskets of clean clothes on their heads; they would whip the chocolate in huge caldrons after grinding it in gigantic grinders; they would get down on their knees to wash; they would give birth to the tortillas in that same servile, maternal posture at the metate, the traditional corn-grinding stone; and one of them, more active than the rest, would seem to take care of everything and everyone at once, her hair a mess, her feet bare, and wiping her nose, which ran because of an annoying cold.

Soldiers in shirt sleeves and with handkerchiefs tied on their heads; troopers with machetes and swords, handsome horsemen like ancient condottieri, sitting on supply crates, vain, with their silk kerchiefs knotted at the corners, floating loosely around their necks, their campaign boots beautifully polished, their bell-bottom trousers embroidered with spangles and gold. Those not sitting on boxes used wicker chairs that were so worn they, too, looked like gold. But none of them could be Quintana—unless Baltasar Bustos's myopic but nervous and rapid eyes were unable to pick out the leader—doubtless because the leader was not any different from anyone else.

Perhaps it was the idea of the wicker and the gold that caused him to turn his head and catch sight of a blond head of hair that quickly hid in one of the tobacco sheds, mixing in with the laughing children hiding there as they played blindman's buff. The blond child came out with a handkerchief over his eyes, whiter than the filth on his rough cotton shirt and trousers. He collided with Baltasar's body and went running back to the shed, as his little comrades' laughter grew louder.

Baltasar was amazed at the serenity of the troops and the women and children that followed them from place to place, overcoming the distances of the vast continent because of the war, perhaps linking the idea of war with the end of a centuries-long isolation, an intimate justification of death, pain, failure, all in the name of movement and of contact with other men, women, and children.

Serenity or fatalism? They barely looked up at Baltasar, answering all his questions in short, almost lapidary, phrases. Only one question was left unanswered: "Where is Quintana? Which of you is the priest?"

They seemed to be saying that if he had managed to get this far, then this young man was one of them, and if he wasn't, they wouldn't let him go alive . . . Meanwhile, why get upset?

"Before he became a priest, he was a farm worker and a mule driver; he knows the land better than any Spaniard or native-born creole. And if he doesn't end up winning the war, the truth is, he's never given a victory to our enemies."

"He was always poor and still is. He's a hand-to-mouth priest. Others have their rents and monies from special fees. Not him. He had only one living, and the king of Spain took even that away from him, just to show his power and his nastiness."

"Go on, Hermenegildo, don't put it to the gentleman that Father Quintana rebelled just because they deprived him of his living."

"No, I think he rebelled against his solitude in the world. Look at him sitting there."

"Careful, Hermenegildo, shut up, we have orders."

"Excuse me, Atanasio. It just came out."

"Let's see you find him," said the man called Atanasio to Baltasar. "Don't believe my eyes. I'm blinder than a bat."

"Did you say solitude? Who knows? He used to like cock-fights and gambling back in his town. He mixed with the people. Who knows if he didn't start fighting just to stop gambling."

"Or so he could go back to gambling after the war," said a man passing by, guffawing, potbellied and merry. But he wasn't Quintana either, Baltasar said to himself as he scrutinized the dark faces, some *zambo*, others mulatto, very few Indian, the majority mestizo.

"I saw some blond children playing. Where did they come from?"

"From right here. Don't you know that Veracruz has been the entrance to Mexico for every foreigner since Hernán Cortés and that there are lots of blue-eyed, fair-haired kids in these parts?"

"All of them children of sleepless nights!"

"Not so. You see, our leader is very good at hiding. Once in Guanajuato he was running away from the Spaniards when we had no weapons, and he wound up becoming the lover of the wife of a famous lawyer of the Crown. He winked and told us, 'No one would ever think to look for me in that lady's bed.' "

"You want to find Father Quintana? What if he's dead and we don't want anyone to know?"

"What if he never existed and we invented him just to scare the Spaniards?"

"But, sir, don't you believe that story, because the people who think Papa Anselmo's dead drop dead themselves from fear when they see him reappear."

"They think they've beaten him, that he's dying of hunger, that he's living in a cave, that he's turned coward. But Quintana comes back to life, returns, and starts over. That's why we'll follow him anywhere. He never gives up."

"Because he's got nothing to lose. A poor parish priest! His living, his Crown privileges, that was the only wealth poor priests had in New Spain."

"How could he have anything when he went to war because he believes the clergy should have nothing, since the laws of Rome forbid them to have anything?"

"Hold on, what about those elegant uniforms he likes to wear? We all know about that."

"So, who doesn't like elegant uniforms? Why should we prove the Spaniards tell the truth when they call us ragged beggars? A man has to look his best once in a while, especially in parades, in battle, and at his funeral. Don't you agree?"

"The best part, sir, is that he makes sure we have good uniforms, too."

"And he won't accept anyone in the troop if he can't give him at least a sword and a gun."

"The ones I'm thinking about are the poor tailors who work for General Father Don Anselmo Quintana, because when the Spaniards capture his coats they're going to shoot the poor tailors who sewed them."

"How they hate him!"

"Don't be a fool. That's why the general's coats don't have labels."

"There aren't even any bills, not a single reference in the ledgers to receipts and payments," said a lawyer carrying a bundle of papers. He'd stopped to drink a steaming cup of

coffee handed to him by the woman with the cold, who offered
to carry the papers from one archive to another. The lawyer
gave her the papers and then turned to Baltasar. "You're looking for Quintana? Well, son, you've been given the counter-
sign, haven't you? You can find him if you want. Or if you are
able."

"Is he here?"

"I can't tell you that, boy. Who are you?"

"I'm not going to tell you. What's good enough for Quintana
is good enough for me."

"You don't talk like a Mexican. But you don't sound like a
Spaniard, either."

"Well, it's a big continent. It's hard for all of us to know
each other."

"Well, boy, let me give you some advice. The general seems
really easygoing, but he's a tiger when he gets his back up. So
watch your step. Don't play with him."

"What do you mean?"

"What right do you have, addressing me so familiarly?"

"What right do you have calling me *boy*?"

"I have a degree in jurisprudence from the Royal University
of Valladolid in Michoacán."

"I see. In that case, what is it your excellency wishes to say
to me?"

"Boy, I want to tell you what happened to a man who looked
like you who was with us in the Oaxaca campaigns. A little
creole officer, about your age, was insubordinate to General
Quintana. He disobeyed orders by visiting a woman. But he
found her in the arms of the Spanish commander of the town.
And the commander, in his underwear, felt ridiculous and
beaten. Without his uniform, what is an officer, whether creole
or Spaniard? Nothing! Our young officer threatened him, and
the commander disgorged some military secrets. Our little
officer then ran out to report what he'd learned, but found no
one in headquarters. So he acted on his own and without

permission attacked the rear guard of the Spanish garrison at Xoxotitlán along the Oaxaca road. His action allowed us to take old Antequera, Mr. . . . ?"

"I see. You, sir, are both curious and impertinent."

"Boy, I want the truth, the whole truth, and nothing but the truth, as we say in court."

"I am Captain Baltasar Bustos. My last posting was to accompany General José de San Martín in the Andes campaign."

"Captain, a thousand pardons. You seem so . . ."

"Callow. Yes. Your story interests me, please finish it."

"Delighted. Let's see now. Sit down on this crate here. We lack amenities."

"Just go on. Quintana was faced with a dilemma: should he punish the officer or not?"

"Exactly, Captain. Your perspicacity is astonishing."

"No more than your malice, Counselor."

"You flatter me, Captain. That was the dilemma. Punish him. Or allow a tradition of disorder and caprice to flourish. The priest Quintana has enough headaches defending himself against edicts of excommunication and anathemas for heresy."

"And he wouldn't add lack of discipline to excommunication?"

"And he couldn't allow aristocratic creoles—sorry if I offend you, Captain—to place themselves above the law."

"Which you, Counselor, represent."

"Exactly. To carry on with their caprices."

"So he had him shot."

"Precisely. It's only fair to warn those who come here alleging they've put aside their social class and become one of us."

"Take a good look at my skin, Captain," said a soldier in a white shirt sitting on a crate across from two bottles of wine, which he studied while making paper cartridges. "You're white, I'm very dark. What does your freedom matter to me if it doesn't include my equality?"

"What are you doing?" Baltasar asked the soldier, whose face, with thick, half-open lips, seemed as flexible and rough as a wrinkled leather wineskin.

"I'm trying to choose between these bottles."

"Why?"

"Because one kind of alcohol is merciful and another is hostile. I look at the bottles and wonder which is which."

"I couldn't have guessed. And what are you doing with those papers?"

"I'm making the edicts of excommunication published by the Holy Inquisition against our leader Father Quintana into cartridges."

"But you are Father Quintana," said Baltasar.

"How do you know that?" The soldier raised his dark, wrinkled face.

"Because you're the only person in this entire encampment who is wavering between two things, even if they happen to be two bottles of wine. And also, you're showing me your bare head, while everyone else has his covered. You don't want to be identified by your cap, which you always have on. Your cap would betray you, but the fact that you take it off betrays you more."

"No," said Quintana without emotion, covering his black, curly head with a tawny cap with long earflaps. "It isn't alcohol that concerns me but Hosts. We're making them out of corn, out of sweet potatoes, out of whatever we have. There is no wheat in this region. And I have to think about the effects of Communion not only on Christ's body but on my own. Understand?"

He fixed his gaze on Baltasar's light eyes without interrupting his cartridge making and added that the boy, if he was going to join them, should know right from the start that every Thursday—tomorrow—everyone had to live in suffering without the Father—only once a week, from Thursday to Friday, but every week without exception, accepting the Host and the wine as the literal body and blood, not only of Christ, but of all those who take Communion: Quintana, Bustos, that toothless man over there, this woman with the cold, the children playing blindman's buff. "Don't try to find out how many are with me, because over the course of the war I myself have lost count. Even those constipated lawyers who fill my head with projects and laws"—Quintana raised his voice so the interested parties could hear—"because they would like to carry out this revolution their way, with order and laws, but without me they would win no battles, not even against their mothers-in-law.

"So all of us, all of us, Captain Bustos, are without the Father because Christ dies on the cross and we only recover Him in the Eucharist; we all have to live this anguish and this hope from Thursday to Friday or we have no right to go on calling ourselves Christians. But only I, Captain, have the pleasure of mixing in my mouth the Host and the wine and of liberating with my saliva and the alcohol two bodies: mine and Christ's. It is not enough to keep the first Fridays because Christ made a charming promise to St. Margaret Mary! This is not a matter of beatitude and grace, it's a question of pain and necessity: every week at least, and not every day so as not to shock anyone."

The priest Anselmo Quintana paused to take a breath, looked around him with a singular mix of arrogance, humor, irony, and unity with his people, and concluded: "That's why I have to choose very carefully which wine I drink at Mass. As you see, with the excommunication edicts I make cartridges and return them like Roman candles to the Spaniards. Now come and eat something and talk awhile. You must be very tired."

He stood up.

"Ah, yes, let me shake hands with someone who fought alongside José de San Martín. But first let's smoke a cigar."

[3]

There was no time to smoke anything that Wednesday morning in Orizaba that smelled of storm. Once the new arrival had solved the puzzle put to him by the entire encampment, the swarm of shysters and scribes descended on the priest Quintana with recommendations, warnings, requests, and news: "If the archives already take up more than ten wagons, what shall we do with them?" "Burn them," says Quintana. "But then there will be no evidence of what we are doing. Your campaign, General, has always distinguished itself not only by winning battles but by setting down laws, freeing land, and giving constitutions and federal guarantees to those who work the land, if not for today, then certainly for tomorrow." "Well, what do you want? To study all those papers, so you can burn some and save others? Your papers drive me mad, do whatever you like with them, but save me two, because I do want to keep them and remember them forever." "Which two might they be, General?"

The priest stopped on his way to the tobacco sheds, where he was going with Baltasar. He took the cigar out of his shirt pocket but didn't raise it to his lips or light it. He waved it like a hyssop or a scourge or a phallus before the eyes of the lawyers and scribes.

"One is my first baptismal act as a priest, gentlemen. In those days it was the custom to conceal the race of newborns. Everyone wanted to pass for Spanish; no one wanted the infamy of being termed black, mestizo, or anything else. So when I baptized that first child, I naturally wrote 'of the Spanish race.' Keep that paper for me also because that first child I anointed with the chrism was my own son. The other paper is a law I dictated to you in the Córdoba congress which says that from now on there will be no more blacks, Indians, or Spaniards but only Mexicans. Keep that law for me: the others deal with freedom, but that one deals with equality, without which all rights are chimeras. And then burn the rest and stop annoying me."

But they did not do it. They formed swift circles around Quintana and Baltasar as the two stood under the wet mangroves, whose smell competed with the rising aroma of the tobacco sheds (which smelled of fertile earth and female thighs, smoky hair and mandrakes, primroses, a wake, and truffles all mixed together, Quintana murmured): "We must take precautions, Calleja del Rey says he's obsessed with capturing you alive before the inevitable defeat of the royalist troops. Executions, the taking of hostages, rewards to towns that refuse to help us, the destruction of those that do—all these things are increasing, General. And the worst is that it's the creole Mexicans who hate you most vehemently; they don't want you on the political horizon when they take power after independence."

"What do you advise me to do?" This time Quintana looked at them with a nervous tremor in his left eyelid.

"Come to terms with them, General, save something of all this and, above all, save yourself."

"Listen to them, Baltasar. That's how you lose revolutions and even your balls."

"Come to terms, General."

"Now, when the final hour is at hand, when my present enemy, Spain, is about to lose, and when my next enemy will be the creole officers? But if for ten years I didn't come to terms with the king of Spain, who at least is a descendant of Queen Isabella the Catholic, why should I come to terms with a ridiculous little creole like Don Agustín de Iturbide? Who do you take me for, gentlemen? Haven't you learned anything in ten years?"

"Well then, what will you do?"

The lawyers asked that question more to themselves than to Quintana.

"The same thing we've done since the beginning. When we had no arms we made up for it with numbers and violence.

We began the campaign looking for weapons. And that's how we'll finish it. If they lay siege, we'll eat tree bark, soap, vermin, just as we did when we joined Morelos in Cuautla. If they capture us and sentence us, we'll commend our souls to God."

He shouldn't be such a fatalist, he should think about them, he should steal a march on Iturbide, and he himself, Anselmo Quintana, because of the sway he held over the people, should proclaim himself Most Serene Highness and with them, his advisers, form a Junta of Notables for the kingdom.

"The only junta I ever hope to see is two rivers joining together, and the only highness I want to experience is the top of a mountain. Mexico will be a republic, not a kingdom. And if there's anyone who doesn't like the taste of that, let him make up his kit and leave. There are lots of others to choose from. With me you know where you're going. And without me we don't go anywhere. Join up with the Spaniards. They'll shoot you. Amnesty's over. Join up with Iturbide. He'll humiliate you. And forgive my arrogance. I know it's a grave sin."

Quintana seized the hand of one of the lawyers, the one who had called Baltasar "boy," and kissed it. Then, without letting go, he knelt before the lawyer with his eyes lowered, asking for pardon for his bouts of pride; he respected them; he was an ignorant priest who respected learned men. He respected them, above all else, because what they did would remain, while what he did would be carried away by the wind and turned to birdshit. "There is no glory greater than a book," he said, his eyes still lowered, "no infamy greater than a military victory. Forgive me, understand that without the revolution my life would have been obscure, with no incidents in it greater than a romance now and then with an anonymous woman. You don't need me."

He stood up and looked each one of them in the eye. "Forgive me, really. But as long as this campaign lasts, the only fat man around here is me."

He guffawed, turned his back on them, and left them

stunned by his rapid-fire Veracruz-style discourse—unlawyer-ish, inspired at times, but ridiculous, the lawyers said among themselves, turning their backs on him and heading for their improvised offices among their mountains of paper. But it wasn't the first time he'd done that to them, and they were still here. Why? Because ten years are an entire lifetime in these parts, where, except by a miracle, no one lives beyond the age of forty, and because the priest was right: at this point they belonged to him, like his children, his women, or, if you like, his parents. No one would believe them if they tried to change sides. But Pascal's bet would not work, because if the royalists didn't win, the creoles would. No one would believe them.

"Well, well," said a lawyer—who wouldn't take off his black top hat and his funereal frock coat even if fighting broke out—as he wrinkled his nose so his eyeglasses wouldn't slide down any farther. "In this New Spain, no act is as certain of success as betrayal. Cortés betrayed Moctezuma, the Tlaxcaltecs betrayed the Aztecs, Ordaz and Alvarado betrayed Cortés. You'll see that the traitors will win and Quintana will lose."

These men, to their own misfortune and despite everything, thought more about posterity than about immediate gain. Which is why, despite everything, they were still with Quintana, and the priest, despite his jests, did respect them. If they wanted an honorable place in history, this was it, alongside the priest. And if the path to glory depended on writing a splendid series of laws that abolished slavery, that restored lands to communities, and that guaranteed individual rights, they would side with him until the moment they were brought before the firing squad.

Quintana knew it, and even though he annoyed them every day with his insults, he would monthly, along with his religious Communion, perform a kind of civil communion:

"Never in the history of Mexico has there been, nor will there ever be in the future, a band of men more patriotic and honorable than you. I am proud to have known you. Who knows what horrors await us. You, the insurgents, will have saved the nation's honor for all time."

They didn't fight. They wrote laws. And they were fully capable of dying for what they felt and wrote. They were right, Baltasar wrote to Dorrego and to me, Varela. Wasn't law reality itself? Thus, the circle of the written closed over its authors, capturing them in the noble fiction of their own inventive powers: the written is the real and we are its authors.

Can there be greater glory or certainty more solid for a lawyer from Spanish America?

"And who, from Argentina to Mexico, Varela"—Dorrego smiled at me as he read this letter—"doesn't have locked within his breast a lawyer struggling to break out and make a speech?"

Quintana, more of a fox than his shepherds, told Baltasar when they'd finally lighted their cigars under the shelter of the entrance to one of the tobacco warehouses: "Perhaps they will abandon me. Perhaps they won't. But they all know that they owe their personality to me. Even if they'd all be delighted to send me back to my rural parish."

"The contradictions in the human character will never cease to astonish me," Dorrego said, sighing, when I read him these lines: he was obstinately engaged in winding a carriage-shaped clock covered with an oval glass dome.

[4]

Dining alone with Baltasar in the kitchen of the tobacco factory, Quintana told more about his past. Thick smoke rose from the braziers fanned by the women as one of them, the solicitous, sniffling woman Baltasar had seen when he reached the encampment, placed Gulf Coast tamales wrapped in plantain leaves on their tin plates. These were followed by cups of Campeche-style seviche, a mixture of oysters, shrimp, and sliced scallops in lemon juice, along with yellow *moles* Oaxaca-style, redolent of saffron and chilies.

Quintana said he shouldn't be judged a rebel simply because of the business of his losing his privileges, although he admitted that had been the original reason for his taking up arms. Rebelling for such a reason seemed too much like taking revenge, while insurrection seemed too much like rancor. And nothing good could come of rancor. Baltasar should also consider that the Bourbon reforms asserted that they were merely bringing reality into line with law. Fine. In that case, not even the Pope had any right to possess more than he needed for his personal comfort. The clergy could not be allowed to own land, treasure, and palaces. Canon law prohibited that.

The independence revolution came along and he, Quintana, began to think it over and to look for a better reason than rancor to become a guerrilla. It hadn't been easy, even when he was ten years younger, to leave the tranquillity of a curacy and start risking his life.

"Should I have stayed there not doing anything? I could have. It was possible. Why did I join the revolution? If I again deny that it was because the Crown took the living away from us poor priests and that my living was my only wealth, I'll bore you. Besides, you'll stop believing me. If I tell you that I took one step too many and told myself that if this was all a matter of respecting the law then we'd have to go all the way, you won't believe me unless I explain something more important. Which is that in order to abandon my peace and quiet or not to stay in my parish like a fool while everyone else chose sides, I had to believe that what I was doing mattered. Mattered not only for me or for the independence of the nation but for my faith, my religion, my soul. And this is where the difficulties begin, because I am going to try to convince you that my political rebellion is inseparable from my spiritual rebellion. I know, because I know who you are, Baltasar, because I see your face and know what boys like you know, how much they've read and all the rest, that for you there can be no freedom with religion, independence with a church, or reason with faith."

He sighed and noisily tossed into his mouth a piece of tamale that was so red with chilies that it looked like a wound.

"But to talk about all that, we need time and opportunity. Now we're short of both."

He grasped Baltasar's impatient wrist. "I know you've come for other reasons and not to hear me talk."

"You're mistaken. I have the deepest respect for you."

"Be patient. One thing leads to the other. You know, in my town there was a blind beggar who was always accompanied by his dog. One day, the dog ran away and the blind man regained his sight."

For a long time, Baltasar stared at the priest, who went on eating noisily and with pleasure, savoring his yellow *mole* right down to the last grain of rice. Finally Baltasar decided to ask him, "Why do you have such confidence in me, Father?"

Quintana wiped his lips and gave the young Argentine a look of candid, friendly complicity. "We've been fighting for the same cause for the same span of time. Doesn't that seem sufficient reason to you?"

"That's only a fact. It doesn't satisfy me."

"Think then that I see in you something more and better than what you see in yourself. I sense that in your heart you feel slightly dissatisfied with everything you've done."

"That's true. I have my guilt and my passion, but I don't have greatness. I find myself laughable."

"Don't worry about greatness. Worry about your soul."

"I warn you, I don't believe in the Church or in God or in the absolute power of absolution that you think you have."

"So much the better. Rest today, and tomorrow we'll meet at midday in the chapel here at the tobacco warehouses. Remember that tomorrow is Thursday and that every Thursday I become very strong, very spiritual. Be prepared to do battle

with me. Then you will have your reward, and everything will
be resolved. I think your ten years of struggle will not have
been in vain."

Baltasar did not allow the conversation to end there. He
had the feeling—he wrote to us later—that the priest was right
and that these would be the final hours of his long campaign
for love and justice.

"What do you see in me, Father, that makes you treat me
with such respect . . . or simple interest? Forgive my boldness
in asking."

Quintana might have stared at him, looking him right in the
eye. He chose instead to scoop up the rest of the *mole* with a
tortilla.

"You have taken charge of other lives."

"But I . . ."

"We've all committed crimes. Shall I tell you something?
Would you like to know mine?"

"Father, in the name of justice I exchanged a poor child for
a rich child in his cradle. The poor child died because of me.
I stole the rich child from his mother and condemned him to
who knows what fate. And, in spite of that, I dared to love
the mother, to pursue her ridiculously across half the Americas. Ten years, Father, with no success, no reward, all to
become, as you say, a fool . . . Do you call that justice? Does
that deserve respect? Does my having abandoned my sister
without a second thought, indifferent to her fate, in the name
of my passion? I didn't give my father a last hope or affection.
Am I worthy of compassion because I survived at Chacabuco
while my comrades died? Wasn't I lacking in mercy when I
shouted a cruel truth at the Marquis de Cabra on his deathbed?
Father Quintana . . . I killed a man in battle."

"That's normal."

"But I didn't kill him as a soldier. I killed him as a man, a
brother. I killed him because he was an Indian. I killed him
because he was weaker than I. I killed him as an individual,

abusing him, even though I don't know his name and can't remember his face."

With a strength that came from total conviction, Quintana told him to be quiet. "Don't force me to confess my own sins to you."

"What, that you're a skirt-chaser, that you like cockfights, that you have illegitimate children all over the country, that you like fancy cassocks? Are those serious sins, Father?"

"Tomorrow I'll make my confession before you," he said with a sudden huge sigh of fatigue. "I'll do it tomorrow. I swear. I'll make my confession before you, even though you don't believe in the power of absolution. I'll confess before my younger brother, who in Maracaibo took charge of a fallen woman and the wounded enemy. I'll do it tomorrow. Tomorrow, Thursday, I shall speak to my brother in mercy."

[5]

That night Baltasar slept in a hammock. He was lulled by the hammock, but even more by a weariness that came not from a single day but from ten years' accumulation. It was the sleep that comes when something is about to end, an imminent sleep that told him: This is where you and I part company; now you will have to change, now you must take account of debits and credits, just as these paymasters and secretaries do who accompany Father Quintana.

Might Quintana be the true notary of Baltasar Bustos's life?

Tomorrow was Thursday. They would meet; the priest had told him to come to the chapel at noon. Did they have anything else to say to each other? Baltasar thought that he had made his confession to the priest that afternoon, and the priest's sins were the talk of Veracruz. What more could they say to each other? To what ceremony had this proud man surrounded by an aura of obscure self-denial invited him?

He had told Baltasar that in the young man he saw someone

who took charge of others. The women in Harlequin House, the Duchess; the slender, disfigured officer . . . That was a slim list of credits next to the column of debits Baltasar had enumerated to Quintana.

But now, drifting deeper into sleep and rocked by the hammock (And who rocked it? There was no breeze, the Orizaba sky was in mourning but did not weep, and he descended, immobile, into sleep), Baltasar only reproached himself for a greater insincerity, which was to have told the rebel priest that everything he'd done, the good and the bad, had an erotic, sexual, amorous (as the priest liked to call it) purpose, which was to reach Ofelia Salamanca, finally to touch her after ten years of romantic passion paraded over the entire continent, the source both of sighs and of jokes, sung about in *corridos, cuecas,* and *zambas.*

To reach her, keeping his passion obsessive and unique, he'd had to sacrifice the love of the beautiful Chilean Gabriela Cóo, since to be unfaithful to Ofelia Salamanca, even if she didn't know it, would be to betray the adorable Gabriela as well.

To see her face to face. To say to her: I love you. To say to her: I forgive you. To which of the two women would he say that? Didn't one feed the love of the other, and didn't both loves drink from a common spring—absence? Did he desire them so much only because he did not possess them?

He opened his eyes. The hammock stopped rocking. He shut them again, overwhelmed by the magnitude of his presumption. What was he going to pardon Ofelia Salamanca for? What did he know of her except, in effect, gossip, idle talk, limericks that often created a new truth only for the sake of rhyme? How did he dare? Hadn't Gabriela told him in Santiago de Chile that acting is insincere, fleeting, that it leaves no more trace of itself than words?

Then he plummeted again from the peak of his aroused consciousness to a pleasant unconsciousness, drugged by the premonition of peace and rest after ten years of exaltation. And in the depths of his sleep he was always on his way back to El Dorado. Holding Simón Rodríguez's hand, he returned to that most high abyss, that deep promontory, the heart of the Quechua mountain, the navel of sleep, and there he accused himself, with rage, with despair, with the terrible feeling that he'd lost his chance, because he hadn't stopped for an instant to watch the passage of dreams in the luminous eyes of the inhabitants of the city where everything moved in light, was born from light, and returned to light.

He scorned dreams. He rejected the possibility of understanding anything through a dream which was not his own, which was not bound to the dream of reason, faith in material progress, the certitude that human perfectibility was infallible, and the celebration that in the end happiness and history, the subject and the object, would become one, once and for all.

The other story, the warning but also the possibility of escape, was perhaps in the eyes of the inhabitants of El Dorado, where light was necessary because everything was dark and where, for that reason, they could see with their eyes shut and reveal their dreams in the screens of their eyelids, warning him, Baltasar Bustos, that for each reason there is an unreason without which reason would cease to be reasonable: a dream that simultaneously denies and affirms reason. That there was an exception to every law, which makes the law partial and tolerable. But his most vivid sensation as he abandoned El Dorado was not that things complement each other, but rather the other extreme, a negation:

Evil is only what our reason hides and refuses to contemplate.

The real sin is to separate the sensible world from the spiritual world.

Then in a dream Ofelia Salamanca ceased to be a visible projection onto the animated wall of an Indian cavern, visible but untouchable, as delightful as his eyes announced it to be from a balcony in Buenos Aires that May night so far away.

Now she was the object of his touch (she was a single, unending animal wearing pulsating silk), of his hearing (she was a Mass in the desert, a voice outside of consciousness telling him from then on, without giving him an opportunity to reply, "You love me!" "You love me not!"), of smell (she was the most delightful stench, the stink without which there is no love, the perfume of a sullied clover leaf), and of sight: Ofelia Salamanca had eyes on her nipples that stared at him furiously, seductively, disdainfully, mockingly, until they made him wake up with a start.

The hammock stopped rocking. Ofelia Salamanca was the owner of the world.

[6]

Anselmo Quintana was standing before the altar. Baltasar Bustos's silhouette materialized in the light at the entrance to the chapel, and the priest waited until the thudding of his boot heels on the floor of flaking bricks, too soft for this rainy climate, stopped. When he was near, Quintana put his hand on Baltasar's shoulder and said to him, "Yesterday you didn't let me say my confession. Today you are going to sit in my place in the confessional, and I am going to kneel at your side and speak in secret through the grating.

"I know you don't believe in the sacrament. So it shouldn't matter where we do this. Yet it does matter to me to be on my knees to speak to you. Today is Thursday, and from now until tomorrow, weekly, Jesus Christ dies again for us. Many forget it; I do not. The most important thing I do is to remind anyone who cares to listen that if we are here and live, it is because Jesus sacrificed Himself to give us life on earth. Bear in mind then, Baltasar, that what I am going to tell you is preparation for the supreme act of faith, which is the Eucharist. The Eucharist is inseparable from Christ's sacrifice. And even though Calvary sufficed, each time I drink the blood and eat the body of Christ, I add to His sacrifice and act in the name of the quick and the dead. The Cross is the confluence of everything: sacrifice, life, death. Calvary, as they taught us in seminary, was sufficient in itself. But for me the Eucharist comes closest to that sacrificial sufficiency. I have no road more certain toward Christ than the Eucharist."

Quintana's words allowed for no response, and in any case the force with which he led Baltasar to the confessional precluded any appeal.

Baltasar fell into the seat of the confessor with a leaden sense that anchored him there as if in a loathsome jail cell, the mortal facsimile of the coffin whose worn-out velvet smelled of trapped cats.

Anselmo Quintana knelt down outside, by Baltasar's unwilling ear.

"Yesterday you did not allow me to confess," said the priest.

"But I told you I don't believe in the power of absolution."

"You think I want to talk about your sins, so you shut yourself off from me. But your sins do not interest me. Your fate does. And what I confess to you is also part of my fate. Let's get started: I confess, brother, to having ordered the execution of a hundred Spanish soldiers held in jails and even in hospitals, in order to avenge the death of my eldest son at the hands of the royalists. I ordered their throats slit. The idea of forgiveness never even passed through my mind. I was blinded. Tell me if you would have forgiven me if I were your father and you my dead son."

Baltasar said nothing. A feeling of growing modesty was taking control of him, inseparable respect and compassion for this man whose voice was becoming black, thick, guttural, reverting to ancient African roots, almost the voice of a psalmodist, which Baltasar did not want to interrupt until he'd heard everything, the same propitiatory act, perhaps, that would permit a believer to repeat the sacrifice on Calvary without taking the slightest bit away from the sufficiency of Christ's martyrdom.

He decided to hear him through to the end without arguing, to listen to him speaking there on his knees, his face like an old ball that has been kicked around: "I understand your silence, Baltasar, I understand your reticence, but understand mine; I share your fear of our weaknesses, and I fear as you do that a word spoken in confidence will be taken away by the one who listens to us, will get lost with our secret in the multitudes, and that we shall be left at his mercy if one day, out of despair or necessity, he repeats it to others; if you don't believe in me, in my priestly investiture or in my power to pardon sins, I shall repeat that I understand you, and for that reason I ask not that you confess formally to me but that you accept my humility as I kneel before you, exposing myself to you as the one who carries away my secret and, not believing in the sacrament, gives my secret to the world. I offer myself to you as an example. I confess before you, Baltasar, because yesterday you said things for which I have to assume some responsibility, and it does not seem right that the burden of our relationship, which has barely begun, which may not last very long, should fall upon me: one day we shall give an accounting not only of ourselves but of each one of the people to whom we have said something or from whom we have heard something. I ask you to accept this and not to believe that yesterday only you spoke, unburdening your conscience, and that today only I will do the same: your responsibility, yours and mine together this morning, is to give an accounting of all the beings who have done us the favor of listening to us. Would you like to know something? I told you my crime against the prisoners, and you should understand that, just as you do when you sin, I committed a crime against universal morality. St. Paul explains that sin is an assault on the natural law inscribed in the conscience of each human being. In my own case, it was also a violation of the vows of the priesthood, which include forgiveness, mercy, and respect for the will of God, who alone is able to give and take away life. Because of what I had done, I feared the punishments of hell that day when I avenged my poor son, a twenty-year-old boy who gave himself to the fight for independence, a gallant fellow with a red kerchief tied on his head, which made it difficult to see the blood when the ferocious Spanish Captain Lorenzo Garrote executed the sentence. Garrote saved his own life and embittered mine . . . But I realized, Baltasar, that I did not fear the ordinary hell of flames and physical suffering but the hell I imagined, and that hell is a place where no one speaks: the place of eternal, total silence forever; never more a voice, never a word. For that reason I kneel before you and beg you to listen to me, to postpone that inferno of silence, even if you do not speak to me, even if there is a hint of disdain in your stubborn silence. It does not matter, my little brother, I swear it does not matter, as long as we do not let our language die. Listen to me, then: I admit that I rebelled because I was unhappy when I lost my living, but now my rebellion has gone far beyond that. My rebellion led me to one gain after another: this is what I want to communicate to you; this is what you should understand. I gained rational faith without losing religious faith: I could have said, simply, 'I am a rebel priest; those who excommunicate me are right. I am going to deliver myself over to independence, to the wisdom of the age, to faith in progress; I am simply going to damn religious faith.' Everything was joining against my faith: my rage when they declared me a heretic and blasphemer, my fear when they denied me the Host, my rancor when they killed my son, my temptation to be only a rationalist rebel. This has been my most terrible struggle, worse than any military battle, worse than all the spilled blood and the obligation to execute: not to give in before my judges, not to admit they were right or give them the pleasure of saying, 'Look, we were right, he was a heretic, he was an atheist, he deserved to be excommunicated.' They ask me to repent. They don't know that that would mean delivering myself to hell. It would mean admitting the absolute evil in me—reason without faith—because I can lose the Church that has expelled me, but I cannot lose God; and to repent would be exactly that, to return to the Church but to lose God—not reason, which can coexist with the Church, but God who can exist without the Church and without reason."

Quintana lowered his head, and Baltasar saw the tawny-colored cloth of his celebrated cap hiding his curly dark hair, which the priest revealed so as not to stand out from the other men in the encampment, but in so doing he revealed himself with more fanfare than if he'd proclaimed it aloud: only Anselmo Quintana wears a cap amid all these top hats worn by the lawyers and the red kerchiefs worn by the troops; thus, Anselmo Quintana is the man who does not use a cap to disguise himself but who, by the same token, does not wear frock coats or tie kerchiefs on his head and who stares intensely at two bottles in order to choose between good and bad alcohol just as he might choose between reason and the Church. But you can't just choose God: God is, with or without the Church, reason, or believers. "That's where I have concentrated my real rebellion," the priest Anselmo continued. "I'm telling this to you, Baltasar, because you are like my younger brother in the world and you are also rebelling against its laws, but you remain open to new persuasions. My real rebellion was to suffer the Calvary of losing my Church but not my God . . . Imagine what went through my soul when I took up arms on the Gulf Coast, angry over the loss of my living. Imagine me pug-nosed and blind, just ten years ago, consumed with lust, in love with gambling, with women, a horse's ass of a priest, with a troop of bastards scattered all over the place, a seducer of women who came to kneel next to me and who thought that, to receive my forgiveness, they had to give themselves to me, and from time to time I did not discourage them . . .

I took up arms, my boy, being the kind of man I was, and then excommunication hits along with the rain of labels: apostate against the Holy Catholic religion, libertine, seditious, revolutionary, schismatic, implacable enemy of Christianity and of the state, deist, materialist, and atheist, guilty of divine and human treason, seducer, impenitent, lascivious, hypocrite, traitor to king and country. They didn't omit a one, Baltasar. The Holy Inquisition did not omit a single crime. They threw all of them at my poor head, and every time an accusation struck me between the eyes, I would say, 'They are right; they must be right. It's true, I deserve this, and my poor, damned motive for rebelling makes me a criminal in all those other things, and that, too, must be true . . .' But I think, brother Baltasar, that the Inquisition, as usual, went too far; they accused me of too many things, some right, others outlandish, and I said to myself then, 'God cannot look on me with as much injustice as my judges. In God's vocabulary there are probably few words for me, but there most certainly must be a dictionary common to Jesus Christ and His servant Anselmo Quintana. They throw so many words at me, but not enough that every week, from Thursday to Friday, you, Lord, cannot still speak, my Jesus, with the most lascivious, impenitent seducer among your servants . . .'

"The word is the only thing that links us when everything else becomes useless, treacherous, threatening. The word is the ultimate reality of Christ, His vigil among us, what allows us, without pride, to say, 'I am like Him . . .' "

Quintana raised his voice as he said this, as if his faith could all be reduced to these few words, and Baltasar, in the half light of the confessional, saw through the grating not the fluttering earflaps of Father Anselmo Quintana's cap but the head of Gabriela Cóo, crowned with clouds and weeds. He had to dispel that adorable vision because the voice of the priest continued, lower now, but more certain as well: "From that time I only spoke with Him, but He was more severe than all

my judges put together, because no one can fool Him. There
are no little tricks with Him. God is the Supreme Being who
knows all, even what we imagine about Him, and steals the
march on us and imagines us first; and if we go about thinking
that it depends on us to believe or not in Him, He steals the
march on us once again and finds the way of telling us that
He will go on believing in us no matter what happens, even
if we abandon Him and deny Him. That is the voice I listened
to during the night when my soul suffered tribulation because
of the edicts of expulsion from the Church and the calls for
me to repent: the voice of Christ saying to me, 'I am going to
go on believing in you, Anselmo Quintana, even if you are a
seducer, lascivious, a libertine, a hypocrite, which you are; why
deny it? But what you are not, Anselmo, my son, is an apostate,
a heretic, an atheist, or a traitor to your country, that you are
not . . .'

" 'Listen to me carefully, your God says to you: there is no
way that I'm going to allow that lie to pass.' "

He raised his eyes to tell Baltasar that all he needed to hear
from God's voice were those words, to fight for ten years, "to
not yield in my battle for my country or in my other struggle
for the love and confidence of my Creator. Imagine what one
thing would have been without the other—neither the nation
nor God; that most certainly would have been my anguish,
and they know it, which is why they call me a heretic, excommunicate me, and ask me to repent and come back to the
sheepfold. But Jesus said to me, 'Anselmo, my son, don't be
a comfortable Christian; make life hell for the Church and the
king, because they adore tranquil Christians. I, on the other
hand, adore rampaging Christians like you; you gain nothing
by being a Catholic without problems, a simple believer, a man
of faith who doesn't even realize that faith is absurd and is
faith and not reason because of that. Reason cannot be illogical;
faith is and has to be, because you have to believe in me against
all evidence, and if I were a logician, I wouldn't be God. I

wouldn't have sacrificed myself. I would have accepted all the temptations in the desert and would be'—are you listening to me, Anselmo, my son, are you listening to me, brother Baltasar?—'the very same long-tailed, incorrigible Devil who invented the statement "I think, therefore I am." ' What pretension! Not even my thoughts are my own, not even my very existence. I neither think nor exist alone. I share each word with God, with you, Baltasar, and each heartbeat as well. Then I learned something else, that it was my obligation, in the name of the simple people of this world, to be complicated; just ask yourself right now as I look at you and listen to you, if you aren't too comfortable in your philosophy, because I think you are being very simple with your own secular faith in reason and progress. You are as foolishly devout as those women who grow old in churches, sweeping and lighting candles every single day. Please, Baltasar, always be a problem, be a problem for your Rousseau and your Montesquieu, and all your philosophers. Don't let them pass through your soul without paying something at the spiritual customs house; don't give your faith to any ruler, any secular state, any philosophy, any military or economic power without adding your confusion, your complication, your exceptions, your damned imagination that deforms all truths.

"Well!" shouted Father Quintana in a flash of good humor. "Wouldn't I have been better off losing my faith and avoiding all that anguish? No sir, because then I wouldn't have fought for independence. It's as simple as that. I would have let myself be beaten in the first fight. My faith in the nation that I want, free, without slaves, without the horrible need for thousands and thousands of bottom dogs, ignorant, dying of hunger, all this, Baltasar, would not have been possible without my faith in God. You may have your own formula. This is mine. I'm not asking you to believe as I do. I'm not that simple. I am asking you to complicate your own secular faith. You've come from far, far away, and this continent is very large. But we

have two things in common. We understand each other because we speak Spanish. And, like it or not, we've had three
centuries of Catholic, Christian culture, marked by the sym-
bols, values, follies, the crimes and the dreams of Christianity
in the New World. I know fellows like you: they've all passed
through here; you've already seen them, although the ones
you saw were a bit more beaten up than you, like the lawyers,
scribes, authors of laws and proclamations in my own company.
I've talked with all of you for ten years. You have given me
the education which, sadly, I never had. My parents were mule
drivers from the coast. I was in a religious seminary when I
was young, and now that I'm grown up, I'm in the secular
seminar with all of you. But let's get on with it. I'm not fore-
telling anything—I have it right under my nose, as pugged and
battered as it may be. All of you would like to put an end to
that past which seems unjust and absurd to you, to forget it.
Yes, how good it would have been to be founded by Montesquieu instead of Torquemada. But it didn't happen that way.
Do we want now to be Europeans, modern, rich, governed by
the spirit of the laws and the universal rights of man? Well,
let me tell you that nothing like that will ever happen unless
we carry the corpse of our past with us. What I'm asking you
is that we not sacrifice anything, son, not the magic of the
Indians, not the theology of the Christians, not the reason of
our European contemporaries. It would be better if we gathered up everything we are in order to go on being and to be,
finally, something better. Don't let yourself be divided and
dazzled by a single idea, Baltasar. Put all your ideas on one
side of the balance, then put everything that negates them on
the other, and then you'll be closer to the truth. Work counter
to your secular faith, brother. Put next to it my divine faith,
but as ballast, weight, contrast, and a part of your secularism.
I do the same thing, working from my faith, with yours . . .
Take me into account more, much more tomorrow than today,
and think seriously that if I not only joined but forwarded the
revolution until the end, it was so that history would not leave

the Church behind—*my* church. See to it that you don't leave
your own church of romantic, anticlerical philosophers behind.
I don't want to find out ten years from now that you became
just one more man made sick by frustrated utopias, by betrayed
ideals. And don't think I don't thank you all for your skepti-
cism, my good company of lawyers. But I have what you lack,
let me say it with forgiveness and humility. I had to burn the
midnight oil reading St. Thomas Aquinas, Albertus Magnus,
St. Bonaventure, and Duns Scotus. Rousseau and Voltaire are
a corrective for me, even an emetic. But you modern fellows,
what will you use as a corrective for what you've learned?
Experience, of course. But experience without ideas does not
become a destiny, a soul . . . And what is the soul, St. Thomas
wonders, but the form of the body? Think about it and you'll
see that that's no paradox: the soul is the form of the body.
Without the soul, the body would not last, would begin instantly to stink and disintegrate . . . Give soul to your body,
Baltasar, and let's hope we see each other again in ten years
. . . Bah, perhaps tomorrow I'll be captured, and perhaps that's
why I felt the need to talk with you today. I want you to think
about me when you hear about my end. I also want you to
take charge of my memory."

The priest was silent for a long time, and later Baltasar
Bustos chastised himself for what, with time, he came to see
as a cowardice that ratified the worst aspects of his character,
argumentative without nobility, envious of what he wasn't,
abusive toward the weak, tempted to humiliate anyone he
thought inferior . . . He did not fool himself later. But in that
moment, when Quintana stopped talking, he thought he was
acting as the priest had asked him to after giving over to him
his soul, while, in his blindness, Baltasar Bustos thought the
priest was only giving him a lesson.

"I was wondering, as I listened to you, what bothered me
most in you—the solitary, chaste priest or the promiscuous
priest with children of his own."

Quintana tried to penetrate with his eyes the grating that

separated them, so that Baltasar would realize the priest was hurt, silenced by a sudden shock more than by overwhelming fatigue.

"Do you want to fight with me?"

"You asked me to be combative. I can imagine that one fine day the Pope will lift the excommunication and you will think that everything you did was useless, a failure . . ."

"Forgive me, I don't follow your line of thought . . ."

"I mean that I hope you aren't alive when the Church forgives you and says 'I was mistaken.'"

"The deed of trying to do something good is sufficient unto itself."

"Even if it fails."

"For God's sake, Baltasar, don't get lost in all this. All I wanted to tell you is that you and I resemble each other. We are both fighting for our souls, although you confuse the soul with matter. It's of no importance. You may be right. The soul is the form of the body. But you and I . . . Later, those who fight for money and power will come. That's what I fear. That will be the nation's failure. And then you and I—or what you and I leave in this world—should help the thieves and the ambitious to recover their souls. That would be my answer to those who forgive me two hundred years from now."

"But you, in part, agree with them." Baltasar tied to guess at the look on Quintana's mistreated face, turned into gridwork and made even uglier by the grating on the confessional door. "You have been lascivious, a hypocrite, and a seducer . . ."

"Do you know what the word *devil* means?" asked the priest, with his eyes lowered and his brow severe. "My problem is that I have not been exempt from the temptations of the flesh. Yours, on the other hand, is that you will not be exempt from the temptations of the soul. *Devil* means *liar*."

"See, you judge me with the same severity with which you have been judged . . ."

"Ah, and it also means *accuser*. I want you to know how they are going to judge me, Baltasar. They are going to humiliate me on my knees before the bishop. They are going to repeat the excommunication and the anathemas. Then they will deliver me to the secular authorities. They will shoot me in the back and then again, down on my knees. I will be decapitated, brother. They will put my head in an iron cage in the public square of Veracruz. I shall be an example for all those who feel the temptation to rebel . . ."

He couldn't finish the sentence because Baltasar was already out of the confessional, where he'd spent an hour occupying the priest's place, and now instead he was embracing the priest, asking his forgiveness, asking him why he did what he did for him, feeling the power, like that of a stormy sea, with which Quintana reined in his own emotion, like the frozen seas where huge tempests seem gigantically immobile, allowing the wind and not the water to be the principal player in the storm.

But the priest embraced Baltasar, kissed his head, welcomed him, and Baltasar understood that Father Anselmo was taking charge of him, so that he, Baltasar, could take charge, finally, of what was awaiting him . . .

[7]

With the strength of a mule driver, the old warrior Father Anselmo Quintana turned the convulsed body of his younger brother, the captain from Buenos Aires, Baltasar Bustos. He made Baltasar look toward the entrance to the chapel.

In the same rectangle of light he himself had occupied an hour earlier, two silhouettes now stood out clearly, a contrast both in gender and in clothing. A woman and a child.

"Come here, come in . . ."

Unlike Baltasar, the two moved forward noiselessly. They were barefoot and said nothing to disturb the silence of the chapel. That silence had not swallowed up the martial thud of Baltasar's heels. He was physically suspended between his two personalities, the fat, myopic young man and the slim, long-haired combatant; the Baltasar of Buenos Aires balconies and the Baltasar of the mountain campaigns in Upper Peru; the Baltasar of the salons of Lima and the Baltasar of the febrile brothels of Maracaibo.

Now, at thirty-five, Baltasar had achieved equilibrium between the half-blind but inquisitive gaze, the robust but agile body, and the lank mustache that gave firmness to his too small but full lips. His hair was indomitable; it seemed to have a life of its own, more than enough life for our romantic century, as we, Dorrego and I, Varela, decided to call it in Buenos Aires, when news of the poems of Byron and Shelley began to reach the New World . . . And his handsome Roman nose always gave Baltasar an air of nobility, resistance, stoicism. His gold glasses rested uncomfortably on the bridge of his nose.

The couple who approached were not at first glance recognizable, however, though the boy was the same one who'd played blindman's buff the day before, a blond child about ten years old, whose fair complexion had to be surmised, because of the tangle of his filthy hair and the dirtiness of his cotton shirt and trousers.

And she was a woman of indefinite age, her hair combed back into a bun poorly held together with pins. Stray hair fell over her forehead creased with wrinkles. The furrows of age around her lips, at the corners of her mouth, and on her chin were not disguised by makeup. The woman, barefoot like the boy, crossed her arms as if wrapping herself in a nonexistent shawl, and her trembling body betrayed the treachery of the tropics in Orizaba, the results of perpetual dampness and rain. Her bad cold was becoming a persistent cough.

"Ofelia," said the priest in his most tender voice, "I've already explained to the captain that you agree the boy should return with him to Argentina."

Quintana looked now at Baltasar—who was a single immobile block, forever locked in the most secret and unshakable of melancholies—as Baltasar stared into the totality of his life; the woman, much too busy blowing her nose, did not even look at him. Quintana told him that the child had been born ten years before in Buenos Aires and then kidnapped under mysterious circumstances. But his mother had managed to get him back from the black wet nurses who had saved him from a fire and who later asked for ransom money. She sent him to Veracruz to be put in the care of the priest Quintana, in the hope that someone would come to get him and take charge of him.

"Yesterday I told you, brother. Your destiny is to take charge of those who need you. And your nation will need both you and this boy. He should go with you. We shall survive here. We are very ancient. You, the Argentines, are the children of the Americas, the younger brothers of this old continent. Take the boy with you and teach him the best there is in the world with your good friends. You will have peace and prosperity. We will not."

"What about her?" Baltasar managed to blurt out.

"Ofelia Salamanca has been the most faithful agent of the revolution for independence in America," said Quintana, staring fixedly at the woman, who seemed dazed and was not listening. "She has kept our struggle alive by creating a network of communication, something so difficult for us on this continent. If I have been in contact with San Martín and Bolívar, it has been thanks to her. Thanks to her, we found out in time what Spanish reinforcements were leaving Callao for Acapulco or going from Maracaibo to Veracruz. She is a heroine, Baltasar, a woman worthy of our greatest respect. She sacrificed her reputation in order to learn secrets, and stained her hands with the blood of traitors who passed themselves off as insurgents while actually serving the royalist cause. One day her story will be written. How ingenious she was so often! She used a network of songs that ran through the Americas faster than a lightning flash to send us news, taking advantage of a rumored love affair between herself and some creole officer from Buenos Aires."

"Father, I am that officer. The songs mention my name. Don't try to fool me."

"Not another word, Baltasar. She ordered another hero of independence to be sent here, a man who, like her, pretended to be a royalist to acquire intelligence and to spread false rumors. She wants that hero, you, to take charge of her son. That is why she wrote to her friend Luz María in Maracaibo, asking you to come."

Quintana threw his arm around Ofelia's shoulders.

"Now she's very sick and cannot take care of the child or work for us any longer. She agrees that her son should return to Argentina with you. I suppose that you . . ."

"Yes," Baltasar said simply. "I agree as well."

The captain from Buenos Aires came nearer just as Ofelia Salamanca left Father Quintana's side. She lost her balance, and Baltasar helped her to her feet. It was the first time he'd ever touched her. She said, in a faint voice, "Thank you."

They separated instantly. She never looked at him. He did not want to see the mortal sadness in those eyes he'd adored so intensely. He put an arm around the boy's shoulders and said something like, "What you need is a good bath. You'll see, you're going to like the pampa. From now on, you're going to be my little brother . . ."

Clutched in his fist, Baltasar held the red ribbon that one night in May Ofelia Salamanca had worn around her neck. The myopic young man had stolen it from the Marquis de Cabra the night of another death in Lima.

He would have liked to return it now to Ofelia, to hang it down on her bosom, but the woman's dazed look held him back.

9

The Younger Brother

Balta's friends Xavier Dorrego and I, Manuel Varela, were standing on the dock waiting for him. We were overflowing with news for him. Eleven years since we'd seen each other! We gave him a rapid summary of what was happening in Argentina. All eyes were on Bernardino Rivadavia, the young prime minister who was fighting for liberal principles, free education, open communication, colonization of the interior, auctioning off of publicly owned lands, creating a public library, publishing books, stimulating local talent . . . One phrase of his seemed to summarize everything: "We are anticipating the future . . ."

But Balta did not seem to be listening to us. He gazed at us with intense seriousness, reading the changes in our features and perhaps guessing at the changes in our souls.

Well, he soon found out that Dorrego was still an inveterate philosophical Jacobin, although his family inheritance obliged him to be a conservative in economics, no matter how anticlerical he might be in his ideology.

Dorrego's close-cropped hair had rapidly gone gray, giving a reddish tint to the porcelain tones of his skin. But he seemed more fashionable with his severe cap of short hair. It was a radical renunciation of the age of wigs. We would never see them again.

I, however, continued to be a printer, and will continue to be one all my life. And now that it was possible to publish modern authors without fear of censorship, I made great efforts in that direction. While I waited for authors of our own to emerge, I already had before me a life of the Liberator Simón Bolívar, a manuscript stained with rain and tied with tricolor ribbons, which the author, who called himself Aureliano García, had sent to me, as best he could, from Barranquilla. It was a sad chronicle, however, and like the story about the blind violinist from Tabay that Baltasar had written to me, it foretold a bad end for the Liberator and his deeds. I preferred to go on publishing Voltaire and Rousseau (*La Nouvelle Héloïse* was the greatest literary success in the entire history of South America) and leave for another time the melancholy prophecy of a Bolívar as sick and defeated as his dream of American unity and civil liberty in our nations.

Yet, being together again gave the three of us immense joy. Baltasar knew that he had written a chronicle of those years— the one I'm holding in my hands right now, which one day you, reader, will also hold in yours—in the stream of letters he'd sent "Dorrego and Varela" (we'd begun to sound like a company).

We let Baltasar take the boy out to José Antonio Bustos's old estate so that he could meet Sabina. He found her a bit mad: she had a mania about sleeping in a different bedroom every night—her father, José Antonio's; that of her mother, Mayté, dead so many years before; that of the absent Baltasar; and, presumably, that of the forgotten Jesuit tutor, Julián Ríos—so she could keep them all warm.

It was useless. Brother and sister could never understand each other, and Sabina, as Baltasar told us when he got back to Buenos Aires, did not even have the courage to find herself a man, not even—he smiled with a malice unusual in him—

now that Rivadavia's modernizing laws had rooted the nomadic gauchos on the estates, forcing them to become agricultural workers and cattle ranchers, as well as a reserve available for conscription.

"Nothing happens for Sabina except in her nostalgia," her younger brother said, sighing. "She is a living recrimination."

By a strange confluence of destinies, neither Dorrego nor I had ever married, preferring to prolong our lives as Buenos Aires rakes as long as possible, though we were both approaching forty. The truth was that carousing was our pretext, a very Buenos Aires pretext to be sure, because our city had always abounded in *vieux garçons* who would not resign themselves to giving up the exciting freedom of their youth. And since Buenos Aires was a city of crossed destinies where thuggish gauchos, fleeing conscription, would jump off their horses—followed by country girls in love with them and cast, as they used to say, into perdition; but it was also a city of Spaniards who had come for business, and of Englishmen who had come to create works of civil engineering, we all met in the brothels, the bars, and taverns. We danced and drank and loved with the calm awareness that our Buenos Aires was a city of foundations, founded twice at the beginning and three, four, even a hundred times each time a foreigner, from the interior or from Europe, came to live here.

We couldn't drag Baltasar to our bordellos, and we ourselves began to give them up. We realized that the real reason for our carousing was that we were awaiting the return of our "younger brother" to see what we would do together. Who would have thought it? In the decade of our participation in the revolution, we had encouraged him from Buenos Aires, had imposed on him that mission to Upper Peru to follow in the footsteps of Castelli, and had thrust him into a life of dangers and adventures that Dorrego and I, well, never in the slightest experienced personally. We soon became disillusioned with revolutionary politics and returned to our hereditary habits: Dorrego, living off his rents; I, a printer. But now Rivadavia was reanimating our hopes.

There was something more, as well. The exciting romantic story of Baltasar Bustos and Ofelia Salamanca, sung from one end of the Americas to the other, had both of us, Dorrego and me (although for different reasons), in suspense. We could not make any matrimonial decisions until we knew how that turned out.

Baltasar did not have to tell us who the child was. Before anyone else, we found out what had happened that night of May 24–25, 1810, in the burned palace of the Royal Court. We showered tenderness on the boy. Why, we began to treat him like a fourth brother, this one really younger. The boy was clever, although melancholy, and he spoke with the charming accent of the Gulf Coast of Mexico. He never mentioned his mother, as if he'd made a vow. But he did speak Spanish, after all, and we could understand each other.

Dorrego had a small estate on the outskirts of Buenos Aires, out toward San Isidro, next to the river, and we would often go there on Saturdays and Sundays. We started calling ourselves the Citizens again, recalling our youthful polemics in that bare but packed Café de Malcos, where it seemed that whether or not the ideas of Rousseau and Voltaire became reality depended exclusively on us.

Dorrego carried his clocks back and forth from Buenos Aires to San Isidro, and the boy was fascinated watching that collection of fantastic, diverse forms—tombs, drums, carriages, thrones, rings, and eggs—while we wondered if, for us, time had in a certain sense stopped. But for the fair boy it was as varied as those clocks, in which he would see a measure of the different suns, so far from each other, that marked his life.

Baltasar adopted the child, whose family name became Bustos, but in my honor Baltasar renamed him Manuel, replacing the Leocadio he'd been given at baptism. The boy and I did not resemble each other in any way, however. My first gray hairs, it's true, softened my dark face, though the ferocity of my mustache did not hide the secret flaw in my face: my upper lip is too big. But neither the shadows under my eyes nor my thinness was repeated in this boy, who must have mirrored instead the youth of his mother, the adorable Ofelia.

We would watch him play on those Sundays we spent together in the country. He liked to blindfold himself and play blindman's buff. Seeing him, so handsome, graceful, and happy, we finally dared to ask his stepfather about his last letter, the one he never sent us after reaching Veracruz and meeting Father Quintana, Ofelia, and the child.

Baltasar stared for a long time at the river that flowed more slowly than the years that were beginning for us that moment, the river that had nothing whatsoever to do with silver plate and seemed, rather, a huge drainage ditch for the jungles and mines of the continent's interior.

He told us that he had always written the truth to us and that he was now finding it difficult to tell us a lie. We already knew by the gazettes that Father Quintana had been executed exactly as he had foretold, shot on the knees and through the back, then decapitated, his head exposed in a cage in the Veracruz plaza.

Quintana was a mysterious, self-absorbed Mexican mestizo, Baltasar added, but he had a spontaneous genius that cut its way through the terrible resentment of that race. He had a sense of the drama he was living, of what military decision entailed, and of historical language. But, above all, he really believed in Christ and in the possibility of establishing a relationship with God through language.

Baltasar took off his glasses and shut his eyes.

They captured him alone in the hills near Cuernavaca, in the middle of the flight of his defeated troops and the terror of his flock of lawyers. He was shouting to all of them: "Don't flee—you can't see the bullets that hit you in the back."

He asked to be shot in his most elegant cassock. They looked in vain for the name of the tailor so they could punish him.

"Quintana was the last real revolutionary," Baltasar said at the end of that afternoon, with its golden stains on the dark grass near the Río de la Plata. "Now what everyone expected in Mexico when I set sail from Veracruz will come about. Compromise, freedom only in law, the nation vanquished and dismembered . . . Can there be liberty without equality?" This was Father Quintana's burning question, and Baltasar repeated it now. And we, his friends, laughed: "Don't start that again, or you'll be kidnapping children once more. We're not as young as we used to be. Settle down . . ."

"There has to be a problem. There always has to be a problem," murmured Baltasar.

"What are you saying?" I asked, because Dorrego wanted to hear no more.

"Nothing," said Baltasar, "but since I've described in detail each doubt that has passed through my spirit, I think I ought to tell you that the worst of all has been not knowing if Quintana told me the truth that afternoon in the chapel."

"Why would you think that?" I asked him in alarm.

"It's very likely he lied out of charity and to take charge, as he put it, of Ofelia Salamanca's memory. It's hard for me to believe that story about her as an agent of the independence movement. She was infamous, from Chile to Venezuela, and the evidence of her crimes was overwhelming . . ."

I asked him not to torture himself and not to be less charitable than the Mexican priest. Besides, he should think about the child—the child certainly was Ofelia's son. In all likelihood, the woman was dead. And he, Baltasar, should accept a respite in this passion that had tortured him for so long.

"But that passion was my reason for being," our younger brother told us then, in his sad, melodic voice.

And we did not plague him with sermons or try to draw definitive conclusions from his experience. We had the bright idea of inviting young ladies of the best Buenos Aires society, accompanied by their mothers or chaperones, along on our promenades down the river, but nothing went beyond the limits of ordinary etiquette.

Nothing happened, except that Baltasar began to upset the equilibrium that Dorrego, with his comfortable compromise between wealth and Jacobinism, and I, with my labors as enterprising publisher (and both of us with our carousing), had contrived here in Buenos Aires, where independence was already consolidated, while in Peru the military campaigns still raged.

I think Baltasar realized this and wanted us to be calm, but without lying to us.

"I lost many things. Echagüe and Arias were as good friends as you two. I really miss them, believe me. What a good time we had together preparing the Andes campaign! There was never a more fraternal or enjoyable moment in the history of the Americas. How grateful I am to have shared it with them. No, I'm not bitter, though I embraced death many times. But I think I came to know myself. Principles became concrete for me. War and independence, respect for others, justice and faith. I know what those things mean. I also know that, having been through it all, I have you, my friends, and with you I may perhaps know the alliance of all souls, united by the sin and the grace that so concerned Father Quintana. But what I want you to know once and for all, to be perfectly sincere, is that there is still a good distance to go from what I've already lived to what I have yet to live. I just want you to know. I'm not going to live that time in peace. Not me, not Argentina, not all the Americas."

He paused and ran his fingers through his wavy, rebellious hair.

"Now that you know this, let's be friends forever."

"What's he saying?" Dorrego asked this time. He was growing impatient with our friend.

"Nothing," I said to him, but we saw that there was that

spark of madness in Baltasar's eyes again. Dorrego told me later he'd noticed—"Did you notice?"—that our friend seemed a bit mad, but I said that he wasn't; that it was enthusiasm. Our younger brother was an enthusiast, that's all . . .

"And I hope he never stops being one."

The eventual reader of these pages, which for the moment only I have the right to read, will now understand why I could not be charitable, then or ever, with my friend Baltasar Bustos and tell him, Yes, Father Quintana didn't lie to you. Ofelia Salamanca was always on the side of independence, ever since the time of Father Camilo Henríquez and the Carrera brothers in Chile, then here with us in Buenos Aires—well, only with me, passing me information about the activities of her old husband, the Marquis de Cabra, during the twelve months they lived in the palace of the Superior Court of Buenos Aires between 1809 and 1810, when she and I fell in love, and I climbed up that vine and entered that room night after night, and I knew the ecstasy of her flesh and enjoyed her until she became large with my son. And yet not a single day passed without her finding out something useful for the cause, communicating it, and making possible, to a great extent, the triumphs of May.

And now I write this and, like the chronicle of the writer from Barranquilla, this manuscript of mine must wait a very long time before being published, for the length of the lives of my friend Balta and the son, Manuel, I had with Ofelia Salamanca, the unknown heroine of the wars of independence, who died of cancer on a forgotten day in the malarial port of Coatzcoalcos, in the state of Veracruz.

I had no one to write with this request: put twenty-five candles around her poor coffin, the same number of years she'd been alive when our son was born, the same age the beautiful Ofelia will always be in my memory.

The legend of Ofelia and her platonic lover, my friend Baltasar, would go on living in the *vidalitas, cumbias,* and *corridos.*

I locked this manuscript away, and Dorrego and I went out on the lawn of the estate along the river.

The boy, whom a singular stroke of luck had saved ten years ago from the flames and from death in exchange for an anonymous black child, was playing blindman's buff, alone, with his eyes blindfolded.

His adoptive father, our brother Baltasar, was watching him in silence, unsmiling, his hands joined under his chin, his index fingers covering his pursed lips and his long, light-brown beard. He was sitting at a comfortable white wicker table, while the lights of summer glimmered on the grass.

It was, I said to myself, as if Baltasar had carried out his fervent desire to have communion with nature, but not on his father and sister's savage pampa, not on the risky sand flats and jungles of Miguel Lanza, not even in the crossing of the Andes with San Martín, not in the besieged port of Maracaibo, not in the final encampment of Father Anselmo Quintana; rather, only now, here, in this civilized corner of an estate in San Isidro, facing the river that reflected the slow undulations of the tops of the willows ruffled by the light summer breeze. Through those trees the clean, strong sun was filtered by a thousand intangible shields.

"These hours of solitude and meditation are the only times . . . I am completely myself, without diversion, without obstacles . . . what nature has wanted me to be."

Was there any reason, in reality, not to accept, with Rousseau, that true felicity is within us?

We looked at Manuel, the child Manuel Bustos, who was playing happily, and the three of us remembered—Xavier abandoning his clocks and walking out to the lawn, I looking with fraternal love at my younger brother, Baltasar, who made his way, passionately, through an entire continent, the same Balta who touched Ofelia Salamanca only once, and then to help her to her feet—that terrible night of May 24 and 25, 1810, when we thought we had lost the child forever, searching for him until dawn in the brothels, meat-salting sheds, and shacks with straw roofs down along the river. Now Baltasar threw into that same river a thin red thread.

The child whirled around several times, playing alone, and then, without taking the handkerchief off his eyes, spread his arms before a wall in the garden, gave the order to fire, shouted *Bang, bang, bang,* and fell to the ground, clasping his hand to his heart.

We were about to laugh at this joke when shock stopped us. We heard a flutter of skirts and saw in the light of summer a woman running toward the child, holding his head, and hugging it to her breasts, a beautiful woman dressed in gray taffeta, gloved and pliant, through whose light veil Dorrego and I could recognize—how could we not?—the adorable features of the young actress who garnered great success in the nights of Buenos Aires, so frequented by Xavier and me: the little mistress, as everyone nicknamed her.

But in fact, the name of this intelligent and beautiful Chilean actress was Gabriela Cóo. She burst unexpectedly into our Sunday garden, tossing aside her drizzle-colored parasol to kneel by my son, Ofelia and my son, Baltasar Bustos's adoptive son; and she turned, this little mistress, to look at us with her black eyes from under those famous, thick, uncensored eyebrows until, lighting up with a smile on her red lips, she fixed them on the face of our friend, our younger brother, Baltasar Bustos.

The campaign was finally over.

Mommsenstrasse, Berlin, June 1989
Paseo del Prado, Madrid, August 1989
Kingsand, Cornwall, January 1990
Mendoza, Argentina, February 1990